Holy Mother. He was pulling her skirt up!

"You can't do this!" she gasped.

"I assure you, your maidenly honor is quite safe. I'm only searching for weapons. I don't trust anyone, especially women as wily as you, my dear. Perhaps a knife strapped to your leg?"

His hand moved up one leg, then another. Her pulse quickened. "How dare you?" she whispered.

Nate removed his hand from beneath the folds of her skirts, then turned her loose.

Ann spun around, ready to give him a piece of her mind. But seeing his raised hand, she backed away. "I don't care who finds me in your room. If you strike me, I swear I'll scream." He brushed back the hair that had fallen into his eyes, and Ann realized her mistake. There had been no blow intended.

Nate leaned against the door. "What's wrong, duchess? Guilty conscience?"

Dear Reader,

What a perfect time to celebrate history—the eve of a new century. This month we're featuring four terrific romances with awe-inspiring heroes and heroines from days gone by that you'll want to take with you into the *next* century!

Antoinette Huntington is the unforgettable heroine in *The Lady and the Outlaw,* a new Western by DeLoras Scott, which also happens to be the long-awaited sequel to her very first Harlequin Historical novel, *Bittersweet.* Here, the pragmatic and English-bred Antoinette has a romantic run-in with a rugged outlaw on a train headed to the Wild West. Don't miss it!

In Suzanne Barclay's new medieval novel, *The Champion,* knight Simon of Blackstone will leave you breathless when he returns from the Crusades to right past wrongs. In doing so, he rekindles a love that was lost but not forgotten…. Wolf Heart is the fascinating, timeless hero from *Shawnee Bride* by Elizabeth Lane. He's a Shawnee warrior who rescues a young woman from certain death. Can the deep love that grows between them transcend the cultural barriers?

Corwin of Lenvil, a Saxon knight, is the handsome hero in Shari Anton's exciting new medieval tale, *By Queen's Grace.* Corwin infiltrates a rebel camp in order to rescue a kidnapped royal maiden who long ago broke his heart. There's passion and danger at every turn!

Enjoy! And come back again next month for four more choices of the best in historical romance.

Happy holidays,

Tracy Farrell
Senior Editor

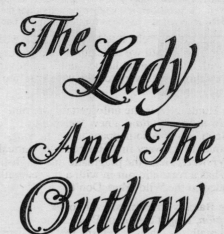

The Lady And The Outlaw

De Loras Scott

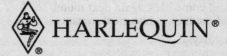

HARLEQUIN®

TORONTO • NEW YORK • LONDON
AMSTERDAM • PARIS • SYDNEY • HAMBURG
STOCKHOLM • ATHENS • TOKYO • MILAN • MADRID
PRAGUE • WARSAW • BUDAPEST • AUCKLAND

ISBN 0-373-29094-2

THE LADY AND THE OUTLAW

Please address questions and book requests to:
Harlequin Reader Service
U.S.: 3010 Walden Ave., P.O. Box 1325, Buffalo, NY 14269
Canadian: P.O. Box 609, Fort Erie, Ont. L2A 5X3

To Tracy Farrell, a very special lady

Prologue

England, October 1875

Having heard the baying of the duke's hounds, the small hunting party spread out. The duke's cousin, Matthew, moved to the left, while Edmund Huntington, the duke of Gravenworth, veered off to the right. The duchess chose to remain in the center. If all went well, the dogs would soon flush a worthy stag from the protection of the forest, momentarily disturbing the morning fog still clinging to the edges of the meadow.

A superb horsewoman, Antoinette set her frisky gray splendidly. As always, her mohair riding habit and hat mirrored the current Parisian fashion. However, her thoughts were not on horsemanship, fashion or the hunt.

As Antoinette drew her rifle from the confines of the saddle scabbard, a momentary frown creased her smooth brow, the only indication of the pain the effort caused. At least her clothes hid the bruises Edmund had inflicted last night.

Resting the weapon across her lap, the duchess glared at her husband's back. Before Edmund had pulled ahead, she had seen his nostrils flare. He was already anticipating the kill. Antoinette's full mouth spread into a contemptuous smile as she curled her finger around the trigger. Finally she raised the weapon to her shoulder and waited for the stag, already desperate to elude the dogs and death. But as if guided by some unknown force, she slowly moved the tip of the barrel until the back of her husband's head came within her line of vision.

Five years of mistreatment flashed through her mind. From Edmund she had learned the meaning of loathing. How many nights had she prayed that some misfortune would befall him? She could end his tyranny here and now. All she had to do was squeeze the trigger.

A stag suddenly leaped into the clearing, not six feet from where Edmund had positioned himself. He fired his weapon, but the magnificent beast didn't falter. The duke had again missed his target.

An unusual calmness befell Antoinette as she looked back down the barrel of her rifle...still pointed at her husband. Could she kill him? Was she capable of such a monstrous act? It would be so easy.

A shot exploded in her ear. Her eyes became large green orbs as she watched Edmund sway in the saddle then slowly slide to the ground, the blood from the hole in his back already staining his yellow hunting jacket.

For a brief moment, Antoinette felt a sense of satisfaction. The next moment she was consumed with the horror at what she had done. The weapon slipped from her hand and fell helpless onto the ground. Pulling her gaze from the motionless body on the grass, she looked at Matthew. She desperately needed to explain that it had been an accident. "I...I..." Words failed her.

As Matthew put his rifle away, Antoinette could see his thin lips were spread in a sardonic smile of satisfaction. Suddenly she questioned whether she had indeed been the perpetrator...or Matthew?

"You murdered His Grace!" she called accusingly.

"I?" Matthew asked, his face mirroring surprise.

No! Antoinette thought. She couldn't have committed the act. There was no sense of guilt within her. Suddenly, she realized the precariousness of her situation. If Matthew *had* committed the crime, he wouldn't want to leave a witness behind. She yanked her mount about. She had to reach the hunting lodge and safety.

A swift kick sent the big gelding into motion, but Antoinette's hesitation had allowed Matthew enough time to close the distance between them. His strong hand grabbed her horse's reins near the bit, causing the animal's head to be jerked about. It took all of Antoinette's skill to keep her seat as the horse tugged, danced and kicked. Desperately Antoinette whipped at the hand holding the reins, but Matthew's grip was firm. Finally she gave up her effort at freedom.

"You shot Edmund in the back!" she again accused.

Matthew's smile didn't reach his steely eyes. "Come, come, my dear. It was a poacher who shot him. Right?"

"There was no poacher."

"Either a poacher," Matthew said, and raised a meaningful brow, "or you."

Antoinette's throat filled with bile.

"Who else hated Edmund enough to shoot him? It certainly couldn't be me. I would have taken care of the matter a long time ago."

Antoinette raised a shaking hand to her throat. "No one will believe me guilty of so vile an act," she said with far more conviction than she felt.

"Ah, but they will. Would it not be easier for the ton to believe that you were ridding yourself of a husband you despised while securing your unborn child's inheritance, than for me, who gains considerably less, to have committed the crime?" He released the reins.

As frantic as she felt, Antoinette knew escape was impossible. "I...I suppose it must have been a poacher." Her mind had become a sea of confusion.

"I'm pleased to see your recollection of this little mishap coincides with mine. I've always known you to be a wise woman, my dear. Actually, you did the world a service by putting an end to dear Edmund." Matthew watched a crow fly by. "Just think. Had my father not been born six minutes later than Edmund's father, I would be the duke. Ah, but as my father always said, trickery abounded that fateful night. He was the firstborn twin, you know, but because his coloring was not dark like the Huntington line, it was claimed that he was second."

Antoinette had heard the story many times. Too many times.

Matthew pressed the soles of his boots against the stirrups and stretched his legs. "Now you carry Edmund's child which again prevents me from claiming what should be mine. That leaves me, or perhaps I should say you, with two choices. Either marry me or die for your crime.''

The duchess opened her mouth to speak, but no words came forth. Marry him? All she could do was nod her consent.

''Good. One week after Edmund's funeral we shall announce our betrothal.''

Antoinette gasped. ''The town would believe the child I carry to be yours!''

''Exactly.''

A shudder crawled up Antoinette's spine, causing the pounding in her head to increase. Her eyes desperately scanned the woods for any sign of help, though she knew none would be forthcoming.

''And of course with the child being mine, I will gain the dukedom,'' Matthew continued. ''I shall become your protector, so to speak. Now, my dear, we must make haste to inform the servants of the terrible atrocity that has taken place this fateful day.''

Chapter One

"Your Grace, there is a messenger here to see you."

"Thank you, Mrs. Cuthwell." Ann went to the narrow entrance and accepted the message. As soon as she returned to the warm parlor she opened the missive and perused the letter from her father. It stated that, after a lengthy meeting between her father and uncle, the duke of Wilmington, it had been decided that she should join their brother's son, Beau Falkner, in America and await the birth of her child. If she delivered a son, he would be the next duke of Gravenworth, thereby thwarting Matthew's attempts to gain the title. Should the child be a daughter, then other arrangements would have to be made. Passage had already been booked on the *Dolphin,* one of the fine sailing vessels owned by W. T. Honeycutt, a close friend of her uncle. Funds had also been provided.

Ann crumpled the paper in her hand and stood watching the heavy raindrops strike the cottage windowpane. The dark, low clouds blotted out the sunlight, making it appear more like dusk than morning.

A perfect cover for the daring plan she had been contemplating. It would be a terribly risky move on her
part, but she would have the advantage of surprise.
And, try as she might, it was the only positive way
she could think of to prevent Matthew from gaining
control of Gravenworth. Ann left the parlor and
headed for Captain Cuthwell's small study.

Twenty minutes later, after half-truths and eva-
sions, Antoinette Huntington had managed to talk the
retired sea captain into finding her a driver who was
trustworthy and had a fast team of horses.

While impatiently awaiting the captain's return,
Ann thought about her escape from Gravenworth. At
Edmund's funeral, a few whispered words to Jonathan
Falkner was all it had taken for him to put his only
daughter in his coach and whisk her away from Mat-
thew.

Ann smiled warmly. During the trip here, she had
told her dear father what had *really* happened during
the hunt. The tall, stately man had been completely
understanding, mumbling something about Edmund's
just reward.

"Perhaps it's because I can't fathom murdering
anyone," she had said, "but in my heart, I do not
believe I fired the shot."

"I understand you were upset at the time, but it's
too bad you couldn't have retrieved your rifle. You
could have found out if it had been fired. Fortunately,
the tale about the poacher was believed by all," her
father had pointed out. "There is a great deal at stake
here if, as you suspect, Matthew did indeed see to
Edmund's demise," he had added thoughtfully.
"Matthew might not hesitate to harm you now that
you are no longer under his control."

"I'll be safe at Seaborne Manor."

"Having you at the manor would indeed lighten my heart. I have been far too lonely since your blessed mother's passing so many years ago and since your brother sailed for India. But it's still not safe. I'm taking you to an old friend's cottage instead."

Her father had placed her chilled hands in his and rubbed them gently. "My dear, you must stay in Bath until it is decided what should be done. Matthew will never find you at Captain and Mrs. Cuthwell's cottage."

Though the following two weeks of confinement had moved at a snail's pace, it had allowed her time to come to grips with her feeling about Edmund's death. She knew she should feel guilty for not caring, but she still hadn't shed a tear and there was no sorrow within her. Edmund had long since destroyed any emotion she might have harbored. For the first time in years, she was free to do whatever pleased her. And if there were tears to be shed, let them be for her and the sin against God she had committed...if she had committed the sin.

Despite her fears, later that morning Ann left Bath, time being her enemy. The *Dolphin* was due to sail in two days, but if she was fortunate, the pounding waves caused by the storm would delay the ship's departure long enough for her to board.

Matthew flung his goblet in the blazing fireplace and curled his lip. Where was Antoinette Huntington? He knew for certain she had never arrived at Seaborne. So where had her father hidden her? He turned to warm his backside. The cold and miserable weather only served to fuel his temper.

What was it going to take to flush the duchess from her hiding place? He had put out word of money offered for her return, but nothing had come of it. Even the men he'd posted at each ship boarding in Bristol had turned up empty-handed. Somewhere, sometime she would have to emerge.

He had thought he had everything under control. He had been convinced that Ann's fear and self-condemnation would prevent her from trying to leave. When she mingled with the guests who had arrived for the funeral, he had remained constantly by her side. But as his cousin was being placed in the ground, she had moved to her father's side and there was nothing he could do to prevent it. He had seen her whisper something to the stately man and knew immediately that he had been tricked. Her apparent meekness as of late had been but a ruse to keep him from suspecting her intentions.

Matthew banged his fist against the thick rock wall. As the closest relative, he would now be the next duke of Gravenworth…if Ann wasn't carrying Edmund's seed. It was without question that she had informed her father of her condition, which meant that her uncle, the duke of Wilmington, was also aware of it. The duke had the queen's ear. Matthew knew that should he make a move to claim the title, Ann's uncle would be quick to inform Her Majesty of his niece's condition. He had no desire to be sent to the guillotine.

Matthew scowled. He had to find Ann and proclaim himself father of the babe she carried. But even that seemed doomed. The duchess was still nowhere to be found!

The door to Matthew's room flew open, startling him. "How dare you barge in here?" he thundered.

"Milord," Thomas, the manservant, said hurriedly, "the kitchen has informed me that the duchess was just here and...she's already left."

"And no one stopped her?" Matthew hurried forward. "I'll see that some heads roll! Get my coat...and my horse!" His heels clicked on the stone hallway as he hurried forth.

Thomas rushed after the taller man. "She took her dog and Hester with her," he sputtered, already out of breath.

Inside the carriage, Antoinette clutched the leather coach strap, trying to maintain her seat. She was so tense her bones were aching. The black overcast skies, the flight for safety, the bumpy ride and the uncertainty of escape had taken its toll.

She released her hold and stretched her cramped fingers. She could barely see the pregnant maid who sat in the shadows on the far side of the seat. Ann worried about the rough road causing Hester to lose her baby, but to slow the carriage would be disastrous.

Antoinette released a suppressed grunt. Had she remained at Gravenworth, it wouldn't have taken long for Matthew to discover her claim of being with child had been nothing more than a means of keeping her husband from her bedchamber.

The whip cracked in the cold night air, reminding Ann of a gunshot. For a brief instant, she relived the sight of blood soaking Edmund's coat as he slid from the—

"If I don't die from this bloomin' ride, I'm as

likely to die from the cold!'' Hester wailed. She pulled the blanket tighter about her shivering body.

Ann shoved the derringer into her reticule then returned her hold on the strap. Threatening Hester with the weapon had been the only quick way she could think of to make the loose woman do her bidding. She still found it hard to believe that at four months into her confinement, the maid's stomach gave no evidence of her condition. Could Hester have also lied about being with child? Enough. She couldn't dwell on it now.

The duchess's thoughts turned to Sir Drake. She wanted to weep. On top of everything else she had lost, she could now include her dog. Even after making it outside the castle safely, she'd had to keep the gun pointed at Hester. Busy hands and haste had allowed Sir Drake's leash to slip from her fingers. The whippet had immediately darted off to relieve himself. To her despair, it would have taken too long to search for him or wait for his return.

''Where the bloody 'ell are ye takin' me?''

Ann's wool cloak failed to keep out the night's dampness. ''Someone should have washed your acid mouth with lye soap a long time ago.''

''Edmund dain't complain.'' Hester toyed with a long flaxen curl hanging over her shoulder. ''At least I ain't barren.''

''You seem to have overlooked something very important,'' Ann said calmly. ''Edmund is dead, and it is because you are pregnant with his bastard that Matthew will see to your demise next.''

Hester gasped. '''E wouldn't do that. Why're you sayin' such? Edmund told me a bastard can't inherit a title, but he said he'd see that his son was well taken care of.''

"And you believed him?" Ann scoffed. "Matthew is Edmund's closest relative. He has slain to secure the title. Why would he allow Edmund's bastard to live? But Matthew isn't going to succeed. I shall see that Richard will become the next duke of Gravenworth.''

"Richard?" Hester asked.

"That is to be Edmund's son's name."

Ann pulled back the curtain and tried to see out the window. Every instinct told her that Matthew was close behind. The momentary break in the clouds seemed a godsend. She rapped on the trap to get the driver's attention. It took several tries before she was successful. "Holbert," she called, when the man on the box finally slid the trap open, "take the coach to the trees! We're being followed at close chase!"

As soon as the team and coach were well hidden, the driver quickly placed scarfs over the team's muzzles to keep them from nickering. Then, everyone waited.

Less than five minutes passed before all heard the cadence of hooves pounding against the earth. Ann could make out only the shadows of riders as they passed, and Matthew was surely one of them.

She let out her held breath. What was she going to do now? After the riders had gone so far without catching the conveyance, they would circle back. Suddenly she remembered an old road that hadn't been traveled in years. When she and Edmund were first married, she'd used it for her morning rides, knowing he wouldn't find her. Ann glanced at the sky. It was clearing. Once past the trees, there would be enough moonlight to see by.

Ann quickly informed Holbert of the road and how to reach it. The driver had already proven well worth his fee. Knowing there was nothing more she could do, she settled against the back of the cushy seat. The clouds were clearing too quickly. Was the storm passing? If so, they would never make it back to Bath in time to catch the *Dolphin* that would have taken them around the cape to San Francisco. She had waited too long to fetch Hester.

But if the ship had sailed by the time they reached the docks, she would be forced to procure another passage to America. The corners of Ann's lips curved upward. She had thwarted Matthew and for the moment she was justly proud of her victory.

"How do ye know it was Matthew who murdered 'Is Grace?" Hester asked, but with considerably less haughtiness.

"I saw him do it," Ann lied. Hester would never know the truth.

"But you told everyone—"

"I said what had to be said at the time."

"Milady, why are you protectin' me?"

"Because of the child you carry. I intend to raise Edmund's bastard as my own." Letting Edmund and everyone else think she was pregnant had proven to be more of a blessing than she had realized. She did, however, feel guilty about keeping the secret from her father. But only by claiming Richard as her own could she secure the title. "You'll have until we reach Bath to decide if you are agreeable. If so, we will sail to the colonies, where I will see that you are financially secure."

Hester had always wanted to go to the colonies. "What if it's a girl?"

"Huntington men sire sons. But should it be a girl, you will still be taken care of." Ann had already concluded that if she had to, she would secretly obtain a boy from an orphanage in the colonies.

They had finally reached the old road. The bumpy road would make traveling even more uncomfortable, but there had been no alternative. Inside the dark conveyance, Ann could feel the abigail staring at her.

Hester sat quietly, absorbing what the duchess had said. It wasn't uncommon for a barren family to raise a bastard child. The duke's death had put an end to all her planning and scheming. Now she'd never be the lady of the castle. Who would have thought His Grace would die at such an early age?

Hester took a deep breath. Since Edmund's departure, she hadn't cared what happened to the brat she carried. But with the duchess now wanting to raise the child as her own, all sorts of possibilities could open up for her. From now on she'd bide her time and do whatever Her Grace wanted. "I ain't gotta think on it, Your Grace. I'm willing to go with you. Richard will be your son."

Ann rested her head on the back of the seat. For now, the Huntington line would remain intact. Only good could come from her decision to become Richard's protector. Besides, the commitment had been made and she no longer had the option of changing her mind. From here on, she must do whatever it took to see that Edmund's son became the next duke of Gravenworth.

Chapter Two

New York, March 1876

Her hands cradling her protruding stomach, Hester continued to pace the creaking floor. Time was running out. Soon she would be giving birth. Who would help her? There was no midwife and she had already determined that the duchess knew nothing of such matters.

Unfortunately, even as near as her time was, Hester knew that they had to get on with their journey. Had they not missed the *Dolphin,* they wouldn't be stranded in New York. But they *had* missed the *Dolphin*'s sailing, and consequently Her Ladyship had booked passage on the next available ship leaving for the colonies. The duchess had reasoned that the colonies were far too small a landmass to be concerned about where they docked.

Hester rubbed her stomach. The baby had kicked. Good fortune had not deserted her. Having the duke's son was going to give her more power than she had ever dreamed of. The ocean voyage had provided ample time for planning her future.

When they arrived at Beau Falkner's ranch, Hester Potter would declare herself as being the duchess of Gravenworth.

Hester smiled and resumed her pacing. While aboard ship, she had waited hand and foot on her seasick mistress to gain her confidence. The single piece of information that had started her thinking about switching places had been the discovery that Beau Falkner had never met his cousin. Bored, and with a minimal amount of coaxing, Her Grace had spent hours talking of her past and willingly answering questions. Hester now knew everything about the duchess, including her life at Seaborne.

Hester's chest swelled with pride. She hadn't been foolish enough to think that was enough to get her what she wanted. Speech and mannerisms were also important. So she had listened carefully to the way Her Grace talked. Then, when off by herself, she had practiced diligently until she could talk with the same sophistication as her mistress and move about with equal grace. Very soon, all her hard-earned efforts were going to put gold in her pocket.

Undoubtedly the duchess's father or uncle had already sent a message to their nephew informing him of Ann's arrival and that she was with child. Though they had different shades of hair, she and milady were both blondes. Yes, she praised herself, she had planned well and was quite prepared to make the transition.

Hester laughed, already anticipating playing the part of a duchess. Of course, she would have to make sure Antoinette Huntington never reached her cousin's ranch.

Hester looked out the window. Snow was starting to fall, but it didn't matter. Knowing she would soon be treated with dignity gave her the strength to tolerate anything. When money arrived from England, she'd be rich. Then she'd stick the brat in an orphanage and go her own way.

The door suddenly flew open and Ann waltzed in. The bellboys trailed behind, each with his arms loaded with boxes. The duchess had been shopping again. Hadn't she already purchased enough clothes for a dozen women?

"Oh, Your Grace," Hester said with mock sweetness as soon as the door had closed, "I can't wait to see what you've purchased."

Ann removed her wool cloak. Her hat and veil followed. Rubbing her arms to rid the lingering cold, she smiled fondly at Hester. Poor woman, Ann thought. How could she move about with such agility while having so heavy a burden? She pointed at two of the boxes. "Those are for you."

Hester tried to act excited about receiving the gifts. "Did you find a wet nurse?" she asked as she untied the ribbons. She pulled a hat from the box but didn't bother putting it on.

Ann frowned. "No. In England it wouldn't have presented a problem. They're everywhere. America is so confoundedly uncivilized. Here women are actually expected to nurse their own children."

Hester plopped ungracefully onto the small space left on the bed. "We're no closer to your cousin's estates, and now you tell me there is no one to suckle the child! You promised that a boat trip was all it would take to reach him." She had to regain control of her temper.

Ann felt guilty. All these months couldn't have been easy for Hester, yet she had never complained. "I'm certain I'll find one soon." The problem was when and where? Though Ann could never forget whose child Hester carried, she had grown quite fond of the maid. Hester had remained by her side when she was seasick and had offered an immeasurable amount of kindness and friendship.

Ann smoothed her hair back and pulled one of the heavy new gowns from its container. It was a lovely brown velvet affair with a long train. At least her new clothes allowed her some degree of satisfaction.

"Have you discovered where your cousin resides?"

"No," Ann replied honestly. "I've inquired at all the fashionable stores, but no one has ever heard of him."

"I believe I have a solution to our problem."

Ann was pleased at hearing how Hester's speech had changed. With such improvements, the abigail might make something of herself.

Hester lowered her lashes. "I understand that the duke's son will belong to you. However, why couldn't *I* be the child's wet nurse?"

Ann's green eyes momentarily glowed with interest, then faded. "It has been proven repeatedly that such matters work best when child and mother are parted at birth," she said kindly. "It causes less hurt."

Ann suddenly wondered what would happen if Hester should change her mind about giving up the child. How could she excuse forcefully taking the boy from her? Hadn't enough wrongs already been committed?

Hester pressed on. "Even you have said Matthew's men are certain to find us if we remain here much longer. I could nurse Richard, and no one would ever suspect that I gave him birth. And, most importantly, we could continue on to your cousin's ranch."

"We can't leave. Richard has to be born before we reach the ranch or everyone will know he isn't mine."

Hester ground her teeth. The closer they were to the Arizona Territory when she had the child the easier it would be for her plan to work. "We can stop at a town on the way. Matthew would be less apt to find us."

Ann pursed her lips. "It wouldn't work. One day you would want to proclaim yourself as his real mother."

"Who would believe my word over Your Grace… especially after the years pass? Milady, how could I, a mere servant, not want my son to become the duke of Gravenworth? I would be so proud."

Ann made the mistake of looking into Hester's blue, soulful eyes and couldn't refuse the request. Besides, what Hester had said made sense. "We do need to be on our way." She sighed. "All right, we'll try it."

When Ann left the suite, her stomach was churning. Every instinct was telling her that she had made a bad decision.

Ann stepped from the hired conveyance and surveyed the building before her. She had read in the *London Times* that Vanderbilt had spared no cost to build Grand Central Station. She had to agree that it was indeed a magnificent edifice.

Fifteen minutes later, Ann continued to stand steadfast in front of the beak-nosed booking clerk, absolutely refusing to move on. She had not yet received an answer that made any sense. She took two deep breaths and tried again. "As I have already stated, I want two tickets to Arizona Territory."

"And as I said, lady, I cannot sell you tickets to there. I've looked at all the timetables and there is no train going to such a place. You can't even tell me which direction you're talking about."

"I believe the lady wants to go west," the man standing behind Ann said impatiently.

"West," the booking clerk repeated. He studied his schedule again. "I can get you to Colorado on the Pennsylvania Railroad. Then..." He ran his finger down the row of numbers. "From there you can catch the Denver & Rio Grande to Pueblo where you can make a stage connection. They'll know how to route you from that point." He handed her the proper tickets. "Your train departs at 8:25 p.m. tomorrow."

Ann's head was swimming with names she had never heard before. "How long will the trip take?"

"Only a day or two, lady," the gentleman behind her again spoke up. "You got your tickets, now move on so I can purchase mine."

Ann paid the clerk, then turned to face the man who had been heckling her. "You, sir, are extremely rude!" With the dignity befitting her station, she left.

Once out of sight of the offensive man, Ann frowned. She had misjudged her money. It was going a bit too quickly. However, she had no idea how she could have spent less. She hadn't bought a thing she didn't need.

Ann was about to leave the depot when someone tapped her shoulder. Expecting to see the same irritant she had just encountered, she turned, ready for battle. But she had never laid eyes on the rail thin man standing in front of her. He was too poorly kept to be a gentleman of substance.

"Madam, please permit me to introduce myself." He removed his worn top hat and bowed deeply. "The name's Jefferson Davis. Perhaps you've heard of me?"

"No."

Jefferson smiled. "I happened to overhear you talking to the clerk. From your accent, I take it you're new in our country."

"Well, yes. I am."

He glanced around as if to be sure no one was listening to their conversation. "What the clerk didn't tell you was that when you leave New York City, you'll be facin' every kind of no-account known to mankind." He tried taking the lady's arm to lead her outside, but she stepped away.

"What does that have to do with you, Mr. Davis?"

"Just trying to be neighborly, ma'am. I wouldn't sleep well if I didn't at least give you a warning. If you and a servant or—worse yet—a child, are traveling by yourselves, you are in grave danger."

Ann's concern increased. Acquaintances had said that the land surrounding the towns was infested with outlaws and Indians. Absolutely no one was safe. "Well...what do you think I should do?"

"I'd suggest you hire someone to travel with you and your party. Someone good with a gun."

"Do you know anyone who would fit that description?"

"You're looking at him, my lady."

"What the hell are you doing here?" a loud voice blared as Jefferson was jerked about.

Jefferson made a run for it. As Ann watched the bear chase the weasel, she caught sight of an entirely different gentleman standing off to the side, seemingly observing everything. Fear shot through her, as cutting as if she had been pierced by steel. Was he one of Matthew's spies? She should have left New York the day after they had arrived. But she had thought to wait for the child to be born. Then there was the wet nurse and new clothes. What choice had she had?

Ann lowered her head and hurried outside. Immediately she spotted another suspicious man watching people entering and exiting the depot. Possibly her imagination was running amok, but paranoia had already infiltrated her mind. It was all she could do to maintain a steady step instead of running to a carriage for hire.

Not until Ann had the red-faced driver take several side streets was she finally convinced that they weren't being followed. Why did one problem seem to compound into another? She had believed Jefferson Davis, which meant she needed to be more suspecting of people. But Mr. Davis had pointed out something very important. Women traveling alone were at the mercy of others. Despite this sad fact she had to continue on to Beau's ranch and pray that along the way she wouldn't be murdered, raped or robbed, or all three.

Ann looked out the window just as the coach

passed a tailor shop with a man's suit on display in
the window. Could she? She thought only a moment.
"Stop!" she yelled to the driver.

The cab came to an abrupt halt, throwing Ann forward. Her hat was pushed to the side, and the hat pin
pulled unmercifully at her hair. After taking a moment
to repair the damage, she turned and looked out the
rear window at the shop.

"You gettin' out, lady?" the driver called.

"Yes, but I want you to wait for me," Ann replied
to the obnoxious man. Apparently the driver had no
intention of helping her down. She was forced to per-
form the service herself. She disliked New York more
and more.

Ann walked back to the shop and stared at the
tweed suit on display. She could fit in it. She was tall,
slender and, unlike Hester, her bosom was small.

Even though the thought of putting on such clothing turned her stomach to whey, a solution to her
problems was taking form. She and Hester could
travel as man and wife. If men performed as women
in Shakespeare's plays, why couldn't a woman pose
as a man? A cold wind stirred, and she felt the added
chill. She moved to the door and opened it.

Hester's gaze shifted from the man's suit to the
duchess, then back to the man's suit. "We are to
travel as husband and wife?"

"Don't look so shocked. We have to do whatever
is needed to protect ourselves."

The thought of the duchess wearing such a suit
threatened to send Hester into peals of laughter.

"I trust you won't have the babe until we find a
midwife."

Hester chose not to point out that it wasn't something she had any control over.

Turning her attention to the suit, Ann held the trousers in front of her to judge their fit.

"After we're settled, I'm certain you'll adjust to the American way of living. I'm quite knowledgeable about the colonies," Ann stated proudly. "Before I married, friends and I often found it an interesting topic for discussion. For instance, you will be glad to know that this land isn't even as large as England. Why we bothered to go to war over such a place is still beyond my understanding."

"You said that sailing on a ship destined for New York wouldn't cause further delays," Hester goaded. "If that was so, why did your father book passage on the *Dolphin* which was to berth in San Francisco?"

"Probably because it set sail sooner. Arizona Territory has to be somewhere in the middle of the two." Ann unbuttoned her gray wool skirt and let it fall to the floor.

"You also said the ocean voyage was only going to take six weeks," Hester reminded the tall woman. "But by the time we reached the islands, waited, then sailed again, another two months had passed."

"The captain forgot to mention the Caribbean Islands," Ann excused.

Hester sneered. The pampered duchess knew nothing. "I'll get my sewing basket from the other room. Adjustments are going to have to be made for the suit to fit properly."

Ann pulled on the trousers. The material was scratchy. "Hester," she said soberly when the abigail had returned, "we have to be very careful. We can't talk to anyone. I had foolishly begun to believe we were safe, today I was reminded of how wrong I have been. I saw two men at the train station. Either or both could have been sentries for Matthew. It reminded me of how precarious our position still is.''

Hester wasn't at all worried. If Matthew caught up with them, he'd have no reason to kill her now. ''What shall we call ourselves?''

''What do you mean?''

''As husband and wife. What names will we use?''

Ann's fingers paused at buttoning the trousers. ''You'll still be Hester…what is your last name?''

''Potter.''

''Very well, we will be Mr. and Mrs. Potter. I…I will be Albert. I have always admired the name. I purchased something else to go with my new look.'' Ann fished about in the hatbox. Finding what she was searching for, she pulled it out and showed it to Hester.

''It's a mustache. I thought my face might be too smooth, so this should take care of that just fine.'' Ann held it to her upper lip.

''It's the wrong color.''

''It's just a little darker, that's all. I've seen lots of men whose mustaches weren't the same exact color as their hair.''

Hester could not hold back the laughter that bubbled forth. ''Did you have to get such a bushy one?'' she managed to ask.

''We can trim it,'' Ann stated defensively.

Hester shook her head. ''What about your hair?'' she asked.

''My hair?''

Hester marked on the pants where she would take

in the waist. "Gentlemen do not have hair to their hips."

Knowing Hester was right, a single tear trickled down Ann's cheek. As Edmund had pointed out, her hair was her only beautiful quality. "You will have to cut it."

Hester forced back a smile. "Such a shame."

"It will grow again," Ann said, more to herself than to the abigail.

The women began their work. They had a lot to do if they were to be ready for tomorrow's journey.

While the bellboys attended to the luggage, Ann took one last look at herself in the mirror. She still had trouble believing that she and the image were one and the same. She really did look like a gentleman— from the suit to the top hat—and even the watch fob and cane that finished off the entire look. Edmund often said her low, raspy voice made her sound more like a man. The mustache didn't look right, but there was little she could do about it now. She turned away and shoved the derringer into her coat pocket. Now she would find out if she could fool others.

As Ann and Hester hurried behind the porter carrying their luggage, Ann had to fight back a sense of giddiness. The man in front hadn't even looked twice at them. Women openly flirted with her—no, they flirted with Albert. Her disguise was working. Ann started to relax. As her confidence grew, she even lengthened her stride, tapping her cane on the floor with every other step.

Ann turned to encourage the huffing Hester to move faster, when she ran into a solid, jarring object.

After some fast handwork to catch her hat, which had been knocked off, she looked to see what she had run into. To her shock, it turned out to be a man!

Ann resented the way the man looked at her with smoldering black eyes. After all, it had been an accident. Then, completely dismissing her before she'd had a chance to apologize, he circled his arms around the woman he was with. His lips captured the redhead's in a kiss that had Ann's cheeks burning from embarrassment. No gentleman would kiss a lady in such a manner, and certainly not in public!

Disgusted at having to witness the man's lack of chivalry, Ann straightened her vest and continued after Hester. Still, she couldn't resist looking back at the man who had towered over her. He and the woman remained locked in an embrace. She had never seen a man wearing a white doeskin frock coat before, let alone one with fringes down the arms. True, it was a bit worn; nevertheless, it was indeed a magnificent piece of apparel. But then she had never seen anything quite like the man wearing it, either. His dark shoulder-length hair, chiseled features and wide breadth culminated in pure masculinity. She found him to be quite intimidating.

Chapter Three

After entering their car, Ann and Hester settled themselves on the red horsehair seat in the Pullman coach. Hester glanced around at the lavish accommodations. Fine wood lined the interior, and brass lanterns with green glass swung from the clerestory. The porter had even informed Albert that there was a saloon car on the train where passengers could relax on soft sofas and men could smoke.

"Are you comfortable?" Ann asked Hester.

"I will be as soon as I catch my breath."

Ann was anxious for the train to be on its way. They wouldn't be safe until they had departed New York.

Seated next to the window, Ann looked out to see if anyone suspicious was stationed about. Her gaze ceased its traveling when it came to rest on the same tall man she'd bumped into. He was again kissing the beautiful redhead but was obviously trying to pull away from her.

The whistle blew and the conductor shouted, "Last call! All aboard!"

The train jerked, then the wheels slowly moved forward. Ann became intrigued. Was it the dark-haired man or the red-haired woman who was supposed to be boarding?

As the train picked up momentum, Ann lost sight of the couple who were obviously very much in love and hated to part. She would never know what happened, or why either had to leave.

"Howdy, sir."

Ann looked up and found herself staring at the very same towering figure she had just been thinking about. His eyes were warm and friendly and so dark they looked black. Though she couldn't call him handsome in the sense of being pretty like Edmund, he was undoubtedly the most magnificent rogue she had ever seen. She nodded her acknowledgment, but made no reply.

"Are you traveling far?" he asked Ann as he took the seat directly across the aisle from Hester.

"Ah...er..." Even his voice was deep and pleasing to the ear. "Just to Coloda."

"You mean Colorado?"

Ann reminded herself that as long as she and Hester remained to themselves, fewer problems would arise. But just looking at the stranger had caused a pleasant fluttering in the pit of her stomach. "Yes. That's the village."

"Village?" He chuckled. "Are you sure you know where you're going? Colorado is a territory, not a village."

"We're *going* to Arizona Territory," Hester inserted.

Ann resented Hester's intrusion.

The man removed his low-crowned hat and placed it on the empty seat beside him. "Looks like we're going to be traveling for a spell together. Name's Nathan Bishop. Folks call me Nate. I'm also headed for Denver."

"Quite a spell?" Hester repeated. "You've been misinformed. Colorado is only a day or two away."

Nate chuckled. "I don't know who you've been talking to, but it's a six-day trip to Colorado."

"Six?" Hester gasped. "But we may not have that long." She turned an accusing eye on her so-called husband. "You said two days! Where are we going to sleep?"

Ann was equally shocked at hearing the length of traveling time. "We sleep here," she defended. "The porter said the seats become beds and beds fold down from above. Curtains are pulled for privacy. I shall take the top. We'll be quite comfortable."

Nate settled himself in the seat. "When did you leave England?" he asked Hester.

"If you don't mind, my wife needs rest," Ann said in a less than friendly tone.

"I feel fine now, Albert." Hester smiled sweetly. "My husband worries about me," she told Nate, teasingly acting as if it were a confidentiality.

Blood surged through Ann's veins when the stranger gave her a knowing smile, then a sense of disappointment followed when he dismissed her and turned his attention back to Hester. This was ridiculous! She didn't even know the man.

Hester smiled at the deliciously handsome man. "We left England nearly five months ago."

"You didn't tell me your name," Nate said.

Her cheeks dimpled. "Hester Potter. This is my husband, Albert."

Nate nodded.

Worried at Hester so easily handing out information, Ann tried to give the woman a pinch on the hip as a reminder of their plight. Unfortunately there was too much material clumped together for her to reach her target, and a verbal reminder would draw attention.

"You must be traveling home to be with your wife and children," Hester said matter-of-factly. She intended to find out right off if the gentleman was married.

"I'm not married."

"How interesting. Why would you want to leave New York and go west?"

"I have a small ranch near the Arizona Territory."

As the stranger and Hester continued their conversation, Ann was wishing she could warn Hester of the stranger's uncouth nature. He'd proven that when he'd stood in the middle of the depot kissing that woman goodbye! And such a kiss. Why, she'd never allow any man to kiss her in such an unacceptable manner.

Ann looked out the window to see if there were any Indians yet, and discovered she could see Mr. Bishop's reflection in the glass. His face was strong, with chiseled features, and his even, white teeth were a pleasing contrast to his bronzed skin. The set of his shoulders indicated a man of confidence. He smiled easily and was friendly, but there was also an unmistakable air of danger about him. Ann suddenly realized that Mr. Bishop was also looking at the window. Had he sensed her watching him? She placed her head against the back of the seat, and the image disappeared. How could she be attracted to such a man? After putting up with Edmund's abuse, she had

thought she would never want to look at a man again.
Yet just now, she had actually been staring at Mr.
Bishop. No, she couldn't call him that. She should
call him Nate. Men generally used another man's first
name.

The following morning, Nate sat with his head
back and his hat over his face, trying to catch up on
his sleep—or lack of. He had already ascertained that
the upper Pullman berths were definitely not con-
structed for a man his size. It was like trying to sleep
on a narrow plank. With his back to the wall, the
movement of the train had nearly caused him to fall
forward on several occasions. Turned the other way,
he was certain he would roll backward off the confounded thing.

Hearing the conductor announce that the train
would be stopping shortly for breakfast, Nate shoved
his hat to the back of his head and straightened up.

"Good morning," a sweet female voice acknowledged.

"Mornin'," he replied to the English lady.

After tying back the curtains, Hester and Ann took
their seats. Though Hester had managed to sound
cheerful, she wasn't yet fully awake. Ann made a
point of not even looking at Nate. She found him to
be entirely too unnerving. Instead of worrying about
his effect on her, she should be worrying about making it to Beau's before Hester had her baby. Still, it
would help if Nate would remain silent for the re-
mainder of their trip.

"I thought you might want to know that when a
train stops at stations for meals," Nate said, "you'll
only have a short time to eat."

Ann squeezed her eyes shut. She should have known her wish wouldn't be granted.

"Why?" Hester asked.

"It's a crooked deal, but there's nothing the passengers can do about it. You see, the cost of a meal is always collected first. On some trains, the conductor will have the passengers board the train the minute the food is placed in front of them. The plates are then collected and handed out again when the next train stops. The conductor gets his share of the take."

"You mean the meal is served over and over again?"

"Exactly. Of course that isn't always true, but it is a guaranteed fact that none of the food along the way is eatable. Nevertheless, to ensure time to eat, I suggest you exit the car as quickly as possible."

"We have managed quite nicely without your assistance," Ann admonished. As she had explained to Hester last night, they had to keep their distance from others. Though they had possibly escaped Matthew's watchdogs, they didn't need word getting out that an English couple had been traveling west and the woman was in a family way.

Twenty minutes later Nate and other more experienced travelers jumped from the train before the wheels even came to a grinding halt.

It wasn't until Nate had gulped down the last bite of food on his plate that Mr. and Mrs. Potter made a leisurely entrance into the eatery.

"All aboard!" the conductor yelled.

Obviously skinny Albert needed all the food he could manage, and in Hester's condition, she could use a meal, also. Nevertheless, Nate thoroughly enjoyed the shocked looked on the couple's faces when the conductor yelled "All aboard!" the second time. Nate considered it ample payment for their ignoring his earlier warning.

Nate went out the doorway, stepped up the steel stairs and into the Pullman car. From here on, the smartest thing he could do would be to keep his counsel to himself.

He took his seat, then watched the other passengers board the train. He wanted nothing more to do with the Potters. He didn't care for Albert's barbed tongue. He'd already felt its cutting edge twice. But it was Hester who bothered him the most. She brought back memories of another gentle, pregnant woman he'd known years ago. Memories he thought he'd long since suppressed.

With no more than a wink of an eye, his mind turned back time and Bright Moon's lovely face came to mind. He had married the Cheyenne princess and had lived with her honorably. Life had been good then.

Nate's eyes focused on the British couple returning to their seats. They seemed such a mismatched pair. Albert looked too young to be Hester's husband. His face was far too pretty for a man. Hell, he looked as if he should still be in a crib. His skin was as smooth as a baby's behind, and it was hard to believe it had ever seen the edge of a straight razor. And that ridiculous mustache Albert was sporting looked as if it were part bear. Did Albert honestly think others would believe it was real? While Albert was tall and lithe, Nate estimated Hester to be only about five feet tall. Other than her protruding stomach, she was quite petite and as cute as a button. She was friendly, Albert wasn't. They both had blond hair, though Albert's was almost silver and Hester's considerably darker. Albert walked with a superior air. Hester didn't walk. She waddled. Another thing. Hester seemed far more common folk than her husband did. Albert had the grinding mannerism of someone who thought himself superior to others.

Ann could feel Nathan Bishop watching as she and Hester moved down the aisle. Not just watching, but scrutinizing. Something she couldn't afford. How long would it take for him to realize she was not a he? She moved closer to Hester, who was leading the way, then leaned down so as not to be easily observed. "I shall not wait for you at the next stop, Hester," she stated firmly. Her mustache had prevented her from eating what little food she'd been able to snatch up. "You deliberately took your time before leaving the train, and we missed our meal."

Hester made no reply. Though on occasion she walked up and down the aisle, she was still uncomfortable and decidedly bored. Now she could add hunger to her growing list of complaints. Nevertheless, she had no intention of apologizing. The pleasure she derived from having Antoinette Huntington wait—then go without food—was as pleasing as eating candy.

Ann sighed dejectedly when Hester settled in her seat and asked Nathan, "Do you travel often?" Last night's talk about protecting themselves had apparently gone in one ear and out the other.

"No," Nate replied reluctantly. He'd deliberately not spoken to her.

As the train stopped at seemingly every small town stretched along the railroad track, Ann kept a constant vigil. She wanted to see who left and who entered their car. Though it was doubtful Matthew would have men searching moving trains, Ann knew she couldn't afford to let her guard down again. She couldn't understand why Hester never showed any concern for their safety. The only thing Hester cared about was hanging on to every word Nate said. Not that Ann could honestly fault that. *She* certainly hadn't failed to notice him, nor had she missed the way his broad shoulders filled out the white leather jacket.

Looking out the window, Ann's full lips suddenly spread into a wide grin. A freckled-faced boy on a bareback horse was racing across a field, trying to beat the train. His face was lit up with joy and excitement. Ann found herself rooting for him. But the contest didn't last long. The young lad finally pulled back on the reins and waved as the train passed him by. Would Richard be able to enjoy such simple pleasures? She hoped so.

Ann sighed. She had never so much as hinted to Hester about her part in Edmund's death. But during the past months, she had spent countless hours deliberating over who had killed the duke. How wise her father had been to send her to Captain Cuthwell's lodgings and now to her cousin. No one had to tell her that Matthew was still searching for her. She and Richard would be in constant danger until they arrived in Arizona Territory and were ensconced in Beau's home.

At noon, Ann and Hester stood with the others, ready to hop off the metal stairs the minute the train came to a complete stop. They only managed to eat a small portion of their food before having to board again. Each was determined to be first in line come supper time.

Chapter Four

Hearing a grunt, Nate jerked his head up, causing his hat to fall to the floor. A quick glance assured him that Hester was only shifting about in her seat, attempting to get comfortable. The way he was acting, one would think she carried his child. But then again, it could be because she seemed so tiny and helpless. Feeling like a damn fool, he reached down and snatched up his hat.

"I'm sorry," Hester said softly. "I didn't mean to disturb you."

"I was only resting my eyes." He gave her an appreciative smile. "I'm not much good at sitting about doing nothing."

"That must be why you persist in talking to my wife." Ann regretted the words as soon as they left her lips. She had no reason to snap at him. She was tempted to retract what she had said, until Nate's cold eyes settled on her. No matter how strongly she felt his masculine appeal, she would not allow him to intimidate her. Her eyes locked with his in a silent battle.

"She needs to talk to someone," Nate said. "You're certainly not offering any conversation."

Ann's mood was already at a low ebb, and the man's cutting words didn't help raise it.

"Mr. Bishop, need I remind you that Hester is *my* wife?" Ann laced her fingers together. "You'd do better to watch for an Indian attack than pay attention to Hester. I'll have you know there are savages everywhere."

"Is that so?"

Nate's broad grin started Ann's heart hammering against her ribs. Why did he have this strange effect on her?

"I didn't realize you were an authority on such matters."

Ann raised her chin a notch. "When traveling, I always make sure I know what to expect from my surroundings."

Hester had to fight to contain her laughter. Her Grace knew nothing.

"I will protect my family," Ann continued. "You, Mr. Bishop, will have to take care of yourself."

"Just how do you plan to protect yourself and your lady?" Nate asked, refusing to let the matter drop. "I see no gun. Or maybe you plan to use fisticuffs." The thought of Albert raising his soft fists in defense made Nate chortle.

Ann's ire had been plucked. She refused to let him have the last word. "I've had enough of your insults," she stated haughtily. "Hester, change places with me. Mr. Bishop can find someone else to talk to."

"But, Albert—"

"Obey me, Hester, and please sit by the window," Ann stated quietly but firmly.

The muscles in Nate's jaw flexed as he settled his gaze elsewhere. He would *not* get involved in this test of wills.

"Sitting next to the window nauseates me," Hester whined.

Ann cleared her throat. "Oh. Well…" She was completely disconcerted. She crossed her legs. She needed to relieve herself and she wasn't going to be able to delay much longer. It was bad enough that a woman of her station had been forced to wear men's clothing. Having to use their closet was absolutely demoralizing.

Later, when Hester was certain Her Grace's temper had calmed, she said sweetly to her husband, "Dearest, Nate knows where Arizona is located." She looked at Nate. "Perhaps he would be willing to escort us there."

Ann gasped. How could Hester suggest such a thing? That would be tantamount to posting a public notice declaring Hester as Richard's mother! "We can discuss it later."

Hester gave a brief nod before returning her attention to Nate. "She's…I mean he's thinking about it."

Ann looked out the window with unseeing eyes. Perhaps she had initiated the confrontation with her comment, but knowing that still did nothing to calm her anger. And who was he to say she never talked to Hester, when Hester was always talking to him! And who was he to speak of a wrongdoing? One minute he had been passionately kissing the woman he loved at the train depot, then he'd turned right around and flirted with a very expectant Hester!

Ann thought of a ball that she had attended a year ago. She had overheard two widows discussing how some men especially enjoyed sex with pregnant women. At the time, she had found the conversation disgusting and had moved. She looked at Nate and sneered. He was no different than other men when it came to leaving one woman's arms and immediately seeking the love of another.

Ann closed her eyes. Her marriage had made her callous, but that didn't change the fact that Nate was in the wrong.

To say she and Edmund made love would be a complete misuse of words. When they were first married, he delighted in hearing her screams as he forced himself on her. It hadn't taken long to realize silence was her best defense. Finally, ignoring the repercussion of what would happen when he discovered she was lying, she had made up the daring story about being pregnant. For some reason the ploy had worked. Edmund had stayed away from her bed. Until the night before his death.

Ann's hands curled into fists. As clearly as if it was happening again, she could see him suddenly appearing in her room, devoid of clothes, his face twisted in viciousness. Her throat had filled with bile, and she had wanted to die. There had been no boundaries of degradation that Edmund didn't try to satisfy his vile lust. That night had been the worst.

Had she really been pregnant, there was little doubt she would have lost the child. Maybe that was what he had wanted. It was likely that he had long since made her incapable of bearing children.

But Matthew was pursuing her. Would it never end?

* * *

After an hour of sitting and watching people getting on and off the train, Ann had developed another throbbing headache. As she rubbed her temples, it occurred to her that Hester had fallen asleep. Ann wished she could rest as peacefully.

The porter had said there would be a fifteen-minute delay at the next stop. That would give her plenty of time to take a walk and work out the stiffness in her legs.

When the train finally made its stop, Ann immediately stepped into the aisle. After a quick glance to assure her she hadn't disturbed Hester, she eagerly hurried to the exit.

As soon as Ann was far enough away from the train, she inhaled deeply. The soft breeze and fresh air immediately lessened the throbbing in her head. She tugged at her fob, then checked her pocket watch to be sure she returned on time.

Ann hadn't walked far before again finding herself facing a broad chest. She backed away. His closeness made her dizzy. "Are you deliberately blocking my path?" she queried. She was tall for a woman, but next to Nate she felt quite small.

"I guess you could say that. I want to know what your problem is."

"I don't know what you're talking about," Ann said irritably.

"Then let me be more specific. You don't know a thing about me, yet when you speak, you deliberately cut me down. I want to know why."

Ann squared her shoulders and stood as tall as her frame would allow. "Very well." She had taken all she could from the man. "I believe you to be an opportunist. A ne'er-do-well. Something neither I, nor my wife, have need of. I strongly advise you to find another place to sit."

Nate pulled a cheroot from his vest pocket and bit off the square end. "And just how did you arrive at such a conclusion?"

"I saw you at the train depot with a woman, acting quite despicably in public. Then, the minute you were seated in the Pullman, you started flirting with my wife. You are a womanizer, sir."

"Flirting?" Nate chuckled. "I thought I was just being friendly."

Ann considered the possibility that he was telling the truth, then immediately tossed the thought away. She could not afford to patronize anyone who knew Richard's true birthright. This was a perfect opportunity to be rid of Nate once and for all. "I don't believe you. I think it advisable that you move to another car."

Nate cocked an eyebrow. "Had you at any time asked nicely, I would have been more than happy to oblige. Except there is only one sleeping coach, and the only empty seat is the one next to me."

Ann watched him strike a match with his thumbnail then hold it to the end of his cigar. She started to go around him, but he stepped in front of her, again blocking her route.

"Oh, no," Nate warned. "You've had your say, and if you're finished, it's my turn. There is no way in hell that I'm going to move, so you might as well relax and listen."

Ann looked up into black eyes that were daring her to try something. "Very well. I've come to realize

that any words we exchange are simply an unneces-
sary waste of my time. If I must, I can tolerate you
until Davers—''

''Denver.''

''Exactly.''

A deep laugh bellowed from Nate's chest.

''May I ask what you find so funny?''

''You, Albert. I'm laughing at you.'' The humor
disappeared from Nate's face. He took several puffs
of his expensive cigar then slowly blew out the
smoke. ''I've met a lot of men just like you. Cowards
who try to intimidate others with threats.''

''I will not stand here and allow you to speak to
me in such a manner!'' Ann tried to push by him.
Instead, she was shoved backward and had to do some
fast footwork to keep from falling.

''I said it was my turn to talk. I'm going to give
you some advice, though I doubt you'll heed what
I'm about to say. Don't try threats out west. I'd hate
to see a nice lady like Hester end up in the middle of
nowhere, widowed, penniless and having to raise a
child. And one other thing. Nice, sweet words don't
cost a thing, and you'd have a lot less trouble with
your woman if you used them.''

''Are you married?'' Ann was fuming.

''Nope.''

''Then don't go around trying to act the authori-
tarian on a subject you know nothing about.''

Nate blew two perfect smoke rings and said, ''I am,
however, a bit of an authority on women, Mr. Potter.
I doubt that you could make the same statement.'' He
turned and walked away, wanting to kick himself. He
had always made it a practice to mind his own business, so why did he continue to ignore his own good

advice? It all centered on Albert. He was like a chigger that gets under the skin, itches like hell and is impossible to get rid of.

Ann continued her walk. Oh, how she would have loved to put a fist in his stomach. An authority, indeed. He hadn't even recognized her as being a woman. Ann suddenly wondered how he would have treated her if he knew she was a female. Would he smile at her the way he smiled at Hester?

By the time Ann was headed back to her car, she had come to accept that Nathan Bishop had every right to feel angered by Albert's sharp tongue. Nor had she any right to be angry with him. He had done nothing but show concern for Hester, a gentlemanly quality that Ann could not fault. And it was Hester who persisted in conversing with him. How could Hester not see the possible ramifications of her actions? At the first opportunity she'd have another private talk with the abigail.

"All aboard!"

Without thinking, Ann reached out for the conductor to help her up the steps. It was the look on the older man's face that made Ann realize her reaction had been that of a woman. She quickly glanced about to be sure Nate Bishop hadn't seen her faux pas. Fortunately, he was nowhere in sight.

As Ann walked down the aisle, she could see Nate and Hester were already conversing. And to Ann's shock, Hester reached across the aisle and caressed his broad shoulder. The turn of the maid's head as she glanced out the corner of her eye and just the right flutter of lashes made her intentions quite clear. Even in her condition, she was blatantly flirting.

Ann continued forward, unexpected anger tearing

through her like a cleaver. Were these the same tactics Hester had used to get herself with child? Ann wondered bitterly.

Positioning herself between Hester and Nate, Ann looked at Hester. ''How could you dare forget yourself?'' she said through clenched teeth. ''Now move next to the window.''

This time there were no arguments. Hester obediently changed seats. She knew exactly what Ann was angry about.

Hearing Albert's angry command, Nate had to curl his fists and force himself not to bound from his seat and attack the yellow-bellied coward. He wanted to tell Hester she could sit by him. He wanted to give Albert a taste of how it felt to be struck. He wanted to break the man's jaw! Unfortunately, none of what he wanted to do was going to change a thing. Still, he couldn't keep from grabbing Albert's coat sleeve and yanking him toward the aisle.

''If you ever talk like that again, or lay a heavy hand on Hester while I'm on this train,'' Nate said quietly, ''I guarantee that an Indian's or marauder's punishment will be welcome, because if I get to you first, you'll no longer be able to call yourself a man.''

Ann jerked her sleeve from his grasp, then looked straight ahead, determined to ignore the warning. How much harm could the man do? Her nerves were already stretched beyond their limits. Neither the anger nor the threats would have even taken place if Hester had kept to herself.

The rest of the afternoon passed in blessed silence. Ann tried taking a nap, but sleep evaded her. Seeing Hester flaunting her feminine wiles had disturbed Ann deeply. She knew that it had not only been Hester's uncalled-for gestures that had caused her fury to explode. Nate's acceptance of Hester's attention had also played a part in it. But Ann now realized there had been yet another reason. As disgusting as it was, she had experienced an unexpected case of jealous outrage.

In truth, when Edmund was alive, she hadn't cared whom he slept with. She had actually been grateful to anyone who kept him from her bed. But when he had dared to seduce her personal maid, Ann had felt betrayed. She had begun to think of Hester as a friend.

It was nearly one in the morning when Ann jerked straight up, striking her head painfully on the top of the sleeper. What had awakened her? Had she heard Hester groan? With little room to maneuver, she scooted around until she could lean over and peek inside the curtain at the bed below. "Are you all right?" she whispered worriedly.

"The child is coming," Hester groaned.

"No, no!" Ann insisted. "There isn't a midwife. Can't you make it wait?"

Hester grimaced at the duchess. "It's not something I have control over." Her face twisted in anguish as she was besieged by another pain.

Ann scrambled to get her robe over her nightshirt. Again she heard a loud groan from below. What was she to do?

She nearly fell from the berth when Hester released a bloodcurdling scream. Somehow Ann managed to grab the ladder and swing her bare feet onto the wooden rungs. Passengers already had their heads poked outside their curtains, either curious or angry at being disturbed.

"Hester…my wife is having a baby," Ann called frantically. "Is there someone who can help?"

Another scream. Ann yanked the curtain back, terrified that she'd find Hester dead. Instead, Hester's eyes were wide-open. Beads of perspiration covered her face and damp tendrils of hair clung to her cheeks. But it was the blood on the bedclothes that proved to be Ann's undoing. Hester was bleeding to death! Ann immediately looked away. Grasping the ladder was the only thing that kept her from swooning.

Nate had heard the quiver in Albert's voice when he pleaded for help. So far, the lanky Englishman hadn't received a reply. Having heard Hester's first groans, Nate had already accepted the inevitable. There was a good reason for a man to keep his britches on when traveling. He never knew what would take him from his bed. For instance, he had thought to be rid of the Potters by getting off in Chicago, then catching a later train. Unfortunately, Hester's time had come too soon. They weren't due to arrive in Chicago until nine-twenty in the morning.

Nate felt his hands shaking. The last child he'd brought into the world had been stillborn.

Nate climbed down from his bed and joined the useless husband.

He shoved the pale-faced man aside and pulled the curtain back to have a look at Hester. She grabbed his hand and squeezed as another pain racked her body. Nope, Hester wasn't going to wait until Chicago to have her baby.

"Albert, make yourself useful and tear up those sheets on your bed," Nate ordered. "And get the porter to bring water, scissors and whiskey."

"Whiskey? What are you going to do?" Ann wrung her hands. "This is no time for imbibing!"

Nate tried to pull forth some sort of sympathy for Albert's nervousness. None was forthcoming. "I'm going to make you a father, though I pity the child. The whiskey is for cleaning. By the way, shaving off that mustache was the smartest thing you've done."

Ann caught herself before she reached up to feel. In her haste, she had forgotten to glue the hair on her lip. Now she was left with no choice but to leave it off.

Much to Nate's surprise, Albert insisted on helping deliver Hester's baby. But he proved to be more in the way than helpful, so Nate told him to just stay by Hester's side. Most of the time Albert's eyes remained squeezed shut. Nate finally told him to go to the saloon car and get drunk. Albert flatly refused, but made a point of staying out of Nate's way.

Though she didn't show it, Ann was weeping for poor Hester. She knew she should be the one to offer soothing, encouraging words...not Nate. She had never seen a woman in labor, nor had she witnessed the pain involved. Why couldn't men be the ones to have the babies? If they enjoyed their pleasure, they should be forced to share the labor.

Nate's laughter caught Ann by surprise.

"That's it, sweetheart," he said to Hester. "Push harder. I can see the head. Come here, Albert, and see your child being born. You can even cut the cord."

Envisioning all sort of horrors, Ann threw her hand over her mouth and rushed to the door at the end of the car. She managed to swing it open just in time to keep from retching all over the pulled curtains.

By the time Ann collapsed onto the grating between cars, she had lost what little she'd eaten that day. She procured a handkerchief from the pocket of her robe and wiped her mouth.

"You have a big healthy boy," Nate said coldly.

Ann groaned and said weakly, "Thank you…for helping deliver the child. I'm certain, Mr. Bishop, that if you knew all the circumstances, you would feel more lenient toward me."

"I doubt that." Nate went back inside the car, snatched up the bottle of whiskey and walked away. The no-account wasn't worth roughed-up knuckles, Nate told himself. To hell with him. Nate had just delivered a boy child. He was due a celebration.

After Nate had walked away, Ann stood in the space between cars, feeling much better. She raked her short hair back with her fingers. When Nate had left his bed to help Hester deliver Richard, he hadn't bothered to comb his thick hair. It had been in a wonderfully roguish disarray and the opening of his shirt had revealed dark chest hair.

Ann suddenly felt a need to be held…to have her insecurities soothed away. She wouldn't have minded if that someone had been Nate. Tonight, he had earned her respect, something she gave to few men.

Chapter Five

Ann sat in the seat next to Nate, wondering at the pleasant odor emanating from his hide coat. Or maybe it was from the man himself…or both. The smell was a combination of dried earth and sun, with subtle hints of wildflowers.

She crossed, then uncrossed her legs. A bad habit she seemed to have acquired since donning men's trousers. Wildflowers, indeed.

She leaned forward and looked past Nate at the drawn curtains across the aisle. Hester and child were still sleeping peacefully. Ann settled back in her seat. She could hardly wait to hold her son in her arms.

A moment later, she caught herself twiddling her thumbs. Nate hadn't spoken to her since he'd marched off with the whiskey bottle last night. She would have said something to him if she could have thought of something to say.

Though they weren't touching, Ann could clearly feel his body heat. The same heat she'd felt in the dreams she'd been having lately. Nate would either be holding her hand, whispering sweet nothings or just staring at her, his black eyes full of hungry passion. It was those dreams that now made her want to lean against him and draw in his strength.

Ann unthinkingly crossed her legs again. There were plenty of things to think about besides Nathan Bishop. She glanced at the closed curtain once more. Why would a woman be willing to go through such pain to have a baby? Not that women had a choice. No wonder there were wet nurses, nannies and such. At least she would never have to go through such an ordeal. She had Richard.

Earlier, she had asked Hester if they should depart the train at the next stop and remain in a hotel for a week or so of rest. Hester had quickly reminded her that money was growing short and, to guarantee their safety, they needed to get to Beau's place as quickly as possible. Ann had considered Hester's sacrifice to be the very epitome of bravery. Never, never again would she question Hester's loyalty and goodness. A horrible thought suddenly entered Ann's mind. Now that Hester had held Richard in her arms, would she decide to keep him as her own?

"I take it you will be getting off the train?"

Ann raised a smooth brow. Had Nate read her thoughts? "Hester has assured me that she can get all the rest she needs on the train," she replied, welcoming the conversation.

Nate nodded. "She may be little, but she's strong."

"Yes, she is," Ann agreed. "Why were you in New York?" Ann asked, in a hopefully friendlier tone. Why hadn't she thought to ask the question sooner? "Is that your home?"

"A relative passed away," Nate said. "Have you picked a name for the boy?"

Albert's sudden, radiant smile startled Nate. He had been caught completely off guard.

"Indeed, I have," Ann spouted joyfully. "Richard. Taken from Richard the Lionheart. Richard Edmund Huntington. You, sir, should be proud."

Nate fidgeted. He was having serious problems with Albert's smile. It had completely transformed the man's face. Nate even found himself avoiding looking at the Englishman. Were Albert a woman, Nate would have described her as a fetching beauty.

"You helped deliver the future duke of Gravenworth."

How come Albert had said Richard Huntington instead of Richard Potter? Nate wondered. Getting the answer from Hester would undoubtedly be a lot easier than getting it from Albert. "I know nothing of titles," he commented, just to say something. He edged his body more toward the aisle.

Ann was shocked. "You know nothing of titles?" She had found a perfect topic of conversation. "How could you not be knowledgeable about something so important?"

"Important to whom?" Nate replied offhandedly. "We don't have titles in America."

"That's what is wrong with your country," Ann stated honestly.

Nate shoved his hat back. He was getting angry. Mostly because of his reaction to Albert's looks, but also because every time they got in a conversation, the confounded man made his blood boil. "I didn't know there was *anything* wrong with this country."

For his own good, Ann decided she should enlighten the gentleman. "Had America remained under English domain, you would have discovered the many benefits. As duchess...'' Ann bit the inside of her cheek. How could she have made such a slip? She had already said too much by giving the boy's proper name. ''Tenants are taken care of.''

''Tenants? I own my own land, sir, as do others. We fought to become a free people and we do not answer to some lord who holds court over us.'' He still refused to look at Albert. ''I don't know what you're so proud of. I met a gentleman from England once, and he couldn't stop praising our vast, open land. He often spoke of the filth and poor in your country.''

His bitter, uncalled-for words stirred Ann's ire. She had been trying to be informative. ''Your friend makes it sound as if all of England is like that. It's not. Your acquaintance obviously liked being around rabble.'' She suddenly realized others in the coach were turning and staring at her. She lowered her voice. ''How else could he be so ill informed,'' she stated in a quiet tone of voice. ''I no longer wish to discuss the matter.''

Nate finally turned and stared at the uppity Englishman, then immediately turned away. Albert's eyes were the deepest green he had ever seen. ''You certainly do have a tendency toward one-sided conversations. But we're not in England and I'm not going to be dismissed. The man I spoke of is from nobility and had been here on a hunting expedition. He is more than qualified to make comparisons.''

''I doubt that your friend was nobility or knew anything about England. He undoubtedly enjoyed listening to himself talk. And how can you sit there and insinuate your country is devoid of the poor? What about the Irish? They are treated as slaves. And what have you done with your Indians? They receive more respect in England than they do here. Why…you don't even have wet nurses!''

Nate stared blankly at Albert. What did wet nurses have to do with anything? It was impossible to follow the man's logic. Albert looked away, undoubtedly dismissing Nate from his mind.

Nate clamped his mouth shut and ignored the festered pimple seated beside him. Last night he would have gotten drunk if he hadn't run out of liquor. Actually, he would have enjoyed having someone to celebrate with. The successful delivery of Hester's child had been a monumental moment for him.

Nate deliberately moved his thoughts to the past. It had been more than ten years since he'd delivered his own son. Some of the memories were faded now. He could no longer visualize running through the forest, searching for his wife, nor could he picture in his mind's eye the bloody trail he had followed. But seeing her by the river, half-conscious and trying to give birth to their child was a sight that would be etched in his mind forever. He had tried to help, but he had lost them both. Fortunately, time did heal. Age also had a way of making a man look at things differently. He no longer blamed himself for what had happened, nor did he lie awake at nights cursing his fate.

Nate smiled inwardly.

This time everything had gone right. For him it was something like redemption. Richard's healthy cry had been the most beautiful sound he had heard in many years.

For the next two days, it seemed that everyone on the train managed to find their way to their car, offering congratulations to the parents. Any hope of keeping herself and Hester secluded had been solidly dashed.

Ann couldn't believe how quickly Hester recovered from her ordeal. The abigail's mood was especially bright, and she gave no indication of how she had suffered. Hester had even said the labor had been brief and there were no aftereffects. Ann cringed at the thought of what a long labor would be like.

She leaned her back against the comfortable seat and permitted herself to wallow in the pleasure of having a son. He was so perfect, even down to his tiny toes. All of her hopes and prayers had been answered. Edmund's son would take his rightful place as the duke of Gravenworth. He even looked like his father, whose handsome facial features had been a perfect cover for his cruelty. But as much as Ann had looked forward to cradling the tyke in her arms, she couldn't bring herself to do it. He was so very small. She was afraid she might do something to harm him. What if she held him wrong and broke something? Surely when he grew bigger she wouldn't be so hesitant.

As for Hester, she had resumed her giggling, leaning closer and reaching across the aisle to touch the man who had claimed to know women. Nate wasn't even aware that Hester was making a fool of him just to satisfy her vanity.

Ann raised her hand to cover a yawn. She wasn't getting much sleep at night. The mattress was too hard and the space too narrow.

She turned her head and looked at Nate. What would it feel like to touch him? What would it feel like to have him touch her? Last night she had dreamed they were copulating. She had awaked covered with perspiration and her unfulfilled passion still painfully alive. Wonderful pleasure had washed over her and she...

Ann felt her passion rising. Embarrassed, she glanced around to see if anyone had notice her flushed cheeks. No. She raised the book of Tennyson poems from her lap. How could she dream about passion when she had never experienced it before? And why? After Edmund, she had sworn never to let a man touch her again. She opened her book and pretended to read.

Nate's curiosity had been eating at him as to why Albert had called his son Richard Huntington instead of Richard Potter. Now seemed the perfect time to find out the answer. Albert might not give information freely, but Hester was an entirely different matter.

"Albert told me your son is a duke," Nate said casually.

Hester was shocked that the duchess had revealed such. "Ah...yes."

"Does that mean you're a duchess?"

"Well, I...yes." Hester knew her supposed husband was glaring at her. She could feel the heat on her back. But she had suddenly realized that she had been given the perfect opportunity to launch her plan. "In truth, I am Antoinette Huntington, the duchess of Gravenworth." Though it hurt, she ignored her mistress's pinch. She had just taken the first step toward switching places with the duchess. "Friends and family call me Ann."

Nate smiled. If Hester was a duchess, Albert had to be a duke. That could possibly account for his prissiness and lack of muscle. That was a big assumption since he'd never known a duke. "Where did the name Hester come from?"

Hester leaned toward the handsome man and whispered, "I didn't want anyone to know my real identity so I took the name of a servant. I had heard so many tales about your country, I feared for my well-being."

Nate thought a moment. "I would say you have every right to feel that way, sweetheart. Do you mind if I call you Ann?"

"Yes!" Hester heard the duchess mutter.

"No," Hester replied, a bit breathy from her sudden excitement at having received such an endearment from Nate.

"Why are you headed west?" Nate asked.

"For a stay at my cousin's estate in Arizona."

"Arizona is a big territory, with Indians and hot desert from Santa Fe to where you're headed. If I were you, I'd convince Albert to find a good guide who can supply plenty of protection before taking you into the wilds."

The baby started fussing and Hester had to attend to his feeding. Nate's words of warning frightened her. As the baby suckled, Hester considered the advantages of getting Nate to take them to Arizona. He seemed to be the only one who knew where it was. And there could also be other benefits. At Beau's ranch, Nate would testify that she was the real duchess and Richard's mother. Milady would declare it was all lies, but who would believe her? The plan was foolproof.

Though it apparently hadn't bothered Hester, Ann had placed a cloth over Hester's breast so others could not observe the nursing. At least Nate had the courtesy to leave the Pullman. He had probably headed for the saloon car.

"Hester, whatever possessed you to tell Nate you are the duchess of Gravenworth?" Ann asked worriedly.

Hester looked shocked. "I had no choice. After you told him Richard's name, I had to be titled."

"You're right. I'm to blame. Well, it doesn't matter, I guess. We'll never see him again once we reach Colorado." Ann looked at the precious baby. She could no longer put off the question that had been tormenting her these past few days. "Hester, you haven't changed your mind about me raising Richard, have you?"

For now, Hester still needed the duchess. She raised her hand to her mouth in mock shock. "Oh no, milady," she whimpered as she feigned humility. "How could you ask? You are the mother." She adjusted her nipple to the baby's tiny mouth. "I'm only the wet nurse."

Ann's concerns faded as quickly as melting ice. She had already come to realize that had Hester decided to keep Richard, she could never take him away. But though that dilemma had been settled, their plight was far from over. Watching who left and who entered the coach had become so automatic that half the time she didn't even realize she was doing it.

"Hester, please be careful about giving information to anyone else. We won't be safe until we reach Beau."

"I fully understand your concerns." Hester smiled sweetly. "Richard is sleeping now. Would you care to hold your son?"

Ann smiled back.

With no further ado, Hester placed Richard in Ann's arms.

Seeing the warmth that had entered the duchess's green eyes, Hester knew she had made the right decision.

"He's so tiny," Ann whispered.

"You won't be awakening him. He is full and content." Hester stretched. It felt so good to no longer be pregnant. And, from all indications, it wasn't going to take long for her body to return to normal. She could hardly wait to welcome Nate to her bed.

"Your Grace, you look uncomfortable. Here, let me lay milord down." Hester placed the baby on the seat between them, making sure the small bundle had enough room. "He will make a splendid duke." She frowned. "Who is going to take care of us once we reach the village of Colorado?" she asked innocently.

Ann's eyes were still on the small, sleeping babe. His long, tiny fingers fascinated her. He was so perfect...so beautiful. "You sound as if you have someone in mind. Would that person happen to be Nate?"

"Please, just listen to what I have to say."

"Can Richard see?"

"Not yet." She hurried on before being told to keep her thoughts to herself. "Nate knows how to get to Arizona. He also warned me that it is a dangerous place. If you offered him money, perhaps he might be persuaded to accompany us. We would at least have a guide and a degree of protection. None of His Lordship's hirelings would be looking for such an entourage."

"Have you forgotten the danger in such a plan? We know nothing of the man. He could easily be lying to take what money I have. No, I won't even consider it. We've managed this far and we can manage the rest of the way.''

''But Nate said the territory is huge.'' Hester could see she was getting nowhere. She had, however, planted the seed of thought. Tonight she would tackle the subject again.

Ann couldn't seem to keep her hands off Richard. She placed him in the crook of her elbow and rocked him. Nate had said that Colorado was only halfway to the West Coast. Would finding Beau prove to be more of a problem than she had anticipated? The miles of never-ending land were beyond anything she had ever seen. None of it fit the descriptions she'd heard in England. Nor had she seen a single outlaw or an Indian riding a painted pony.

Thirty minutes later, Ann stood and placed Richard on her seat. Though she would have been quite content to hold her son for the rest of their journey, she had to use the gentleman's closet. She dearly resented no longer being able to squat and hide what she was doing beneath the folds of a full skirt as proper ladies did.

Ann expelled a sigh of relief when she discovered there wasn't a line of men waiting to use the closet. She stepped inside, but before she could close the door behind her, a hand reached out, bracing it open. Ann found herself face-to-face with Nate. She stared in disbelief as he folded his arms and leaned comfortably against the doorjamb.

''Leave here immediately,'' Ann demanded.

''Why? I want to talk to you about your trip to Arizona.''

''Anything you have to say can certainly wait. I want my privacy!'' She had to watch her temper. Was it her imagination, or did Nate seem to avoid looking at her?

Nate grinned. He was in just the right mood to give Albert a bad time. "Would you feel less emasculated if I turned my back? Perhaps you don't want your lack of manliness to be seen," he ribbed.

Ann stiffened. Did he know the truth? "What do you mean by that?"

Nate slowly shook his head. "I thought it was pretty obvious."

Ann's cheeks burned when she realized what he had alluded to. At least he still mistakenly took her to be a man. "Move out of my way. If you must, I shall let you go first. I will wait outside." She tried to move back out of the way, but Nate continued to block her path.

"That won't be necessary, Albert," Nate said with considerable disgust. With that, he backed out of the gentlemen's closet, shutting the door behind him.

Ann made sure it was locked. What other humiliations would she have to suffer before this trip was over?

"I'll meet you in the saloon car when you're finished," Nate called through the door. "Don't make me wait too long."

Ann could hear his chuckle fade away as she proceeded to unbutton her trousers. How could he cause her heart to race when they were always at odds with each other?

By the time Ann entered the saloon car, she had managed to regain her composure. Her eyes were immediately drawn to the virile man seated with a drink in his hand. Just looking at the way his clothes hugged his strong body made her knees weak. But from the look on his face, Ann knew she was about to have more problems. She decided to attack first this time. "I don't like threats," she stated when she joined him.

"Nor do I. Here." Nate handed Albert a partially filled glass. "It's whiskey. Maybe it'll put some hair on your chest, though I doubt it."

Ann thought to refuse but held her tongue. The sooner Nate said what was on his mind, the sooner she could leave. She raised the glass to her lips, but the smell of the brew caused her to lower her hand. She preferred good Irish whiskey.

Nate shook his head. "Albert, you're such a greenhorn it makes me almost embarrassed for you."

"I don't need the sarcasm. What was so important that you felt the need to converse with me?"

Nate curled his lip but somehow managed to contain his temper. "I made a decision."

"I am not the least interested in any of your decisions."

"Dammit, I seriously suggest you contain that mouth of yours!" Nate stood. The easiest way to handle the duke would be to avoid him. He took a deep breath and looked down at His Lordship, who had taken the same chair he'd just vacated. "I have grown quite fond of your wife—"

Ann leaped to her feet, only to be shoved back down.

Nate placed his hands on the arms of the chair and leaned down into the duke's face, his eyes boring into Albert's. "Not the way you think. And," he continued, "since I have agreed to be Richard's godfather—"

"You what?" Ann gasped. "No! I forbid it! I was

not consulted.'' Not until he suddenly stood did Ann realize she had been holding her breath. Why was he looking at her so strangely?

''Have you ever shaved?''

Ann's hand flew to her cheek. ''Oh...a...well, you see, I'm rather fortunate. I have never had many facial hairs. I hope we have an understanding about you being Richard's godfather. I have someone else picked out.''

''As I started to say, as Richard's godfather, I have decided to accompany you to Arizona.''

Ann tried to control her panic. How could this be happening? ''Listen to what I am telling you. You are not his godfather!''

''You no longer have any say in the matter.''

''Of course I have a say. I am his father. Besides, you would never find Cousin Beau's ranch.''

''Beau?'' Nate asked, startled. ''Beau Falkner?''

Ann groaned. ''You know him?'' she asked weakly.

''I doubt there's a man in Arizona Territory who hasn't heard of the man. New Mexico, as well. He's a mighty rich man.'' Nate frowned. ''Had I known your destination, I would have volunteered my assistance sooner.''

Nate had backed away and Ann seized the opportunity to stand. She felt as if she had been run over by a herd of stampeding cattle.

''We'll catch a train from Denver to Pueblo, then travel to Santa Fe by stage. From there—''

''You are not listening to me,'' Ann said desperately. ''Your company will not be needed.'' She eased away, ready to depart as quickly as possible.

Nate shook his head. ''I've made up my mind. Like

it or not, I am going to be your guide. But rest assured, Albert, I'll see that you reach Falkner's ranch quickly and with as few inconveniences as possible.'' Nate spun on his heels and left the saloon car.

Ann collapsed onto the chair, picked the glass back up and downed the contents. Something she should have done in front of Nate instead of listening to his barbs. The brew wasn't as strong as the Irish whiskey she drank to numb the pain of Edmund's blows.

Nate's words meant disaster. He'd tell everyone that he delivered *Hester's* son! She had to find a way to change his mind! After having already traveled so great a distance by train, even a fool could tell that getting to Arizona Territory wasn't going to be as easy as she had originally thought. Hopefully she could find help in Denver or Pueblo. She had to be rid of Nate once and for all.

The wheels continued to click away the miles, and passengers still arrived to see how the newborn was faring. In Ann's opinion, Nate acted more the proud father than she did. He often held Richard and wasn't the least shy about showing him off. Was he also planning to steal Hester from Albert? The nerve of the man!

Ann spent her time frantically trying to devise a plan that would rid her of her nemesis, should she have trouble locating another guide. So far, nothing short of murder had come to mind. A terrible waste indeed for such a ruggedly handsome man to die early in life. Why, he probably hadn't even reached thirty.

What nonsense! What difference did his age make? Richard's entire future was at stake. She had asked

Hester what had possessed her to make Nate Richard's godfather.

Hester had replied, "Since Nathan was kind enough to help deliver him, I thought it would be a nice way to express our gratitude."

Ann couldn't remain angry with Hester for what she had done. As usual, the act had been one of kindness. Hester had no way of knowing that Richard's safety would become Nate's obligation.

When Nate returned to his seat, Hester was still sleeping. Being asked to be Richard's godfather had had a strange effect on him. He found himself taking the responsibility seriously. He knew he had to make sure that the pup and his mother made it safely to their destination. He'd been headed to his land between Santa Fe and the Arizona Territory anyway, so a few more miles was of little consequence.

Nate thought of Beau Falkner. He'd heard a lot about Falkner's spread, and he was already looking forward to seeing the big ranch and meeting its owner.

Chapter Six

Colorado Territory

As the hired coach made its way toward the hotel where they would spend the night, Ann feasted on the view. Denver most assuredly was not the quaint village she had expected, nor did it look like New York. This was a raw, backward, growing city. Clapboard stores gave way to tall, impressive brick buildings. Fine carriages vied with old buckboards on busy streets. Ann paid special attention to the women's gowns, which were at least ten years out of fashion.

Ann was breathless from it all. She had actually stepped into the American frontier. The wilds. The untamed land that, until now, she had only heard of. It had been years since she'd felt such exhilaration.

"Tomorrow morning we'll catch the train to Pueblo," Nate informed the ladies. "The following day we'll leave by stagecoach for Santa Fe."

Ann looked down at the sleeping baby in her arms, then returned her attention to the marvelous parade passing before her.

To Ann's delight, the hotel proved to be a grand affair. After agreeing to meet Nate for supper, the women retired to the apartment to rest and refresh themselves.

The rooms seemed huge, though Ann knew they weren't nearly as large as her quarters at Gravenworth had been. Of course, it was all an illusion. After the ship, the small rooms in New York, then being cloistered in a train, anything would have appeared large.

Richard began to fuss. Ann smiled as she turned the child over to Hester. "He's gone a long time without food," she commented.

A quick inspection assured Ann that the furniture was of a good quality, polished and dust free. She then entered the first of the two bedrooms. She pulled back the coverlet and inspected for bugs. The linen was clean, crisp and devoid of pests. Even the feather mattress was fluffed to perfection.

With a wide smile and eyes glowing, Ann turned to Hester, who had followed her into the room. "At least for tonight, we're going to have real beds to sleep on."

"And bloomin' good it'll feel," Hester replied, not realizing her speech had slipped. Richard's fussing had become louder, but she paid scant attention. She was too busy gaping at everything. Never had she been in so grand a tavern.

"Aren't you going to feed Richard?" Ann asked.

Resenting the intrusion, Hester collapsed onto a deep red velvet chair. It took but a moment to open the front of her dress and expose a breast for the child to suckle. She would be glad to be rid of the brat when the time came.

"You know, Hester, if Nate goes with us, it will

be impossible to convince Beau and his family that I'm Richard's mother.'' Ann placed her top hat on the walnut chest of drawers. ''Thank heaven he isn't aware of the trouble he could cause.''

You haven't even begun to experience trouble, Hester thought bitterly.

''Hester, are you listening to me?''

Hester looked up. ''Yes. We must find a way to leave Nate behind.''

''Exactly. I have an idea.''

So have I, Hester mused. *Get out of my life!*

Ann sat on the bed and bounced up and down. Tonight there would be no gawking eyes. ''Tomorrow,'' she continued, ''when the train takes us to…''

''Pueblo.''

''Yes. Pueblo.'' Ann removed her coat and stretched. ''While we await the stagecoach, I want you to keep Nate occupied. You can get him into one of those incessant conversations you've been having. It will give me an opportunity to gather information and try to find someone who can take us from Santa Fe to Arizona. You shall then inform Mr. Bishop that he is no longer needed.''

''Hopefully you'll be successful.'' Hester assumed her practiced look of meekness. ''I know I'm to blame for the predicament we're in, but Nate is so handsome, friendly and considerate that I found myself immediately drawn to him.''

Ann rose from the bed. She knew exactly what Hester was talking about. She rubbed her temples. Her mounting concerns were taking their toll.

She moved to the window and looked down at the wide street below. The streets in London were narrow. Not so in Denver. ''Hester, sometimes I feel that you aren't concerned about our plight. Are you thinking about running away with Nate? If you are, please allow me to find a wet nurse first.''

Hester forced herself to remain calm. ''No, Your Grace. He hasn't even mentioned such a thing. If he had, I might be tempted.'' She smiled sweetly. ''I was only fooling. I would never do anything without letting you know first.''

Ann made no reply.

Though milady tried to hide it, Hester knew she had to be jealous. Nate was too beautiful of body and face for the duchess to not have noticed, and he made no secret of his dislike for her—Albert. Hester swallowed a giggle. Her Grace had to be boiling inside, knowing that such a man preferred the servant to a duchess.

Satiated, Richard's eyes closed and he quickly drifted off to sleep. Hester rearranged his blanket before laying him on her lap.

After an excellent supper and a filling breakfast, Ann found herself enjoying the train ride to Pueblo. According to the porter, it would be a short trip. She spent most of her time caring for Richard, or in thought. And she realized, with some relief, that when they reached Pueblo or Santa Fe, she wouldn't have to listen to Nate's sarcasm. But in all truthfulness, she would remember Nathan Bishop for a long time to come.

Ann crossed her legs and looked down at the child on the seat beside her. Did all babies sleep so much? Hester acted as if it were normal. But other than attending to the feeding, Hester spent little time with

Richard, a good sign that she had come to accept Ann as his mother.

How long should they remain in the colonies before returning to England? Should she wait until the boy was old enough to watch his hind side? But by then he would have made many attachments and wouldn't want to leave. On the other hand, traveling across the ocean with a tiny baby was entirely too risky. There were so many things to consider. Being a mother carried a multitude of responsibilities.

Antoinette sighed. Tomorrow they would travel in comfort. And the fine coach—or stagecoach as Nate called it—would surely stop at fine inns that offered the best of food. All of which should have made her happy. But for absolutely no sensible reason, she suddenly felt like bursting out in tears. This entire voyage had been harder on her than she had cared to admit, even to herself. She reached up and fingered the ends of her hair. How she wished she still had her long mane of silver.

Following the duchess's instructions, as soon as they debarked in Pueblo, Hester requested Nate walk with her to the nearby hotel. She excused her plea by stating she felt the need for fresh air.

Nate and Hester strolled away at a leisurely pace, enjoying the crisp air. After Hester's comment about never having seen such mountains, Nate was more than happy to provide information about the Rocky Mountains as well as the wildlife residing there.

"From the way you talk, Nate, I have a feeling you are very fond of the Colorado Territory. If that's so, why don't you live here?"

"I did once."

"Why did you leave?"

"That's a long story."

Hester placed her hand on Nate's arm, bringing him to a halt.

"I…" Hester took a deep breath. "Nate, you have been so good to us and I feel so…"

Seeing the concern on her face, Nate asked, "Is something wrong?"

"No. Well, not really. Oh, never mind. Let's continue on and you can tell me more about the shaggy white animals you call mountain goats."

"If there's something you want to say, just spit it out." He smiled.

Hester laughed nervously. "Let's sit under that tree over there."

As soon as they were settled and Richard lay comfortably on a clump of grass, Hester glanced over her shoulder to be certain the duchess wasn't already headed in their direction. Satisfied that there would be no intrusions, she looked sweetly at Nate then quickly away. A practiced movement that had always caught men's interest.

"As I had started to say, you have been ever so kind to us." She swished a ladybug from Richard's arm. "I don't know what would have happened to me when Richard arrived had you not been there. I could never thank you enough. It's because of your kindness that I feel I should be completely honest with you."

He gave her a lazy grin. "Oh, come, come. What could possibly be so serious."

"You're not making this any easier for me."

Nate plucked a piece of grass and stuck it between

his teeth. "Very well, I'll be serious. Now, what terrible secrets do you have to reveal?"

Hester glanced at the depot again. She had given a lot of thought about what she should tell Nate. She had decided on half-truths and half-lies. All lies never worked. "Albert is not my husband."

It took a moment for Nate to absorb what he had just heard. "What do you mean Albert is not your husband?"

His voice was low and quiet, and more deadly than if he had yelled. Hester's news had produced exactly the response she'd hoped for. "You, see…please, let me try again. This is very difficult for me." She pulled a handkerchief from the waistband of her skirt. "My husband was murdered at our hunting lodge by a poacher. Albert and I were the only witnesses to the crime." She bowed her head and raised her handkerchief to her nose. "Edmund, my husband, was a cruel man and I'm sorry to say the crime was justified. But that is another story." She brushed a tear from her eye. "Albert tried to stop the poacher, but he escaped. Everyone knew of Edmund's heavy hand where I was concerned, and Albert warned me that I might be the one accused of the crime if we didn't leave. At the time, what Albert said made perfect sense." She sniffled. "I was so confused. I had no one else to turn to."

"So Albert brought you to America."

"He assured me we would be safe. But Albert accidentally discovered my husband's cousin, Matthew, was searching for us and had paid men to keep an eye out. Albert insisted we leave New York and go to my cousin where I would be safe."

Hester looked up through heavy lashes. "In the beginning I was grateful. Albert had given up everything to bring me here. I thought he had truly saved my life. But when we reached New York, he began dropping comments about how he should be rewarded and that, after all, he was the only one who could prove my innocence. At first I agreed. I said that after the child was born, we would return to England and he would be justly rewarded. You see, by this time I was beginning to question the wisdom of so abrupt a departure. When he started mentioning marriage, I became truly worried.''

Hester lowered her head again. "Nate, I'm afraid I shall never reach Cousin Beau's ranch. I'm certain Albert plans to force me into a marriage somewhere along the way. I've tried to make him leave, but he only makes more threats.'' Hester waited for a reaction. "I'm helpless," she added. "I'm a mere woman with a baby to think of, and my money is low.'' His stony expression left her unsure as to what he was thinking. She certainly didn't expect the sudden burst of laughter.

"I don't see what's so funny," Hester stated indignantly. She reached out to snatch up Richard, but Nate's hand on her wrist prevented it.

"I'm sorry for laughing," Nate finally said. "It's just that it explains so much. I know now why Albert never acted like a husband. I hope he never—''

"Oh, no," Hester quickly assured him. She leaned forward and whispered, "I had hoped that you might have a…solution.''

Nate stood. "Your so-called husband is headed our way. You have nothing more to worry about. I'll take care of the matter.'' He took Hester's arm and helped her to her feet.

Hester was having a hard time hiding her elation. "While I have the chance, I want to thank you for any help you can provide," she whispered before picking up her son.

"The depot master said the luggage will be delivered to the stage office," Ann informed the pair. She had found out she would have to wait until Santa Fe to find someone to replace Nate. She looked at him briefly and realized she truly would miss him once he was gone. But it was best it ended this way. She was falling in love with a man who didn't even know she existed.

"I suggest the two of you continue on to the hotel," Nate said.

"And what about you?" Hester asked anxiously.

"I, my dear lady, will retire to the saloon."

"But—"

"You have nothing to fear. I have no intention of abandoning you." Nate turned and headed down the street. He'd started to feel some respect for Albert. He'd surmised that a man who bestowed so much attention on his son couldn't be all bad. Or at least that was what he had thought until hearing the duchess's story. Now he was curious to know if it was all an act.

Nate was ready for a good, stiff shot of whiskey. How had he managed to get involved in all this? It was hard to admit, but Albert had been right. He should have kept to himself.

Chapter Seven

Ann stared in disbelief at the coach they would be traveling in to Santa Fe. It bore little resemblance to the fine coaches in England. And the team of six were certainly not proud-stepping geldings. This vehicle was a two-seated affair lacking the soft leather comforts. Besides the people crammed inside the coach, there were others that would be riding on top. The entire affair was reminiscent of the milk wagons in England.

Ann turned to complain to Nate, but seeing his set jaw, she clamped her mouth shut. She didn't care to become involved in another argument. Obviously this was not going to be the pleasurable trip she had envisioned.

Nate helped Hester into the coach, then took the seat beside her. By the time Ann climbed in, she had been left with no choice but to take the seat by the window, across from Hester. She would have preferred sitting next to Nate.

By the second day of travel, Ann had discovered that a stagecoach driver paid no heed to menial things such as passenger comfort. The traveling was back-breaking and the roads primitive and bumpy. After fifteen hours and the forty miles they'd crossed yesterday, plus the sixty miles they were supposed to cover today, Ann was convinced death would be far more acceptable than being thrashed about by wheels that continually bounced over rock outcroppings.

Ann pulled the leather curtain back and looked at the sky. Supposedly the curtains were to help keep out dust, but the dirt the wheels churned up still managed to float through the open window. At least the low dark clouds were keeping the heat down today. Yesterday had been stifling.

She let the curtain fall back in place. Rain was imminent. She could smell it. The men riding on top were going to be drenched.

She looked across at Nate. "With all this bouncing about, I can't understand how the men on top keep from falling off," she commented.

Neither Nate nor anyone else made a reply. Ann looked away. Since departing Pueblo, she had caught Nate glaring at her on more than one occasion. Not the warm looks he gave Hester, but with eyes reminiscent of obsidian. What was the reason for his anger this time?

Hearing hoots and whistles, Ann raised the curtain again—as did everyone else. The stage was about to pass two covered wagons transporting women. Some were walking while others rode.

The men cheered and Ann was astounded when the women waved, made obscene gestures, flashed their boldly colored skirts and exposed bare legs.

"Light skirts," Ann thought aloud. She dropped the curtain just as the driver swung the stage off to the left, apparently trying not to leave the women in the wake of dust.

Every time Nate looked at the rail-thin critter across from Hester, it added to the slow boil that was barely hidden behind a thin sheet of human veneer. When he had learned what Albert had done to Hester, Nate's first reaction had been to just shoot him. Later he had concluded that it would be too merciful an ending. Since *Lord Albert* wanted to travel west, it only seemed fitting that he should see the *real* frontier.

"Must the driver persist on traveling at such a reckless speed?" Ann asked after another crushing blow to her side.

Nate's lips curved into a slow grin. "Perhaps you'd prefer walking."

Before Albert had a chance to guess what Nate was up to, Nate grabbed the Englishman by the arm while at the same time opening the stage door. One strong jerk sent Albert flying. Nate paid no attention to the passengers' astonished looks as he closed the door. It had been years since he'd felt such total satisfaction.

"A man fell out of the stage!" someone said from up top.

The driver pulled back on the reins. Nate stuck his head out the window. "Keep going," he yelled. "The gentleman felt a need for pleasure."

Everyone laughed as the horses quickly picked up their pace.

Hester giggled, unable to hide her burst of joy. "That was terribly cruel," she said with no conviction, "but I guess he did deserve his punishment."

As soon as she stopped rolling, Ann scrambled to her feet, screeching the entire time. Seeing the stage slow, she ran toward it—only to have it speed back up. She screamed at the top of her lungs, waved her fist, stomped on her hat now resting on the ground, and turned furious, frustrating circles. Finally she kicked the hat as hard as she could, then stood watching the stagecoach disappear into a cloud of dust.

"You no-account…miserable…snake. So help me, Nathan Bishop," she seethed, "you are not going to get away with stealing my wife and son!"

Ann looked at her clothes. One coat sleeve was barely hanging from the seam. She pulled it off and threw it.

"You…you bastard! To think that I gave you my admiration! I should have stuck to my first opinion of you."

Shoulders slumped and her breathing heavy, Ann started walking. "You're not worth—"

A clanking cowbell caught Ann's attention. She turned and stared in dismay at the "light skirts'" wagons headed directly toward her.

"Hello, sweetie," a well-rounded woman called as the first wagon came to a halt. "Ooh. He's so young."

"Need a ride, you gorgeous man?" another woman spoke up.

Ann had temporarily forgotten she had on men's clothing.

"You…you don't understand," Ann replied nervously. "I'm not—" The words stuck in her throat when a dark-skinned man rode from the far side of the wagon. She wanted to turn and run but her feet refused to move. The black braids hanging past his shoulders, his beaded headband and painted horse left no doubt that she had finally come face-to-face with an Indian.

Ann fainted dead away.

"I tell ya, there's nothin' there!" the redhead shrieked.

"How would you know about, Jezebel?" Agnes asked.

The older madam shoved her girls aside. "What's going on here?"

"Mae, Jezebel thinks this ain't no man." Agnes snickered. "She's so used to seein' men without clothes that she doesn't recognize one dressed."

The women riding in the wagons and the ones walking started running forward to see what was going on.

"Everyone back to where you were," the madam ordered. "I'll handle this." Mae shoved her henna-dyed hair from her face and stared down at the prone man. His clothes declared him to be a gentleman, but he did seem a bit too pretty for a man. "Agnes, unbutton his britches. We'll settle this right fast."

Just as the thin brunette leaned down, the stranger's eyes flew open. The strumpet quickly jumped away.

Ann glared back at the three painted women standing over her. However, it was the Indians seated on their horses less than ten feet away who made her bolt upright into a sitting position.

The obvious fear on the young man's face caused Mae to turn and see what he was staring at. Her throaty laugh made her full bosom shake. "You got no reason to fear them boys," she assured the gentleman. "I pay 'em to keep me and my girls safe."

"Stand up," Agnes crooned, already smitten with her find. "We're gonna let you ride in our wagon."

"I can walk to where I'm going." Nevertheless, Ann still didn't stand. No matter what reassurance the big woman had tried to give her, the men still frightened her.

"Walk?" Mae placed her beefy hands on her well-rounded hips. "How do you plan to do that? What about the Apache? And what would you do for water and food?"

"Why should I worry about...Apaches when I'm staring at three Indians!" She hated the quiver in her voice.

Mae shook her head. "Honey, Apaches *are* Injuns." Mae's harsh features relaxed. "These boys are good Injuns," she said kindly. "Why, Zachariah, the light one, is half Injun and half white. You come with us." She gave the young man a wink. "We'll take good care of you."

Gnawing at her bottom lip, Ann cautiously rose to her feet. She tried to hold back the fat tears that were already gathering, but it was futile. The clap of thunder wreaked the final blow. She plopped back down onto the ground and wailed uncontrollably, her heavy sobs racking her body.

Their mouths hanging open, Mae and the others stared in disbelief. They were oblivious to the light sprinkles of rain that had started to pepper the ground. None had ever seen a man cry in such a fashion.

Mae cleared her throat. "Mr.—"

"I'm no man," Ann sobbed. "Can't anyone see that I'm a woman?" She leaned her head down and bawled all the harder, the tears leaving streaks down her dirty face.

It was the drop of water landing on her nose that brought Mae to her senses. She looked at the sky. At any moment the ground and everything else was going to get soaked. "Everyone in the wagons!" she commanded.

Now that it had been established that the stranger wasn't a man, Mae knew exactly what to do. She had been handling temperamental women for nearly fifteen years and this one was no different. "Get up!" She grabbed the woman by the arm and snatched her to her feet. "I'll not be caught in a storm just because you're feeling sorry for yourself."

By the time Ann was in the wagon, her sobs had been reduced to sniffles. She sat on one of the benches that ran the length of the wagon and tried to ignore the staring women. Her behavior and obvious vulnerability embarrassed her. What could have possibly come over her?

The rain didn't last long, even though dark clouds still hovered overhead. Mae had not ordered the wagons to move on, so as soon as the rain stopped, the rest of the women either moved into the first wagon, or stuck their heads in the back opening. All wanted to hear why the woman with the strange accent had on a man's suit.

Ann noticed that even the three Indians and two drivers had strategically positioned themselves.

"All right," Mae said kindly. "What is this all about?"

Perhaps it was the anxiety on everyone's face, or maybe the concern in the big woman's voice, but Ann would never quite understand why she opened up to these women of pleasure. Nevertheless, for the first time, the words poured forth. She told of Edmund's death, she told of the trip, and she confessed all her worries, angers and doubts.

By the time Ann had finished, except for the men, there wasn't a dry eye in the place. Including Mae.

"We can't let that Nate get away with that!" one of the girls said. "He tried to kill her!"

The others joined in agreement.

"But what can we do?" another asked.

Mae looked at her Indian guards. What with the drivers, she didn't need more than two other men. But Zachariah, who had already been hired, had talked her into taking on two of his friends. She and Zach had known each other for years. He was not only a good lover, his winning smile and personality made it impossible to refuse him a thing. She looked back at Ann. "Do you know how to ride a horse?"

"Quite well."

"Mae's thought of something," someone whispered.

Everyone became silent as they waited in eager anticipation.

"Zachariah, I want you to help Ann catch up with that stage, then see that the man named Nate gets his just reward."

All eyes shifted to Zachariah.

Ann started to protest but decided to hold her tongue. She needed help and she had nowhere else to turn.

"Then what?" the man with gray eyes asked. "Kill him?"

"No, no," Ann protested. "I want revenge," she said bitterly, "but I do not want blood on my hands. He should be left stranded, the same as he left me.

And I want him to know that I'm a woman. I want him to know how blind he has been.''

There was a chorus of agreements.

''Then you and Hester can continue as planned,'' someone spoke up.

The women wanted to see Ann get her revenge. It was apparent to Ann that the ladies thought taking Zach was the ideal solution. Mae had even assured her several times that the Indians could be trusted. There was no choice. She had done everything in her power to secure Gravenworth and she couldn't give up now.

Ann straightened her back. ''I have money,'' she declared.

Zach's gaze settled on the questionable woman. ''Is that right?'' he drawled.

His whimsical smile was contagious. She would never have expected to see such perfect white teeth, nor had she realized just how handsome he was.

Zach asked, ''And does keeping me satisfied come with the deal?''

''No,'' Ann said sharply. ''The job offers no bed privileges.'' She looked at the other two men. ''Would either of you be interested in earning a considerable amount of money?''

Zach chuckled. ''Neither one speaks English.''

''Fine. Since you are obviously not man enough to handle the task, I shall do it myself.'' Hunched down, Ann made her way to the back of the wagon.

''You can't just leave,'' Agnes whined.

''Mae, you asked if I can ride. Can I assume you have a horse I can take.''

Mae nodded. She kept watching Zach out the corner of her eye. He still hadn't made his decision. "Zach, have Joe saddle Star."

Zach said something in a language Ann couldn't understand. But the minute he had finished, the Indian called Joe slipped away.

"And would you by chance have a rifle?" Ann asked.

Mae was impressed. "So you can also shoot?"

Ann nodded then climbed to the ground. This time she was steady on her feet. Mae followed, as did everyone else.

"Do you plan to stay in Santa Fe?" Ann asked as she brushed at the grime covering her clothes.

"Sure do," Mae answered. "Before long I hope to have enough money to open a gambling hall."

"I shall see that your horse is returned safely," Ann said, smiling.

Joe came from the other side of the wagon, leading a saddled mare. The sorrel filly was breathtaking. She had a beautiful head, flowing mane, and legs that were long and muscled. Though Ann had never ridden astride other than bareback, she couldn't foresee any problem. The other Indian handed her a rifle. A canteen had been slung over the pommel along with a hide bag filled with what she assumed was food.

Tears welled in Ann eyes. "Thank you, Mae, and all the rest of you for your concern. I only wish everyone could be as compassionate as you."

Ann swung up in the saddle. Joe quickly adjusted the stirrups. Choked with emotion, she could hardly speak. "Which direction should I go?" she managed to ask.

"Straight west," a driver called out. "You'll find a way station some fifty miles ahead."

Ann smiled, waved and then sank her heels into the mare's sides. It was going to take hard riding to catch up with the stage, and she would have to watch the pace she set for the mare. She had to be sure she didn't wear the mare down.

Ann had only traveled a mile or so when she heard someone approaching from behind. Somehow she wasn't surprised when she turned in the saddle and saw Zach headed toward her, his buckskin in a full gallop. She slowed the mare, waiting for Zach to catch up.

Zach brought his horse alongside the sorrel, a devil-may-care grin spread across his face.

"Want company?" he asked.

Ann smiled. "Only if you can get me to that stage."

The taste of revenge was sweet. Nathan Bishop hadn't escaped her yet.

Chapter Eight

◈◈◈◈◈

The stagecoach passengers were exhausted, Nate being no exception. The broken wheel that had needed repair, the extra miles they'd had to traverse due to the swollen streams, plus the persistent deluge of rain had played havoc on everyone. Because they had missed the way stations, they'd had to stop often to let the team rest. And when they were on the move, the horses were kept at a slow pace.

As dawn streaked the sky in hues of yellow and orange, Nate took a good look at the motley travelers. The wet stench of wool suits, body odors and loud snores added to his discomfort. The only one who had taken the constant delays without complaint was Richard. The tiny baby seemed totally unaffected by the hardships.

Nate tried moving his feet. Four of the men who had been traveling on top of the stage were now squashed inside. Hell, Nate silently complained, there isn't enough room for a man to think. Of course the realization that Albert had undoubtedly fared better than the rest of them didn't help Nate's already surly disposition.

The wheels struck another bump. Hester's hand curled over his. Her deep breathing told Nate she had somehow managed to fall asleep. With Richard secured by her arm, the duchess's head had slowly drooped to the side until it was now resting on Nate's shoulder. He chuckled gruffly. A woman had a way about her when she wanted a man, and Hester had made sure he hadn't missed any of her signals.

A few years ago he might have given more than a little thought to the advantages of a liaison with such a woman. She was attractive, nice and round. However, he wasn't interested. Not that he lived an exemplary life. Quite the contrary. But age had mellowed him somewhat, and easy conquests no longer had the same appeal as when he was younger. Unfortunately, time had not improved his lack of patience and he still had no qualms about killing a man if he deemed necessary.

Maybe he was more like his father than he had realized. More than one man had accused him of being cold. Yet baby Richard had somehow managed to slip past all that. The tadpole had touched his heart.

Nate thought about his own childhood. Affection had not been a part of his rearing. His mother was too busy being the wealthy socialite and his father used money to buy and rule others. Fed up with his father's cruelty and bitterness, he had run away from boarding school, knowing full well that his father would disinherit him. But at the young age of fourteen, wealth and a shipping empire had no appeal. The West, however, did. Stealing money from his father, he'd left home and had never looked back.

Until his father died of a heart attack.

Something the older man obviously hadn't expected. He hadn't taken time to change his will. To his mother's delight, she ended up a widow with a fortune to keep her from being lonely. When he had been living with the Indians, his mother had somehow managed to get word to him of his father's death. She had also said that it wouldn't be necessary for him to come home as his father had been cremated and she was moving to France. Martha Bishop wanted for nothing.

When his mother had suddenly become ill, she returned to New York. Knowing she could reach him through his uncle living in San Francisco, she had sent word that she wanted to see her son—a command that had surprised him since they had never been close.

Nevertheless, he had gone to New York. Though there was little if no love shared, the two had made their peace with each other before his mother passed away. It wasn't until she had been buried that he found out he had been left everything, including the huge mansion his father had built to show off his wealth. Nate smiled bitterly. He had left New York with instructions for the family lawyer to sell it.

The duchess moved her head to a more comfortable position. Nate looked at her for a thoughtful moment. Should he inform her that the man she was running from was waiting for her in Santa Fe?

Nate watched a devil wind whirling about some distance away. He had always enjoyed women's company, but perhaps because of his mother or his own experiences, he wasn't a man inclined to trust them. For instance, how did he know that the duchess's tale was nothing more than a pack of lies? If he was convinced of her innocence, he'd make sure Matthew Huntington left them alone.

The duchess suddenly sat up, almost toppling the baby from her arm. She had to make a quick grab to keep him from falling. She nestled him to her shoulder, murmuring sweet words. Nate grinned. Richard didn't release so much as a whimper.

"We should finally be reaching the way station in less than an hour," Nate said.

Ann's green eyes shone with evil delight. Finally she could see a way station in the distance. A man was hitching a fresh team of horses to the coach.

Ann and Zach rode down a deep grassy hill, and when they came up on the other side, the man had disappeared. Ann assumed he had joined the others inside.

Thanks to Zach, they had caught up with the no-account Nathan Bishop. He was about to discover what it felt like to be on the other end of a rifle. He was a wife-and-baby stealer, and he deserved a lot worse than he'd be getting.

Ann and Zach rode up in front of the log cabin, then dismounted. Ann removed her rifle from the scabbard. Zach drew his pistol.

"I'll cover your back," Zach said.

With an air of self-assuredness that surprised even Ann, she moved to the heavy wooden door and opened it. Her gaze immediately fell upon the pair seated at the long table, their backs turned. She leveled her rifle at the man wearing the white hide frock coat.

"You should have killed me, *Mr. Bishop.*"

The eating ceased as one passenger then another

looked up from their plates. It was the guilty look on
Hester's chalk-white face that suddenly planted a seed
of suspicion in Ann's head. Had the maid betrayed
her again? Nate, on the other hand, showed no sign
of surprise, fear or regret.

"Stand up," Ann ordered the big man. "You're
going to pay for what you did to me." She nodded
toward Zach, who was now standing by her side.
"My friend assures me he has a special treat just for
you."

Nate shoved his chair back and slowly rose.

Ann sneered at the man now standing straight and
tall. She would never forgive him for what he had
done to her. He wasn't any different than any other
man who used women. At one time she had thought
that perhaps...well, it didn't matter now.

"Ah..." Zach tried to say.

Ann waved a hand to silence him.

Again Zach tried to get her to listen to him. "I
need to speak to—"

"Hush! I have this man exactly where I want him,
and I intend to savor every moment."

Though Nate appeared calm, Ann clearly recognized the anger in the dark brown eyes glaring back
at her. Her gaze didn't waver. It occurred to her that
at some unknown point in time, she had shed her
rabbit's fur and had donned a wolf's cloak. She
wasn't afraid of Nate.

"Zach," Ann hissed, "escort the gentleman outside. But before you kill him," she added, just to put
fear in Nate, "find out why he chose to throw me
from the stagecoach." Her gaze shifted to Hester.

Hester transferred Richard to her left arm. It was
Her Grace's cold, unwavering countenance that

caused Hester to worry. Not a speck of mercy showed on milady's face. Had she guessed the truth? "No," Hester uttered. She couldn't allow all her well-laid plans to turn to dust. She was so close. "You can't kill him. He helped deliver Richard. Surely you can afford him a kindness."

Hester nervously twisted a stray strand of hair behind her ear. Even though she knew the gesture to be foolish, Hester glanced at the door, weighing the possibility of escape. Somehow she had to convince Ann that she was innocent of any wrongdoing.

"I'm so relieved to see you're unharmed." Hester's voice was shaky. Why hadn't she thought to show concern first? "I had nothing to do with any of this. I wanted to join you, but I couldn't. I had to protect Richard." She lowered her lashes so as not to appear brazen. "I'm so ashamed of myself. You were right all along. I should never have spoken to Nate." Hester knew her attempt at appearing sincere wasn't convincing.

Nate slowly turned and viewed the two-timing vixen. How many times had he said "A man should never turn his back on a woman. She'd stab him every time?" This was a perfect example. Not more than an hour ago, the duchess had been declaring her undying love for him.

"I'm trying to tell you," Zach persisted, "that this—"

Zach's mouth remained open, but no words were forthcoming. Ann's eyes became large green moons as Zach slumped to the floor. Only then did she see the arrow embedded in his shoulder. But where...

"Indian attack!" someone yelled.

Ann was torn between helping Zach and keeping

an eye on Nate. When Nate turned away, ignoring the rifle she still had pointed at him, she wanted to pull the trigger. Instead she fell to her knees. Placing the rifle on the floor beside her so it was within reach, she helped Zach sit up. Blood was oozing from around the shaft of the arrow. It reminded her of Edmund's death, yet her strength remained intact.

"What can I do to help?" she asked Zach. "Should I pull the arrow out?"

"No. Diablo will take care of it when he has time."

Ann sat back on her heels. "Diablo?"

"Nate and I used to ride together. That's what I kept trying to tell you."

Ann stared at the fallen man in disbelief. Of all the men, why had she been given one who knew Nate? Her misfortune was boundless.

"All the women huddle in the center of the room," Nate commanded as rifles and shotguns were being handed out.

"Join the women," Zach told Ann. "I'll be all right."

To Ann's amazement, Zach pulled himself to his feet. "Give me a gun," he called.

"But you're in no condition to do anything," Ann protested.

"We're going to need all the help we can get."

As Zach made his way to the other side of the room, tales of Indian massacres began racing through Ann's mind. At the moment, she could think of nothing more soothing than being clustered with the other women. But as she crawled on her knees toward Hester, she was suddenly jerked to her feet by a strong hand grasping the neck of her shirt.

"Where the hell do you think you're going?" Nate demanded.

"I—"

"You're nothing more than a yellow-livered coward from the bottom of your feet to the top of your head. Well, you'll not be running away this time. You're going to one of the gun portals and start shooting, or I swear to God, I'll gun you down myself!" He kicked her rifle to her.

Ann didn't think this was the right time to point out that she was a woman.

Nate drew a pistol from beneath his coat. Before he could point it, Ann snatched up her Winchester and scrambled to the nearest opening. Not until she peered out the gun slit did she fully realize the precariousness of their situation. Mounted, yelling Indians were circling the cabin, their faces grotesquely painted and their bows and guns raised in war.

Ann was certain every bone and muscle in her body had ceased to function. She wasn't even aware of raising her rifle, or shoving the barrel out the hole…until a yellow-faced warrior rode by, his rifle aimed directly at her. For a brief moment, their eyes met. Ann tasted fear. She pulled the trigger and watched the brave fall from his mount. She reached up and wiped the perspiration from her brow.

Everything happened so quickly that time became a blur. All Ann could think about was survival. Not just hers, but Richard's…yes, and Hester's, as well.

Ann pulled off a shot before stealing a glance at Hester and the baby. Ann was overcome with fury when Hester placed the child on the floor. But it was the look of open loathing on Hester's face as she scooted away that turned Ann's heart to ice. How could Hester hate a child she had birthed?

Ann was about to go to Richard when a bullet shattered the wood near her head. Nate had been right. If any of them were to survive, they had to defend their positions. The renegades had already absconded with the stagecoach horses and the coach was nothing more than a huge flame. As much as she wanted to cradle the crying infant, she knew she could not leave her station. At least for the moment, Richard was out of harm's way.

Hester frantically glanced about the room. The men who hadn't taken up arms were busily handing out shells, and the stationmaster's wife and daughter were now attending to wounds. Already two men were down with injuries. Why didn't they attend to her? How could they expect her to sit alone, waiting to be claimed by death?

A faint whistling sound caught Hester's attention. To her horror, a flaming arrow had landed only a foot away. Momentarily dazed, she sat staring at the quivering shaft and the flames licking at the plank floor.

Collecting her wits and disregarding her son, Hester quickly scooted away. To her relief, a man finally rushed over and stomped out the flames.

Another blazing arrow cleared an unattended slot, this time catching the corner of Hester's skirt. Frantically she glanced about for help. Everyone had his back turned. She tried to scream. Her throat was too dry.

Hester tugged desperately at the material with her clammy hands, attempting to free herself from the flaming hell. Her eyes blurred, and she could smell the stench of burning cloth. The moment her skirt came loose, she jumped to her feet. She had to find water! The flames! She had to kill the bloody flames!

Before anyone realized what she was about, Hester shoved back the bar bracing the door and, with unexpected strength, opened it.

The horse trough. She had to make it to the horse trough.

Her cheek pressed against the gun stock, Ann again pulled the trigger. She had no idea how many times she had shot, nor could she remember being handed bullets...or reloading.

Suddenly Ann lowered her weapon and stared in disbelief out the portal. ''No,'' she uttered as she watched Hester run into the open, fire licking at the bottom of her skirt.

Ann glanced in the other direction. The attackers now were closing the space and headed toward Hester, their bullets peppering the ground around her feet. Then, from seemingly nowhere, Nate appeared. Ann held her breath as he ran in a zigzag motion toward Hester. The moment he was close enough, he made a flying tackle. Knocking the panicked woman to the ground, he scooped up dirt and doused her with it, successfully smothering the flames. Scrambling to his feet, he hoisted Hester up in his arms and darted back toward the station. The Indians pushed their ponies, trying to cut off his escape.

Ann raised her rifle and began shooting at the pursuers, trying to give Nate enough time to reach safety. She didn't start breathing again until she heard the door slam shut and the bar shoved back into place.

''They have built a fire in back!'' a man yelled.

Ann turned and saw smoke seeping into the room from under the door. Others were already running in that direction. Was there no escape? Was this how they were to die?

"Albert!"

Ann turned and saw Nate headed toward her. There was a hole in his leather frock coat. When had he been shot? He didn't even appear to be aware of it.

Nate pulled up in front of Albert, who looked as if he were about to fall on his face. "If you ever wanted to be a hero, I'm about to give you your chance."

His stern voice prevented her from saying a kind word to the wounded man.

"You're the skinniest one of the lot, so you're going to have to be the one to save us all."

Ann already sensed she wasn't going to like his next words. To be a hero was the least of her desires. "I'm sure someone else—"

"There's a narrow tunnel leading to a corral of horses. The Sioux haven't got to them yet. You have to crawl through the tunnel, mount a horse and head due west to Fort Bennington. You'd better get the cavalry back here damn fast, 'cause if you don't, we'll all be dead."

Ann swallowed loudly as she followed him to the side wall. He stopped, leaned down and lifted a trap in the floor near the inside water pump. She wanted desperately to refuse. She wanted to make Nate get someone else, or at least someone who knew the location of the fort. She wanted to scream out that she was a woman who feared closed places. She wanted…she glanced toward Richard on the floor. He had cried himself to sleep.

As Ann crawled through the seemingly endless hole, her body became soaked with perspiration due to apprehension and lack of air. Had this been Nate's way of making her pay for pointing a gun at him? Her face was again covered with cobwebs. She quickly brushed them away. She wanted to go back, but there wasn't even enough room to turn around. And what was there to return to but certain death.

Ann was convinced that spiders and other creatures were crawling all over her face and hands. But the thought of Richard gave her the courage to push on and keep her wits intact. Somehow, some way, she had to make it to the fort.

Ann cautiously climbed out of the hole and lay on the ground, humbly thankful for the air she pulled into her lungs. Rolling onto her stomach, she hugged the ground and looked at the cabin down the hill being savaged by Indians. Under cover of bullets, the bald-headed man who had sat beside her in the stagecoach rushed out the back door and threw a bucket of water on the fire. Another man followed.

In the other direction, not five feet away, stood the corral with the horses nervously huddled in one corner.

Ann crawled forward then ducked between the pole logs. There were no saddles or bridles, just team trappings. It had been a long time since she had tried to prove to her brother she could outride him bareback.

After selecting a horse, Ann put her hands out and slowly moved forward. "Easy there," she crooned. "I'm not going to harm you." When the horse didn't shy away, she gathered a handful of coarse mane, then swung her long legs up and over the sorrel's back.

After a couple of quick turns to determine if the

gelding could be mane led, Ann leaned off to the side and released the leather hoop holding the gate shut. What had Zach told her about knowing which way was west?

Chapter Nine

Propped against a chair, Hester tried to clear her throat. It hurt too much. She placed her hand on her chest then raised it high enough to be seen. It was covered with blood. She was dying. Bitterly she cursed the woman she hated. All the injustices that had plagued her life had been Antoinette Huntington's fault. "She should be lying here instead of me," she muttered.

After closing the trapdoor behind Albert, Nate surveyed the room. Most men, including the wounded, were still holding their places, but he was well aware of how things could change in a matter of minutes. At least Richard seemed satisfied. Warm and tucked safely in a blanket, the child had ceased his crying. He was now eagerly sucking on his balled fist, but it was going to be a long time before the pup had his next feeding.

Nate moved to where the duchess sat on the floor. She was dying, and there was nothing he could do.

"Hold me," Hester pleaded when Nate kneeled beside her.

Nate carefully cradled her head and shoulders with

his arm. Her eyes were already glazed. She had been shot several times when she had run outside, once near the heart.

"Nate, lean down. I must tell you somethin' and it's bloody well hard to talk."

"Shh."

"I lied about Albert." Hester clutched the front of his shirt.

Wondering if he had heard her correctly, Nate leaned closer.

Hester fought to keep her eyes open. "I was desperate." She coughed again, causing blood to seep out her nose and the corner of her mouth. "Albert..." She took several short breaths. "Albert is Antoinette Huntington, the real duchess of Gravenworth."

"But—"

"She's posin' as a man."

Nate was stunned. If that was true...no, he couldn't believe it.

Hester's hand momentarily slipped down his blood-stained shirt, and her eyes closed. She forced them open. She couldn't die yet. Her Grace had to pay. "Me real name's Hester. I'm a simple maid who was seeded with the duke's bastard child. Because the duchess is barren..." She tried to swallow.

Nate noticed that Hester's speech had changed. The accent she now had left no doubt that she was who she claimed to be.

"She forced me to come with 'er to the colonies so she could take Richard from me when he was born. But she couldn't find no wet nurse. I've bloody well lived in fear for what she'd do when she no longer needed me."

Nate's gut tightened at the injustice. "Try to rest."

"No! I have to finish." Hester's breathing had become shallow, but she had to hang on a little longer...just a little longer. Her grip on the front of Nate's shirt suddenly tightened. "She plans to declare him...her own so 'e will become the duke. That way she can keep her power and wealth and prevent Edmund's cousin from taking the title."

Nate brushed aside the straggly hair clinging to her mouth.

Seeing the doubt on Nate's face, Hester tried again. "I swear on me deathbed that I'm tellin' the truth. I've nothin' to gain now." More coughing and more blood. "Swear to me that you won't let 'er have me son."

"Hester—"

"Swear to me!" Her words were fading. She tried pulling him closer. "Don't let 'er have Richard," she pleaded. "She'll destroy him. Swear!"

Nate didn't have to answer. Hester was dead. He gently laid her on the floor, the sounds of shots, pony screams and moans suddenly enveloping him again. He couldn't linger a minute longer.

A deep fury was building, the likes of which Nate hadn't known in years. Unless something happened, the duchess would never lay a hand on his godson. He grabbed his rifle. If Hester had told the truth, the duchess would come back just to get Richard, even if it did mean bringing the cavalry. The lady was interested in only money and power.

Ann followed the charging cavalry down the hill, certain her heart would burst from joy. The cabin was still standing, and there were shots coming from inside! She had visualized finding everything burned to the ground, and all the occupants dead. How wonderful to know she had been wrong.

The moment the Indians heard the bugle and saw the soldiers descending on them, they turned their ponies and fled. The cavalry continued their deadly pursuit of the renegades, but Ann pulled up in front of the cabin. As she slid from the gelding's back, the cabin door swung open. Three jubilant men rushed out. Each congratulated her for bringing help, then cheered the cavalry on.

Ann hurried inside, eager to find Richard. The terrible hate she'd seen on Hester's face when she'd looked at Richard was branded on Ann's mind.

Any joy Ann had felt disappeared when she saw men sitting and lying on the floor wounded or dead. The single-room cabin was now filled with the sounds of expletives and groans. It was Richard's crying that drew her to him. He was being rocked by the station master's daughter. Seeing he was safe, Ann scanned the room for Hester. Richard only cried when he was frightened or hungry. Obviously he hadn't been fed.

A knot twisted in Ann's chest as her gaze fell on the woman lying near the door, her hair spread like a fan around her head. Her eyes were closed and her lips were spread in a strange smile.

Ann started forward. No. She had to be mistaken. Hester couldn't be dead.

''Indian bullets caught her when she ran outside. Nothing could be done to save her.''

Though Nate's words weren't loud, Ann could hear them clearly. She paused, still staring at Hester. Was death following her? Ann worried. First Edmund, now Hester. She should never have taken the abigail from England. For the first time, Ann questioned her reasoning behind her actions.

Brushing the tears from her cheeks, Ann's eyes skirted the room in search of Nate. She spotted him in the shadows, his back resting against the wall, his rifle lying across his legs. His once beautiful doeskin coat was now crumpled and lying off to the side.

Ann hesitated to go to Nate though the blood on his once white shirt reminded her that he had been shot when he'd run out to save Hester. There was no indication that he was dying, and she refused to offer him sympathy. This was the very same man who had thrown her from the stagecoach and had tried to run away with Hester and Richard. She also blamed him as much as herself for Hester's death. She headed back toward Richard.

"Just a damn minute," Nate barked, his throat parched and aching. Of all the times in his life, he couldn't have picked a worse time to take a second bullet. It had happened only minutes before the cavalry bugle had blown. Damn it all. The duchess had won again. The shot in his side had left him completely incapacitated.

Ann turned and stared at him. For some unexplainable reason, it occurred to her that this was the first time she'd seen Nate with a shadow of a beard darkening his jaw. The dirt and soot smeared across his face and clothes made her wonder what she must look like.

"I want to talk to you."

Ann hesitated. But remembering how he had risked his own life to save Hester, she finally relented. And while she was at it, she might as well see if she could stop his bleeding. No matter how much she hated him, she couldn't bear the thought of someone else dying.

As soon as she was close enough, Ann squatted and reached out to open Nate's shirt.

"Don't you lay a hand on me!" Nate growled.

Furious at the unwarranted verbal attack, Ann stood. "I didn't want to help you anyway," Ann snapped at him. "What did you want to talk to me about? I find it hard to believe that you're going to thank me for bringing back the cavalry."

"You're right. I'm not going to. As far as I'm concerned you're useless. I had to make you fight, and I had to force you to go for help. You only came back for one reason. To get Richard."

Seething with anger, Ann was about to walk away when she saw three soldiers enter the room.

"I'm a doctor," the major announced.

"Should I call him to come to your aid?" Ann asked contemptuously.

"He can check the others first."

"How magnanimous," Ann said scathingly. "But you weren't exactly magnanimous when you tried to abscond with my wife." Nate's eyes were as black as midnight on a cold winter's day, but Ann paid no heed. Nothing was going to stop her from finally being able to rub salt in his eyes. "I would have given anything to see your face when you discovered the duchess had no money," she taunted.

As quick as a striking snake, Nate lunged at the duchess, but his wounds had left him weak.

Ann's face paled as she jumped back. Nate had come too close to wrapping his steel fingers around her leg.

"You keep your hands off Richard," Nate warned.

Ann glared at him. "Richard belongs to me," she stated firmly.

"You lay a hand on that boy and I swear you'll regret it."

"Ha! Look at who is making threats. You can't even stand."

"I won't always be in this shape." Nate's jaw muscles twitched.

Ann's green eyes had turned nearly as dark as his. "If I ever see you again, I shall have you shot." Head high, back straight, Ann turned and walked away.

Nate's inability to prevent her from leaving with Richard was maddening. "Hester told me everything," Nate called after her, his words starting to slur. "If you take Richard," he raged, "you'd better keep looking behind your back, Duchess, because one of these days I'm going to be standing there!"

A shiver ran up Ann's spine but her steps didn't falter. Had Hester really told him everything, or was he bluffing? But if he was bluffing, why did he call her duchess?

Bitterness and pain eating at his insides, Nate watched Ann walk out the door with Richard. There was no longer any doubt that Albert was a woman. It now seemed so blatantly obvious. But being a female wasn't going to save her hide.

As Ann and Richard left the way station for the last time, the soldiers were digging graves. Though the needless deaths lay heavy on Ann's shoulders, she tried to remember that except for the loss of Hester, she had been very fortunate. She and Richard had escaped unharmed.

She said a silent prayer for Hester and the others,

the first of many that would be said during the coming days. But Hester's hatred of an innocent child would haunt Ann for a long time.

Ann straightened herself in the saddle. She still had a long way to go before her travels would end, and probably even more problems. First she had to find a wet nurse, then she had to figure out a way of getting to the Arizona Territory and Beau. She had hoped Zach would take her at least as far as Santa Fe, but an arrow had put an end to that. And then there was Nate.

How could she have been attracted to another infuriating man? Being married to Edmund hadn't taught her a thing. She obviously had a weakness for the lethal combination of virility, humor, straightforwardness, gentleness and, yes, even bravery. Once again she had been drawn in by a man who was an artist at hiding his real self.

Ann shuddered. It was enough to have Matthew looking for her. She certainly didn't need to add Nate to the list.

Hearing Richard hungrily sucking on his fist gave Ann cause to smile. He was her future.

Ten minutes later, Ann watched the sun disappear behind the horizon, leaving streaks of pink and orange splashed across the sky. Today would remain with her forever. Not just because of the sorrow she carried in her bosom, but also because she had again witnessed just how quickly a life could end.

Chapter Ten

Fort Bennington, New Mexico Territory

After only two days at the fort, Ann stood transfixed in the open doorway of Sergeant King's house, watching the cavalry returning with the way station casualties. Unfortunately, the house was on one side of the parade ground and the hospital on the other, preventing a clear view of the men on the litters.

How bad was Nate's wound? Ann wondered as the soldiers began carrying one litter at a time into the hospital. Bad enough to keep him in bed for three more days? Ann crossed her fingers. She'd get her answer from Mrs. King tonight. Just three days. By then the preparations would have been completed for her continuance to Santa Fe.

Unfortunately, Ann's determination to concentrate on the future and push Nate's threat to the back of her mind hadn't been successful. That thunderous look on his face when they had parted had stayed with her. More than once she'd caught herself turning to see if he was following.

As the third from the last litter was being taken inside, Ann felt her hackles rise. She was being watched. She could feel those dark eyes boring into her as surely as if Nate were standing before her. Neither the dim light nor the comfortable room made her feel safe. All her senses were warning her to leave Fort Bennington as quickly as possible.

She was reminded of what Inez King had told her after supper the previous night. Inez had insisted they sit on the porch rocking chairs to visit, and Anne had finally relented, hoping their conversation would be short.

"You're probably not aware of it," Inez said as soon as they were seated, "but the man you know as Nathan Bishop is known all over these parts as Diablo. The only reason I know this is because Major Oxford told another officer, who told his wife, that Bishop and Diablo were one in the same." Inez shook her head. "A rogue if there ever was one."

Inez fluffed the ruffles adorning the neck of her gown. "Why, I heard tell he killed his folks when he was young and ran away to live with the Indians. After that he turned outlaw. That's a bad one, that is. Wouldn't trust him an inch. The only reason he's being allowed to stay at the fort is because he and Major Oxford are old friends."

"If he's an outlaw, why hasn't he been put in a prison?"

"No one could ever prove anything against him. None of us are going to be safe until he leaves. Especially the women. He's notorious with them, too."

In bed last night, Ann had mulled over what Inez King had said. Nate's patience and kindness toward Hester had been exemplary, but there had been a purpose for that. It was her guess that he thought the duchess had money. But he had tried to save her life, as well as the others at the way station. No one could question his bravery. True, he was a black-hearted opportunist, but was he a man of wild intent, a killer who had murdered his parents?

Ann peeked around the doorjamb. All the wounded had been taken inside the hospital. She rubbed her arms for warmth. After feeling Nate's eyes on her minutes ago, she was already rethinking last night's conclusions.

Satisfied that Nate could no longer see her, Ann stepped outside, welcoming the sun's warmth. Perhaps there was something she could do to hasten the preparations for the trip to Santa Fe. She took off toward the supply room at the other end of the fort.

As Ann passed another house, she heard a baby cry. What would I have ever done without Blossom? she wondered. When she had arrived at the fort, the fort commander had dismissed any possibility of Albert taking quarters in the barracks because of the baby. Sergeant King had offered to let Albert stay in the extra room at his house.

Originally Ann had thought to tell Inez King of her deception. She had quickly changed her mind when it became apparent that the small brunette woman was excited at having the Englishman stay at her house. Not just any Englishman, but Mr. Potter. The very same Mr. Potter who had single-handedly delivered the cavalry to the way station and saved the lives of all those people. In only one day she had informed everyone at the fort that the brave man was staying at her house.

Inez might be a gossip, but she also was a woman

who knew how to get things done. When Ann and Richard had first arrived at the house, Inez already had a wet nurse waiting. A big Indian woman by the name of Blossom. Ann's first reaction was to refuse the offer, but Richard's crying left her with no choice but to turn him over to the dark woman with the full breasts.

Ann smiled. What a blessing Blossom had turned out to be. She not only fed and took loving care of Richard, she saw to the supplies needed for their trip. Knowing nothing about such things, Ann could only offer to help. Now she had to inform Blossom that haste was of the essence.

Three days later, the doctor stood in the hospital looking down at Nate, who lay prone on the bed. After a thorough examination, he was quite pleased with the results of his operation in the field. "You're going to be as fit as ever," he said, smiling. "However, you will be spending some time here."

Nate made no reply.

A low groan came from the far bed in the corner. Zach was having a bad time of it. "Is he going to make it?" Nate asked.

"He still has a little infection, but he'll be out of here as soon as that hole in his shoulder heals. He wants to go to some woman named Mae. He swears she'll take better care of him. Do you know who that might be?"

Nate shook his head, the motion sending sharp pain through his shoulder and side. The sooner he got out of this place the better.

Later, when the doctor had finished his rounds and walked out into the sunlight, he caught sight of Albert

Potter and his wet nurse riding away from the fort. They were a strange-looking pair. The Englishman wore an army forage cap and was seated on a prancing sorrel, while the Indian woman trailed behind astride a donkey.

Blossom, the Indian wet nurse, clutched the lead ropes of two other donkeys carrying trunks and supplies. As her back came into view, the doctor could see the cradleboard strapped to her back. Tucked snugly inside was the infant.

The doctor headed toward the officer's quarters.

As one day slowly followed another, Zach and Nathan grew stronger. The other men who had been injured had already left, one with a limp, but all with smiles, gratitude and well wishes.

On a particularly hot afternoon, Nate called, "Zach!"

"Yeah?"

"How come you were riding with Albert?"

"Albert? I don't know anyone called Albert."

Nate propped himself up on an elbow and looked over at the other bed. "I may have been shot, but I'm sure as hell not addle-brained. Do you honestly expect me to believe you were going to kill me at the way station without even knowing the name of the Englishman who hired you?"

Zach suddenly realized whom Nate was talking about. He would never have thought Diablo would wait so long to broach the subject. "Some friends and I were escorting a couple of wagons for Mae Hoffman and her girls when you shoved 'Albert' off the stage."

Nate remembered passing the prostitute wagons. "Did you know Albert was a woman?"

"I knew it a lot sooner than you did, my friend." Zach chuckled. Just the idea of a scrap of a woman pulling the wool over Diablo's eyes was too amusing not to enjoy. "She told everyone her story."

"The child she took was my godson. I intend to get him back."

"Why? The boy needs a mother."

"A boy needs a father. She only wants to use him to get her land back in England."

"For a hundred, I agreed to ride with her and see that a man called Nate got left out in the middle of nowhere. Course, the only name I ever knew you by was Diablo." Zach had come to admire the woman's bravery and determination as they raced to catch up with the stagecoach. "Can't say as I blame her for wantin' to get even after what you did to her."

"You've only heard her side of the story. I should have waited until there was no one in sight before kicking her out of the damn stage."

Chapter Eleven

Ann wiped the sweat from her brow, though it did little good. New beads of moisture quickly replaced the old. Even after discarding her vest, her clothes still clung to her damp flesh as if she had leaped into a pond of water. Though the traveling had been more difficult in the mountainous areas, at least they hadn't had to suffer from the unending heat the flat land offered.

On the train she had counted the days until she could don feminine finery again. Little good the clothes she'd had made in New York were going to do her. They were all winter wear. What was her cousin going to think when he saw her disguised as a man?

She wrinkled her sunburned nose. Was Nathan Bishop up and around yet? No. Impossible. Inez said he would be confined to his bed for quite some time, and it had only been a week since she'd left the fort. What was he doing right now? Try as she might to forget the heartless man, he continued to invade her thoughts. Just like Hester and countless other women, she had been spellbound.

Near sunset, Ann saw Santa Fe in the distance. The hardest thing she'd had to deal with had been the vast, open land and the constant silence. But finally they would be among people again. And even if her funds were low, she wanted lodging and good food for the next two nights.

When they rode into the dusty town of Santa Fe, the heat was still insufferable. It seemed to come from the ground, the buildings and even the air she breathed. Ann was relieved at finding a hotel right away. It wasn't as fine as other hotels she had stayed at in the past, but there would at least be a bed and hopefully a tub to bathe in. She dismounted and entered the small lobby. Moments later, she was staring in disbelief at a short, potbellied clerk.

"We would be more than happy to give you accommodations, sir," the clerk assured Ann. "However, as I have already stated, the squaw and papoose will have to sleep in the stable."

Ann marched back outside.

It was another hour before Ann found a place that would take the three of them. Though dirty and off an unsavory-looking alley, it would have to do.

After the lantern had been extinguished that night, Ann lay on the bed still fully clothed. Her eyes were wide-open as she hummed a soft lullaby to her son. She brushed at her cheek, convinced a cockroach had slithered across it. Feeling nothing, she rubbed Richard's tiny arms and legs to be sure nothing was crawling on him. This was going to be another sleepless night.

Only minutes later, Ann was fast asleep.

The following morning, after a surprisingly tasty meal of beans, tortillas and spicy roasted chicken,

Ann left the room in search of a guide. Perhaps the man at the livery stable could suggest where she should start.

From the directions given by the old man at the livery, Ann had no trouble locating the Overland Stage office. It had been his suggestion she go there.

Ann was about to bring the spirited filly to a halt in front of the building when two men stepped out of the building. Her heart slammed against her ribs as she sank her heels into the mare's sides. She had not only recognized the stagecoach driver, she also recognized the man offering the driver a cigar.

Matthew's angry gaze fell on the narrow back of the man who had just put his mount into a gallop, causing the horse to kick dirt all over him. His gaze quickly traveled upward to the army hat the man was wearing. "You would think an ex-army man would have more consideration," he chafed as he brushed his coat with a gloved hand.

The stage driver grinned. "I reckon we just have more dirt here than you're used to in England," he drawled. Gus lit his cigar then cupped his hands around the flame and extended the match to Matthew.

Matthew nodded his thanks. "Now let me see if I understand this correctly." He took a strong puff and impatiently blew the smoke back out. "You said there was an English couple with a baby?"

"That's right." Gus never did like having to repeat himself. "Like I said, the woman got killed by the Indians when she ran outside, and it was her husband that brought back the cavalry and saved most of us." He tipped his hat back. "Yes sirree. He was a mighty brave feller. Real good shot with a rifle, too."

"And what happened with the baby and the father?"

Gus looked toward the bathhouse, eager to climb into a tub of hot sudsy water and be scrubbed down by the women. "Don't know. Now if you don't mind, I'm aimin' to take me a bath."

It was apparent the stage driver had no other information to give. "Thank you for your time and information."

Gus was about to walk away, then paused. "I take it thems was your family."

"Ah...yes, they were."

"I'm real sorry about the woman. She was a pretty little thing." He started across the hard-packed street.

"Wait a minute," Matthew suddenly called. He hurried forward. "You called her a pretty little thing." He stopped beside the whiskered man.

Gus frowned. "That's right. She didn't even come to my shoulder." He walked away perplexed but determined not to be stopped again.

"What color hair did the man and woman have?"

"Both was blond!" Gus called over his shoulder just before he disappeared from sight.

Matthew returned to the boarded sidewalk, his mind racing. Could Ann have been the husband and Hester the wife?

Before making his way to America, Matthew had discovered secrets that had hitherto been untold. After threats, Ann's personal maid had admitted that Her Grace hadn't been pregnant when she left. Rose had sadly informed Matthew that it had been nothing more than a simple ruse to keep the duke from his lady's bed.

It wasn't until a few days after discovering the

duchess and her old abigail had sailed to America that Matthew finally fit the pieces of the puzzle together. Ann needed a child, and the maid she had absconded with was carrying Edmund's bastard. It was so simple that it angered him to know he hadn't figured it out sooner. The duchess intended to pass the child off as her own.

The duchess was cleverer than he had given her credit for. A mistake that wouldn't happen again.

Nate lay in bed wide-eyed. He'd had his fill of Fort Bennington and doing nothing more than watching the Eleventh Cavalry performing drills on the parade ground. His wounds had kept him down longer than he'd anticipated. Or maybe the doctor had been right about the older you got the longer it took to heal.

Had the duchess headed straight for Arizona Territory, or had she changed her mind about going there? It was possible she had remained in Santa Fe since he knew about Falkner and might follow her. Nate had done many things in his life, most of which he'd as soon forget. And he'd known every kind of man, woman, gunfighter, outlaw, whore and lady, but never had he been so completely duped as he had been by what Antoinette Huntington had done.

He reached for the glass of water sitting on the stand beside his bed, then downed the contents. Whiskey would have been more satisfying.

His thoughts flashed back in time. After procuring his train ticket in New York, he'd stopped to let a boy shine his boots. An English lady with a heavy veil had been arguing with the ticket master. The raised voices had drawn his attention. He now realized the woman had to have been Ann.

Though he'd only been in New York a little over two months, he had heard of the reward being offered for information leading to the whereabouts of an English lady, possibly with child. He even knew that the man offering the reward was Matthew Huntington, and that he was in Santa Fe with cash for anyone who could supply him with the right information.

Had Ann and Matthew Huntington met in Santa Fe? Nate's lips twisted into a wry smile. He would have liked being a fly on the wall so he could have overheard their conversation.

Nate replaced the glass and rolled onto his side. No matter what his condition, in another week, he was getting out of here. First he'd head for Santa Fe. If he had no success locating the duchess and child, he'd head for Beau Falkner's ranch. One way or another he'd get Richard back, even if it meant going to England.

Dawn had barely broken when Nate climbed from his bed and reached for the clothes neatly stacked on a bench by his bed. He'd waited five days. It was time to leave.

"Diablo," Zach called. "You headed for Santa Fe?"

"Yep."

Zach sat up. "I'm going with you. There's a woman named Mae who was supposed to be opening a saloon there. Once I find her, I'll have all the care a man could need."

Nate's chuckle faded. Pulling on his boots hurt like hell.

Their saddlebags draped over their shoulders, the two men walked out of the hospital toward the stable.

Nate could still feel his injuries, but his steps were steady and the discomfort bearable. It was something he'd have to put up with for a spell. Zach hadn't said a word, but Nate knew his lanky friend wasn't feeling any better.

Even as early as it was, Nate could feel the sun's heat on his face. He sidestepped a pile of horse dung, entered the stable and quickly located the chestnut gelding he'd secretly purchased last week. As promised, the trappings were on the stall rail. The animal was far from the best he'd ever owned, but until he reached Santa Fe, he'd have to settle for what he could get.

Eight days and Ann still hadn't recovered from the shock of seeing Matthew. Even after two days of travel, she continued to turn in the saddle to see if anyone was following. She had thought time would again be her enemy. It had taken three days for Blossom to locate a guide and another three to stock provisions for the journey. That, added to their slow travel because of Blossom's donkey, continued to worry her. What if Matthew discovered their departure and caught up with them? What if Nate should come out of nowhere?

Ann pivoted back around and stared at the man on lead. Their guide was a lanky, grizzled old soul with sun-darkened skin stretched tightly across bone. He wore soiled buckskin clothing. A rawhide strap held back a thick head of long white hair and his wide-brimmed hat usually shaded his small, keen eyes. He was of a grouchy disposition and seldom spoke. Blossom had been quite proud of her selection, and had stated that Will—he claimed he had no last name—

was trustworthy and had been recommended by the local Indians.

Ann passed the time with mental pictures of Nate hanging from a tree by his neck. Besides everything else he had done, Nate was the only person who could have informed Matthew that they would be arriving in Santa Fe. That even explained why Nate had wanted to get rid of her. The circumstances would have undoubtedly been different had he known at the time that she was the one Matthew was searching for. He would never have thrown her out of the stage-coach.

When they stopped to set up camp on the fifth night, Ann felt that all was finally going right for her and Richard. Will and Blossom never seemed to tire, but Ann was proud of her own accomplishments, as well. At night, her thighs and back end no longer ached from hours, days and weeks in the saddle. Even her nose was now brown instead of constantly red and peeling. Will had called her "trail broken." Richard was so content that on more than one occasion she'd had to prove to herself that he was all right. Life had settled down to a routine, one which Ann was starting to enjoy.

Chapter Twelve

Matthew twisted his soft leather gloves and inhaled the slight but pleasing odor of freshly waxed furniture mingled with cigar smoke. A man had recently been in the large study.

Feeling a soft breeze, he moved toward the open French doors and looked out at the tall trees that provided welcome shade. He glanced back at the heavy wooden door. How much longer before Beau made his entrance?

While being escorted to the study, he'd had quick glimpses of other rooms. From what he had seen, the entire house appeared to boast impressive furnishings. Something he would never have expected in so remote an area. Of course there was no comparison to Gravenworth's opulence.

"Matthew?"

The Englishman turned and faced his host. Though it had been several years since their last meeting, the tall half-breed was as striking as ever. Matthew never had cared for him. He'd always considered it a total abomination of etiquette for the ton to welcome a savage into their midst during the years that Beau had lived in England with his uncle.

"Beau!" Matthew smiled as he walked forward to shake hands. "I would never have thought a gentleman of your sensibilities could exist in so hot and isolated a place. Whatever do you do for pleasure?"

Beau's broad grin allowed Matthew to relax a bit.

"Nor would I have expected to see you here, Matthew. I'm seldom fortunate enough to be blessed with visitors from England. Please, be seated." Beau motioned toward the two chairs facing each other. "Would you care for something to drink? Either liquor, or perhaps you would prefer a cool glass of lemonade on so hot a day."

"Lemonade would be most welcome."

Beau pulled a cord and a moment later a servant entered. As Beau ordered their drinks, Matthew seated himself, then ran a finger around the inside of his stiff shirt collar. Fortunately the room was cooler than outside, but it was still damnably uncomfortable.

"You're looking quite fit," Beau commented.

"Thank you. I feel splendid." Under the circumstances, Beau's trousers and loose painter shirt seemed quite appropriate. "Surely you do not spend the entire summer here?"

Beau chuckled. "I'm used to the weather."

The maid returned with a pitcher of lemonade and two crystal glasses, then left. Beau poured their drinks and handed Matthew his.

"How is Edmund?" Beau asked as he took the chair across from his guest.

Matthew stiffened. Was the question a ploy? "Edmund is dead."

Beau cocked a dark brow. "Oh?"

It was impossible to read any emotion on Beau's face. "A hunting accident." Matthew took several long swallows of the refreshing drink. "My reason for arriving at your door isn't a pleasant story. I'm embarrassed to admit there might be problems—"

Matthew glanced toward the French doors and suddenly realized it was beginning to get dark outside. He pulled a watch from his vest pocket and opened it. "I have arrived much later than planned. My sincere apology for my lack of manners. I must not keep you from your meal." He finished his drink and stood. "If you're not too busy, may I call upon you in the morning?"

Beau also stood. "Have you arranged for accommodations in Prescott?"

"No. I came directly here. In my haste, I didn't stop to think how tactless that was. I should have sent my valet with my calling card first."

"We don't stand on formality here, Matthew. Guests are always welcome. I would be offended if you didn't accept my hospitality for the duration of your stay."

"Thank you. That would be most appreciated."

"I'll have rooms prepared and send a servant to fetch your valet. Because of the heat, we prefer to eat late. If it's agreeable with you, after supper you can tell us what brought you all this way."

Matthew nodded.

Beau headed for the door. "While you wait, why don't you relax on the veranda?" Beau grinned. "Help yourself to another drink."

As soon as Beau left the room, Matthew began to pace. Beau had been courteous in every respect, but he still maintained an aloofness that Matthew had always found most irritating.

Matthew poured another drink. Did Beau Falkner know what had transpired in England? Had Ann already arrived? Perhaps Beau was playing a game, hoping for some slip of the tongue. Matthew licked his dry lips. He would have to wait for any forthcoming answers.

Matthew heard a buzzing noise. From the corner of his eye he caught sight of an insect flying toward him. He felt the sting in his neck before he was able to brush away the offending creature.

"Milord, your rooms are ready. I have inspected them myself."

"Confound it, Thomas, I've been stung! Do something!"

"It must have been a wasp." Thomas hurried to his master's side. "I see the barb, milord. Stand still and I shall attempt to pull it out."

Though Matthew's neck was swollen to the point of not being able to button a collar, he was prompt for supper. After an excellent meal, he, Beau and his wife, the beautiful Danielle, retired to the parlor. Matthew was feeling considerably more self-assured. It was now apparent that Ann hadn't yet arrived, nor was there any indication that he was looked upon as a villain.

By the time the maid had served their drinks, Danielle's curiosity had gained considerable momentum. "Beau told me you had arrived with a purpose other than a visit."

"Yes. It concerns Beau's cousin, Ann," Matthew

replied. "Until Santa Fe, I had feared she may have perished at sea."

"Ann?" Danielle asked her husband. "I don't remember you mentioning a cousin by that name, darling."

"I apologize. Her friends and family call her that. Her name is Antoinette Huntington, the duchess of Gravenworth." Matthew pulled a lace handkerchief from his sleeve and dabbed his damp cheeks. "I can't remember if you've ever met her," he said to Beau.

"No," Beau replied, "I haven't. Was she headed for America?"

"Yes. My hasty trip was because I wanted to be sure I arrived here first."

"Isn't that a bit of a contradiction?" Danielle impatiently tapped her fingers on the arm of the sofa. "First you say you thought she had been lost at sea, then you tell us you wanted to arrive before her."

Matthew gave her a toothy smile. "I've started this all wrong." He ran a finger along the rim of the crystal glass. "The problem began when a poacher shot Edmund during a hunt. Ann and I witnessed everything. It had a profound effect on Ann. She became...deranged. The servants and I kept agreeing with her fantasies, hoping she would regain her faculties. Of course, I said nothing to her father about her condition because of the embarrassment involved. No family wants to admit to insanity and paranoia within their ranks," he quietly informed Danielle.

Beau opened the humidor and offered Matthew a cigar. Matthew shook his head.

"Soon Ann was accusing others of committing the crime and swore she was being plotted against. Eventually the accusations were even turned toward me.

"To add to the problem, Ann decided she was carrying Edmund's child. Her abigail assured me that Her Grace had started her monthly time the day after the hunt. But in Ann's mind, she now had two people to protect. Herself and her child."

Matthew gently patted his swollen neck. "At the funeral, she told her father some tale. I do not know what it was she said because he refuses to talk to me. I was helpless when he took her away in his coach. I should not have kept her problem a secret."

"So she caught a ship to America?" Danielle encouraged.

"I'm certain her father arranged it." Matthew stood and strolled to the French doors. "The odd part is that, before sailing, Ann returned to the castle then took off again with a pregnant maid who used to be her abigail." He turned and looked at his audience. "I discovered this too late to prevent her departure."

"Why didn't one of my uncles inform me of Ann's arrival?" Beau asked.

"They may have tried, darling," Danielle said. "You know how difficult it has been to receive messages with all the Indian uprisings."

Beau nodded. Matthew continued sadly. "I followed as soon as I discovered she had left England. I have traveled all this way and have had only one possible clue as to her existence."

"Clue?" Danielle asked excitedly.

"A stagecoach driver told of an English couple who had traveled with him. They were caught in an Indian attack and the woman was killed."

"What kind of clue is that?" Danielle persisted.

"I found myself wondering if the couple could have actually been Ann and her abigail. I did everything I could to find Ann. I spared no expense. However, it never occurred to me that Ann would pass herself off as a man. The couple even had a baby with them.''

''You said Ann wasn't pregnant,'' Danielle reminded him.

Matthew turned and looked soberly at the beautiful redhead. ''But the abigail was. She was carrying Edmund's bastard.''

Danielle stared at him, wide-eyed.

''Though Ann may be dead, I came here to wait, knowing that if she were alive, this would be her destination. My concern was that she would arrive first and tell you lies, making me less believable.''

''How do you know she will come here?'' Beau asked.

''Where else can she go? On several occasions she mentioned her cousin in America and spoke of his great deeds. If I'm right and the couple were indeed Ann and Hester, then that means Hester is dead and Ann has the child. There is little doubt in my mind that she will insist the babe is hers.''

''Not being a close relative, I'm curious as to why you have gone to all this trouble to find Ann?'' Danielle asked.

Matthew mopped his forehead. ''I am in love with Ann. I have dedicated myself to finding her and bringing her safely home.''

Danielle was excited at the possibility of a romance taking place. However, their guest seemed to be looking paler with each passing moment. ''Beau, I believe Matthew is feverish.''

''I'll be fine,'' Matthew protested.

''Danny is right. I think you should lie down in

your room." He pulled the cord for a servant. "Maria," he said as soon as she entered, "get Mr. Huntington's valet. I'm afraid either the heat or the bite on our visitor's neck has caused a fever."

"I'll tend to it right away, then I'll go mix some herbs to take the fever down."

Beau nodded.

After their guest had been seen to, Danielle and Beau retired to their own quarters for the night.

Chapter Thirteen

Ann kept her horse flanked by Blossom's donkey and Will's mustang, even though the five men on horseback who were escorting them had assured her she was on Falkner land. She had made sure her pistol was in easy reach. How did she know these men could be trusted? Perhaps they were a band of outlaws taking them to their camp.

Ann looked across the land. If all this really did belong to Beau, he was indeed a fortunate man. They were in a beautiful green valley surrounded by mountains, and the air was blessedly cooler than it had been on the flat desert.

A sprawling one-story house came into view, and Ann let her laughter peal forth. Such a fine structure had to belong to her cousin. Against all odds, she had come out of this victorious. No longer would she dress in men's clothing. She could finally shed all her worries. From now on, Beau would be her protector.

Danielle lay on the bed, staring at her husband stretched out beside her. She had always loved the way his thick, tousled hair hung in his eyes when he awoke. Actually, she couldn't think of a thing she didn't love about him, unless it was his occasional stubbornness.

"How can you believe Matthew?" Danny had changed her mind about Matthew. "He's entirely too...too—"

"Pompous?"

"Exactly! He loves himself too much to love anyone else."

Beau kissed his wife on the nose, then climbed from their bed.

The loud knock startled them both.

"Yeah?" Beau called.

"Jake just rode in," the servant replied from outside the door. "He came ahead to let you know a woman is being brought in. She claims to be your cousin. They figure she's the one you told them to watch for."

"I'll be out as soon as I'm dressed. In the meantime, waken our other guest." Beau looked at his wife and grinned. "Apparently Matthew was right. She didn't die at sea." He walked over and snatched his britches from the back of a chair. "Better get dressed, love, I think there is going to be a need for you."

Danielle jumped off the tall bed, laughing. "This is proving to be quite exciting. Just think about it, Beau. We're not only watching a love story unfold, we're now right in the middle of our own little mystery! The question being, how did Edmund really die?"

As they neared the house, Ann's happiness abounded. The tall, handsome man with black hair standing in wait had to be her cousin, Beau. Now she knew why the women in England had spoken so highly of him—behind spread fans.

Ann was about to make a proper greeting when Matthew stepped from the house. Traveling by ship, all the hardships, and even Hester's death had been for nothing. The one person she had tried so desperately to escape had already arrived.

"Matthew," Ann gasped. Telling herself she no longer had to be afraid, she braced her left foot against the stirrup and dismounted.

"Cousin Beau?" Ann inquired once her feet were firmly planted.

Beau smiled. His cousin had been doing a lot of traveling. Her skin, hair and clothes were covered with trail dust. Though much taller and the coloring all wrong, he was reminded of his first encounter with Danny. "You must be Antoinette." He reached out to take her hand, but she moved away.

"That man murdered my husband!" Ann accused.

Beau looked at Matthew for a brief moment before returning his attention to Ann. "You must be exhausted. Why don't you come inside and we'll discuss this later."

Danielle came rushing out of the house and went directly to Ann. "My dear, we've been so worried about you." Danny placed a firm arm around Ann's waist and guided her toward the house.

Ann drew up short. "My baby." She looked toward Blossom.

So did the others.

Ann was slow to awaken. How long had she slept? She stretched lazily, then opened her eyes.

She sat up suddenly, her concerns returning with

the force of a hurricane. Where were Blossom and Richard? And what had Matthew told her cousin? Most assuredly not the truth, or Beau wouldn't have seemed so passive when she had accused Matthew of murder.

Ann tried combing her hair with her fingers. She hadn't had an opportunity to speak to Beau about Matthew, his crime, or why she had come to the ranch. A servant had whisked her to her rooms, where her bath was drawn and her things unpacked.

A light knock on the bedroom door drew her attention. "Yes?" she called anxiously.

Danielle stuck her head inside. "May I come in?" she inquired.

"Please do." Perhaps now she would find out what lies Matthew had spread.

A chubby servant followed Danny into the room.

"Where is my baby?" Ann asked anxiously.

"In the nursery," Danny replied calmly. "The door over there leads to it." She pointed to the corner of the room. "Blossom is standing guard. The woman absolutely refuses to leave the child's side." She heard Ann's sigh of relief.

"And Matthew? Is he gone?"

"No, nor has he been asked to leave." Danielle was quite taken aback by the woman who climbed off the bed. Now that the dirt had been washed away, a tall, willowy woman had emerged a butterfly and a vision of grace.

"Then I must leave. I had been told that Beau would be my protector. Apparently that's not so." She glanced around the room for her clothes.

Danny's heart went out to the duchess of Gravenworth. She understood Ann's fears. "Please, you have no reason to be concerned. Beau takes his obligations very seriously. You and your child are quite safe here.''

"Not with Matthew in the house!" Ann stepped forward. "You don't know him," she said in a hushed voice. "He's evil. He'll do anything to become the duke."

Danny made herself comfortable on the green velvet chair. "But he can't very well accomplish that if he's dead."

"Dead?"

"Out here there is no law. Beau is judge and jury. I'm certain you are aware of his past."

Ann nodded.

"Then perhaps you can understand that when Beau told Matthew he would be a dead man if anything befell you or Richard, Matthew took the threat quite seriously."

A half-unbelieving laugh escaped Ann's lips. "Beau said that?"

"Right after you were brought to these rooms." Danny looked toward the maid who had been standing silently by the door. "Come here, Juanita."

As Juanita moved forward, Ann could see the servant had a yellow bodice and matching broadcloth skirt draped over her arm.

"Earlier, when Juanita took your gowns out to be hung and aired, I noticed they were all winter garments." Danny moved on into the room. "I thought you might like something cooler to put on for supper. I hope you don't mind that they are some of Beau's sister's old clothes that she left when she married and moved to the East Coast. They're quite serviceable."

"How I've longed for the day I could wear a dress again, no matter how old it is."

Danielle laughed. "I must warn you, they aren't made to be worn with petticoats or a girdle. Andrea long discarded such items because of the heat."

Ann's eagerness to look like a woman again quickly faded as Juanita dressed her. She felt naked. There was no corset, no bustle and only two petticoats. But after she had stepped into the dress and it had been tied in the back, Ann had to admit it was far lighter and cooler than anything she'd worn in a long time.

Ann suddenly realized she had undergone an amazing transformation during her travels here. In the past, she would have been appalled at the prospect of wearing another woman's clothes, and certainly not something as unfashionable and lacking in all the proper undergarments. Now, after going so long in men's clothing, the dress almost looked beautiful.

"Thank you, Juanita," Danielle said when the servant had finished dressing Ann. "You can go help in the kitchen."

Ann looked in the mirror, not at all displeased with her reflection. The skirt came only to her ankles, but everything else fit amazingly well. "Thank you," she said again.

Danny smiled warmly, but she could stand it no longer. Her curiosity was itching away at her, and she'd waited long enough to find out if Ann's interpretation of what happened to Edmund agreed with Matthew's.

"Supper isn't quite ready, so I thought we could take this opportunity to get to know each other."

Chapter Fourteen

Squatted on his heels and hidden in the shade of an ancient oak, Nate studied the scene spread out before him. Ahead was a rambling Spanish-style house, well surrounded by shade trees, and nearby a fancy brick stable where the better horses would be kept. He chuckled softly as a big goose…wings spread…came from around the side of the stable, chasing a skinny dog with its tail tucked between its legs.

The rest of the numerous outbuildings were set well away from the house. These included a bunkhouse and kitchen for the cowpokes, smokehouse, tannery, blacksmith's forge and anything else needed to make the large spread self-efficient.

As Nate scanned the area, he counted eleven ranch hands tending to various chores. The count included the five men standing by an exercise corral. There were undoubtedly more men about the compound, but they were out of sight. The women must be in the house.

Nate took one last look around the area, making sure he'd put the layout to memory. Should he have to make a quick getaway, he wanted to know which direction to take out of here. The duchess had said she'd have him shot if he ever showed his face. But the lady had said many things, most of which hadn't amounted to a damn.

Nate stood, then swung himself up into the saddle. The time had come to make his presence known.

"I am an excellent judge of horseflesh," Matthew stated proudly, "and I assure you, that mare is as fine an animal as I've ever seen. Where do you suppose Ann came by her?"

Will tapped Beau's shoulder. "Looks like you got yourself another visitor."

Beau turned to see what the old scout was talking about, then groaned. The man headed in their direction was definitely a predator. Having been one himself, it wasn't difficult to recognize another. And the stranger was well versed in how not to get shot. His hand was well away from the pistol resting in the holster by his side, and he was moving his horse slowly, letting everyone know of his presence and that he wasn't here to make trouble.

"Well, I'll be damned." Will removed his floppy hat and scratched his head. "I recognize that feller. He's the gunman they call Diablo."

"I thought he was dead," one of the hands said in awe.

"I heard that, too." Will shook his head. "But that's him all right. He wasn't named the devil for nothing. Got a draw that's as fast as I ever saw. I seen him shoot a gambler some years ago. 'Pears the feller was dealing from the bottom of the deck."

"What would bring him here?"

Nate brought his horse to a halt and tipped his hat. "Howdy. Mighty fine morning."

The men nodded in unison.

"Aren't you Beau Falkner?"

Beau pushed away from the corral gate. "That's right. What can I do for you?"

"You've changed somewhat since I last had a glimpse of you. As I recall, you were a Cheyenne dog soldier at the time." He dismounted and extended his hand. "Name's Nate Bishop. Years ago, I was married to Bright Moon, Chief Howling Dog's daughter."

The two men shook hands.

"I remember Chief Howling Dog very well. How is his daughter?"

They were feeling each other out, and both men knew it.

"She died in childbirth. I buried her and the baby, rode away and never returned."

Beau nodded. He'd heard the story and knew Chief Howling Dog and his people often wondered what had become of Bright Moon's husband. It had happened years ago, and it was doubtful that anyone would know or care about the story except the people involved.

"A lot of time has passed since then. Why have you come to me?" Beau asked.

"I'm on a quest. I had hoped you'd allow me to stay a spell. Perhaps I could even hire on."

Beau heard a crow calling. It was a good omen. He could not deny a quest, as long as it was honorable. "Will said you're the man known as Diablo. I would kill any man who endangers my family."

"As would I if I were standing in your shoes. As

you said, a lot of years have passed. I'm no longer a young bear cub testing my claws. I seek only knowledge.''

''Then since we understand each other, you're welcome to stay in my house as long as it suits your purpose.''

''The bunkhouse will be fine.''

Beau chuckled. ''No, my wife would never hear of it. Having you in the house will help round out the table. Besides, I can keep a better eye on you.''

''Round out the table?''

''Just a saying. We have other guests, and you'll make an interesting addition to the supper table.'' Beau made the proper introductions. The young ranch hands were obviously still in awe.

Though surprised to find Matthew Huntington here, Nate gave no indication of ever having heard the name. Had the Englishman and the duchess arrived together?

Beau said to the towheaded stable boy who had joined them, ''See that our guest's horse and gear are taken care of. Come along, Nate, I'll take you to the house. You can meet my wife and get settled in.''

Nate realized he had just been given an opportunity to kill two birds with one stone. He'd tag along with Beau and Matthew, see the ranch and learn all he could about Matthew before facing the duchess.

When the three men finally rode from the compound, Nate settled himself comfortably into the saddle. Unlike the crow-bait gelding he'd been riding, the fresh horse had a smooth, comfortable gait.

Originally Nate had thought to sneak into the house at night and escape with Richard. But while traveling here, he had realized that there were obstacles. Feeding the boy was one of them.

Matthew Huntington was nothing like Nate would have expected. He was almost as tall as Beau, slender, and a man women would probably consider handsome. However, the way Matthew had mounted his horse had told Nate a lot. Matthew wasn't as inept as his prissiness would indicate. While Beau was in the house talking to his wife, Nate had managed to have an informative conversation with Matthew. He had learned that the duchess of Gravenworth and her son were here. According to Matthew, the lady was still in her rooms when they had left, and it had been her horse in the corral that the men had been admiring. Nate was more than a little curious to know how Matthew had finally caught up with the woman, but he didn't want to appear too interested.

Hester had said Ann was going to claim Richard as her own. Matthew had verified that was exactly what she had done. Nate chuckled inwardly. If he had guessed right, the duchess wasn't going to be the least bit pleased to see him.

Ann spent the morning playing with Richard, and warned Blossom that they had to be watchful with Matthew in the house.

It was the wonderful aroma of freshly baked bread that later drew Ann to the kitchen. It was a spacious room with a large round table and chairs off to one side, and dried herbs and pots of every description were hanging about. There were cutting tables and worktables, one with a big rack full of fresh eggs, a pie closet and even a hand pump. One woman was raking the ashes from the deep stone fireplace that covered one wall, while another cleaned vegetables freshly picked from the garden. Danielle stood near the stove, taste-testing something from a large pot.

"Excellent," Danny complimented the cook.

Having seen Ann enter, Danny walked over and joined her. "My son Kit is going to be so excited when he sees Richard."

"I didn't realize you had a son."

"Kit is two. How would you like some tea and cookies?"

Ann rolled her eyes. "That would be delightful."

"Maria," Danny called over her shoulder, "have tea and cookies brought to the sitting room." She took Ann by the arm and guided her out of the kitchen.

As they strolled down a hall, Danielle debated whether she should or shouldn't tell Ann what Matthew had said that first night. She finally decided that Ann did have a right to know.

Thirty minutes later, Ann clanked the teacup down on the saucer, then stood. She was trying to remain calm, but it wasn't working. "For him to say he loves me is the most absurd thing I have ever heard! The man knows no bounds to his underhandedness." She started pacing then abruptly stopped. "But I have no way of proving he's lying, do I?"

"No," Danielle said softly.

"Matthew is very clever. No matter what I say, he has already provided an answer. Danielle, can't you see that this is all a ploy to get me back to England?" Ann heard a dog barking. "That...that sounds like Sir Drake."

"It is. Matthew brought him to make you happy.

The dog has certainly enjoyed his stay. He runs all over the place and likes to get petted by the hands.''

Ann clapped her hands with excitement and grinned.

That afternoon Danny gave a party for the boys with a big cake, all decorated, and Blossom, Richard, Ann and Sir Drake being the guests. Kit and Sir Drake took to each other immediately. Ann was enchanted with the boy who already had his father's charm and handsome looks...and his black hair. Watching the boy, Ann thought that if Nate had a son, he'd probably be very much like Kit.... What had made her think of Nate?

Chapter Fifteen

Ann sat staring into the mirror, trying to figure out why, at first glance, she hadn't recognized herself. True, after spending so many days in the sun, her skin was much darker...and quite unfashionable...and after Juanita's magic with the curling iron, she looked like a woman instead of a man...but none of that had anything to do with what she was seeing. It was more elusive...more subtle. Gradually she recognized what it was. She had developed maturity and bravery she was justly proud of. It was all there in her face. She smiled, quite pleased at her admirable traits.

Ann rose from the stool, then adjusted the pink neck-high bodice and flounced skirt. Andrea's gown was perfect for dining...and most becoming even if it was outdated.

Ann glanced at the clock. Surprised at the time, she hurried out of the room. As soon as she entered the parlor, Matthew stepped forward. His false expression of concern infuriated Ann.

"Ann, you look wonderful," Matthew spouted.

"Why do you say such things, Matthew?" She

struggled to maintain an even, conciliatory tone. "You know I have seen better days."

"I find you absolutely stunning. I didn't know what to expect. For months I've been beside myself with worry. We have so many things to discuss. Perhaps after dinner—"

"Surely it can wait until another time," Beau stated. "Perhaps in a day or two, after Ann has had a chance to recover from her travels."

Matthew's cheeks reddened. "Yes...well..."

"I've done a good deal of traveling myself lately," a deep voice said. "I know how tiring it can be."

Ann's mind ceased to function. That voice. It couldn't be... As if in a fog, Matthew turned aside and Nate Bishop came into her view. Her ears ringing and certain she was going to have a seizure, she fell onto the nearest chair.

"Ann, are you all right?" Matthew asked worriedly. "Your face is absolutely ashen."

"See, you've upset her," Danielle accused. She started to rise from the sofa, but Ann's raised hand detained her.

"I'm fine," Ann assured everyone. She drew a deep breath and forbade herself to tremble. "Truly. I just lost my balance." What more could possibly befall her? It would take an iron will to control her nerves.

Ann thought of the first rule of decorum she'd been taught when she was a little girl. Fold your hands in your lap. It helps contain any uncalled-for emotions. Ann folded her hands. Edmund had also provided her with ammunition. How to recover quickly from unexpected circumstances, and more importantly, how to contain inner feelings.

"Nothing Matthew could say is going to upset me, Danielle." Ann's stomach was fluttering badly and caused her words to sound less convincing.

Satisfied that his cousin's momentary dizziness had been caused from confronting Matthew, Beau gestured toward Nate. "Ann, permit me to introduce another of our houseguests. This is Nate Bishop. Nate, this is my cousin, Antoinette Huntington, the duchess of Gravenworth."

"How nice to finally meet you. Matthew has been singing your praises most of the afternoon." Nate hadn't missed the momentary look of fear that had flashed across the duchess's face. Her threats had all been a bluff. Instead of insisting he be shot, she was acting as if they had never met.

"And am I what you had expected?" Ann asked with what she considered to be an admirably calm voice.

Knowing now that he definitely had the upper hand in the situation, Nate's lips spread into a full smile. "Not at all." Nate moved forward, his eyes taking in every line of her face...her shoulders...small perfectly molded breasts...tiny waist. What had been tall and lanky was now slender and regal. "Believe me, seeing you is quite an enlightening experience." The lady was a rare beauty. He had known the minute she walked into the room that he would not leave until the duchess shared his bed. "Please forgive me for staring, but something about you reminds me of a man I knew," he mocked as he stopped in front of her.

Ann's hands tightened. "Are you implying I look like a man?"

A faint smile played on Nate's lips. "Not at all. I

assure you, your beauty is unmistakably feminine. I simply meant that Albert...that was his name... looked enough like you to be your brother.''

Ann wanted to scream. Why didn't he come right out and say they had traveled together and that it was Hester who had birthed Richard?

''Ann's brother is in India, last I heard.'' Matthew toyed with a shirtsleeve ruffle. ''However, when Ann arrived, you could have mistaken her for a man what with her clothing and cutoff hair.''

Nate chuckled. Matthew didn't know the half of it.

''It was a matter of survival, Matthew,'' Ann stated sharply. Anger was threatening to take over. She, Matthew and Nate were each playing foolish, convincing rolls. Even Nate, dressed in evening clothes, could have easily been mistaken for an extremely attractive gentleman instead of the cur he really was.

Convinced that Ann was quickly losing patience with Matthew, Danielle announced, ''Supper is ready. Why don't we all move to the dining room?''

Upon seeing Matthew headed in their direction, Nate extended a crooked elbow to the lady before him. ''It would be an honor to escort you to supper, Duchess.''

Ann wanted to refuse but couldn't. For the present, Nate was going along with her pretext of never having met her.

''I told you I'd come looking for you,'' Nate whispered when she took his arm. ''I don't care how you do it, but find a way to come to my room tonight.''

''You can't expect—''

''Duchess,'' Nate said, loud enough for the others to hear, ''you're shaking. Should I have a servant fetch your shawl?''

"I do not need a shawl, Mr. Bishop," Ann hissed.

"Please, call me Nate."

"Tell me, how long do you plan to avail yourself of the Falkner hospitality?" She was furious at herself for having allowed Nate to see how his presence had upset her.

"As long as it takes to satisfy my quest," Nate answered smoothly as he escorted her from the parlor.

By the time Nate had Ann seated at the table, her mind was a desperate hodgepodge of thoughts. But one thing was quite clear. Nate had come after Richard.

While the soup was being served, Beau gave Matthew a good-natured warning. "You should be careful what you say about women wearing men's clothes, or you might find yourself on Danny's bad side. It's not uncommon to find her tending cattle in her britches and chaps."

"My profound apology." Matthew started to say something more but realized he would only be getting himself in deeper trouble.

"That's quite all right," Danielle said graciously, though she wanted to hit him.

Ann found it impossible to make light conversation when she could feel Nate's eyes boring into her. Why couldn't he have been seated somewhere other than directly across from her?

"How did the two of you meet?" Nate asked Danny, his eyes momentarily off Ann.

"On a stagecoach," Beau answered.

Danny looked lovingly at her husband. "It was love at first sight," she teased.

"This is quite superb, Danielle," Matthew said between sips of soup.

"Nate, you said you came here from Santa Fe," Danielle said. "Too bad you hadn't known Matthew at the time. The two of you could have traveled together."

Ann's bowl was empty. She couldn't even remember tasting the soup. How dare Nate expect her to come to his room!

"Actually I wasn't in Santa Fe. I had been visiting a friend at Fort Bennington."

The servants cleared away the bowls and began serving the main course.

Matthew and Nate! Ann suddenly knew the significance of both men being here. It was all so clear. Nate had planned to deliver her to Matthew, but that had gone awry. So when Nate was well enough, he had headed for Santa Fe where he'd met with Matthew. Nate then told Matthew everything that had happened on the train and stagecoach. But there was still a thin ray of hope for her. Two could play Matthew's game. Nate had done all this for money. Why couldn't she bribe the snake into refuting Matthew's claims?

Matthew continued his compliments. "This meat is excellent."

Danielle's smile was weak. Feeling an air of hostility among their guests, Danielle said, "Beau dear, why don't you tell Matthew how beef became so marketable a product in America?"

Beau looked at her questioningly. Danielle shrugged her shoulders.

"Yes," Matthew said. "I've been curious about that."

"Not much of a story." Beau buttered a thick slice of bread. "Used to be pork and game were the only meats eaten in the East. The gold rushes changed all that. By the time the miners returned home they'd acquired a taste for beef. The selling price per head quickly escalated, and started cowpokes to thinking.

"There were hundreds of thousands of wild cattle, so men began rounding them up. Huge herds were driven across hundreds of miles to the nearest buyers, and big money was exchanged. Those same mavericks were also how most big ranches got started."

Ann was beginning to think the meal would never end when the dishes were finally removed and the dessert placed before her.

Nate swallowed a bite of blackberry cobbler. "I understand you have a son, Duchess."

Ann's green eyes flashed with anger.

"A very handsome son," Danielle said. "His name is Richard."

"He looks like his mother," Matthew added, his voice laced with sarcasm.

Nate finished his dessert. "Richard? Since you're from England, can I assume he was named after Richard the Lionheart?"

Ann gritted her teeth. How dare he play cat and mouse with her! "How very intuitive of you. Yes, he was named after King Richard. Is there anything else you would care to know about me, Mr. Bishop? Perhaps you'd also like me to tell you how Matthew murdered Richard's father."

Matthew mopped his damp forehead with his napkin. "Ann, you know I had nothing to do with Edmund's death! He was killed by a poacher!"

Danielle started to say something, but the slight shake of Beau's head silenced her.

"Please forgive me, Duchess," Nate said with

deliberate innocence. "I had no intention of upsetting you. I was simply trying to make conversation."

"You..." Ann snapped her mouth shut. She took a long look at him, then gave Danielle a tight smile. "The meal was excellent, but please excuse me. I'm quite tired."

"Of course. I'm sure you'll feel more rested tomorrow."

The men stood, and with a dignity derived from a life of training, Ann majestically rose from her chair.

"I do apologize, Mrs. Falkner," Ann heard Nate say as she left the room. Nate and Matthew's lies dripped of honey. Nate had deliberately baited her.

"Apparently I have unintentionally upset your guest and disturbed your fine supper," Nate continued.

"It's not your fault, Nathan," Matthew excused. "Ann's mind has been confused since the death of her husband."

"Confused?"

"I'm certain that over a period of time...and plenty of rest, she will be fine. I assure you, I was not my cousin's assassin."

"Excuse me," Danielle said. "I want to be sure Ann is all right."

The men again stood.

"Gentlemen," Beau said, "why don't we retire to the study and enjoy a good drink and a fine cigar?"

As soon as Ann was out of hearing distance from the others, she scurried to her room, then straight to the nursery. Blossom was asleep in the rocking chair, and Richard asleep in the crib. Ann gently shook the plump woman. Blossom awoke immediately.

"I want you to go to the kitchen and find out where

Nate Bishop's room is located. Act as if you're just curious. I don't want the servants to suspect you're getting the information for me.''

A wide grin spread across Blossom's broad face. ''You find man you like?''

''No. This man brings trouble.''

A few minutes later, Danielle arrived. To Ann's relief, the lovely redhead stayed but a few minutes. As soon as she departed, Ann lit a bayberry candle and nervously waited for Blossom's return.

Chapter Sixteen

Ann silently stepped into the dark hallway, one hand cupping the candle flame. According to Blossom, Nate's room was only three doors down from her quarters.

Ann wasn't certain how much time had lapsed since she'd left the dining room, but hopefully the men had finished their after-dinner leisure. She wanted to get this over with as quickly as possible. Since Nate obviously had no morals, getting him to accept her money shouldn't present a problem. She'd double whatever Matthew was paying, no matter what the amount.

Ann stopped at what was supposed to be Nate's bedroom and rapped lightly on the door. Receiving no answer, she knocked again...a bit louder. Still no answer. Not wanting to be caught by one of the servants, she turned the knob and opened the heavy door. The room was dark. "Nate?" she called anyway. A hand suddenly circled her wrist and she was roughly yanked into the room.

"I'm right here, sweetheart," Nate muttered. Holding her tightly against him, he shut the door. "I wouldn't miss our little meeting."

Nate's deep, sarcastic tone was unmistakable. "Unhand me!" Ann ordered.

"You're shaking again. I wonder what it is about me that frightens you, Duchess?"

Ann tried kicking him on the shin. She missed. His hold was so tight around her waist that the effort had been painful.

"If you scream or do anything to draw attention," he said as his hand glided over her breasts, "you're the one who's going to have to make an accounting."

"What are you doing?" When his hand continued to travel over her body, Ann opened her mouth to scream. His cupped hand prevented any sound being released.

"Remember, Duchess, you came to *my* room, not the other way around." He took his hand off her mouth.

"You ordered me to come here!"

"Can you prove it?"

He was pulling her skirt up. "You can't do this!" she gasped.

"I assure you, your maidenly honor is quite safe. I'm only searching for weapons. You see, I don't trust anyone, especially women as wily as you, my dear. Perhaps a knife strapped to your leg?"

His hand moved up one leg, then another, her hips...her pulse quickened. "How dare you?" she whispered.

Nate removed his hand from beneath the folds of her skirts, then turned her loose. How in the hell had she managed to keep hold of that damn candle?

Ann spun around, ready to give him a piece of her

mind. But seeing his raised hand, she backed away. "I don't care who finds me in your room. If you strike me, I swear I'll scream." He brushed the hair back that had fallen into his eyes, and Ann realized there had been no blow intended.

Nate leaned against the door. "What's wrong, Duchess? Guilty conscious?"

"You had no right to take such liberties." Having him trail his hand over her body had been degrading, but at the same time it had excited her. She could still feel the sensation.

"And you've misjudged me," he said softly. "I always get even for an injustice. But just to set your mind at ease, I don't make a habit of slapping women around."

"What injustice are you accusing me of? I did nothing to you except pose as a man. We could, however, discuss what all you did to me?"

Nate chuckled. "Albert had it coming. Had the sassy, prima donna of a man you created continued his line of logic, he would have undoubtedly ended up with a bullet between his eyes. So you see, I did you a favor." He lit the lantern near the door. "But that has nothing to do with why I'm here. I've come for Richard."

Ann's heart turned to ice. "You can't have him."

"You're mistaken." Nate's jaw tightened. "It's *you* who can't have him. Hester told me why you want Richard."

"Did she tell you that she was quite willing to give up her son?" Now she understood why Nate hadn't been surprised to see her. "I have told everyone I am Richard's mother."

"I'm sure you have."

Ann bumped against a high, long bed with heavy mahogany frame and thick posts. She quickly moved away. "I did not come here because you ordered it. I came with a proposition."

Nate's gaze slowly, deliberately dropped from her eyes to her shoulders to her breasts. "And just what kind of proposition would that be?"

"Ouch!" Ann almost dropped the candle. She quickly brushed away the hot wax that had dripped onto her finger, then blew out the flame and placed it on a table. "I know why you and Matthew are here," she said, proud of how clever she had been. She moved behind a nearby chair.

"I told you why I was here."

Her eyes widened in alarm. Had she just heard the key turn in the lock? His hands were still behind him. "I…ah…" She looked toward the open window. "I didn't come here for…" She choked on the words.

"I didn't say you did."

He was patronizing her. "I'm here to offer you money. I wish you would stop staring at me like that."

"I enjoy the view."

"I'm quite aware that I lack the qualities men find attractive or interesting in women, so don't bother trying to convince me differently." Why did she continue to blabber? "I am here on business."

"All women have a certain beauty." He pushed away from the door and began removing his coat.

"What are you doing?" Ann hadn't meant to be so loud. The key was still in the door lock. Had he locked her in or had it been her imagination?

"I'm getting comfortable. Does that bother you?"

"Yes, it does. It isn't a gentlemanly thing to do in the presence of a lady."

He hadn't expected her to be so jumpy. He'd thought that when she found out he knew about her little scheme, she'd be cold and calculating. Instead she was worse than a Mexican jumping bean. "Since you seem concerned about protocol, perhaps you can tell me if it's permissible for a lady to be alone with a man in his bedroom?" He tossed his coat onto the bed.

By circling to the other side of the chair, Ann managed to keep the heavy piece of furniture between them. She didn't trust him. He was starting to talk to her the way he'd talked to Hester. "You told me to come! If you would just let me—"

Nate chuckled. "I must admit, I never thought you had the guts to—"

"Blast it! Would you let me speak?"

Nate shrugged, sat on the edge of the bed and waited.

"You've made me forget what I was prepared to say." Ann rubbed her temple. "First, I want you to know that I have no desire to...I do not find you attractive in any way...so you can just erase any thoughts of...what I'm trying to say is—"

"You didn't come here to ask me to make love to you?"

"Yes. Exactly."

"I'm devastated." He broke out laughing.

"I hardly find this funny."

Nate stood. "If, as you say, men find you unappealing, why would you think I would take you to my bed?"

"All men—"

"Never, 'all men,' sweetheart. Or perhaps you're fishing for a compliment."

"Absolutely not."

"I find you very appealing."

He was walking toward her. "I warned you that I'll scream—"

"And wouldn't your face be red? I'm sorry to disappoint you, but I was merely going to get a cigar." He stopped at the end table next to the chair she hovered over, and pulled a cigar from the humidor. "I wonder what you would be like in bed? It would probably take a man all night to thaw you out."

"How dare you!"

He turned his back to her, then sat in the very chair she had been using as a barrier. "Now, what is this proposal you want to discuss?" He lit the cigar.

Left with no choice, Ann made a wide circle until she was again facing the impossible man. "I realized tonight that both you and Matthew being here is no coincidence. When I saw Matthew in Santa Fe, it wasn't difficult to figure out why he was there. He was waiting for me. When did you send the telegram? Chicago? Earlier or later?"

Nate was finding her theory quite interesting. He grinned. "You know, you have a very devious mind, Duchess."

"Very well, then keep your secrets." She walked to the bed, then turned. The room seemed so warm. Even her cheeks were heated. "I'm sure, when you did get together with Matthew, you were more than happy to report everything that happened during our travels together. Now Matthew has proof that Richard is nothing more than Edmund's bastard."

It had been a long time since Nate had found himself being so thoroughly entertained.

Head bowed in thought, Ann began pacing the short distance between the bed and the commode. She finally stopped and looked at the virile man relaxed on the chair. "At first I considered appealing to your honor, until I remembered you have none. So here is my proposal. Since this is all about money, I'm willing to pay you twice what Matthew has offered."

"To do what?" Nate asked.

His deep, resonant voice brought back the tension she had almost managed to rid herself of. "To swear you helped birth *my* child."

Nate's eyes narrowed as he slowly let the cigar smoke trail from his lips. "Why?"

"Why? The only important thing you need to know is that you'll be getting twice the money you'd planned on."

"I want to know why."

Ann slapped the side of her skirt in frustration. "Matthew murdered my husband. If he can prove that Richard is not mine, he becomes the heir to the title of duke and obtains all lands, monies and everything else that goes with that title. If *I* can prove Richard is *mine,* Richard will be the heir and Matthew gets nothing."

"And you get everything."

"That's not the point."

"Isn't it?"

Ann's anger was quickly replacing bad nerves. "Matthew cannot be allowed to gain from his crime." She released a heavy sigh. "You wouldn't understand."

Nate tapped his ashes into the spittoon near his

foot. Her conjectures had been totally wrong, but other than the part about Matthew killing Edmund, her story coincided with what Hester had said. To what extent would she go to achieve her purpose?

Ann couldn't stand his silence any longer. "Aren't you going to say something?"

"I'm almost sorry to have to dispel such wonderful detective work, however, my being here has nothing to do with Matthew."

"But...you did meet Matthew in Santa Fe, didn't you?"

"Nope. Never laid eyes on the man until I arrived here."

Ann was at a complete loss. "Then why are you here?"

"To take Richard from a woman whose sole purpose is to use him for her own benefit."

"That's not so!"

"Then it's going to be up to you to prove me wrong, Duchess. As I see it, it would only take a few words to Beau and Matthew to put an end to what you're up to. You see, I don't give a damn what Matthew does or doesn't get." He stood, dropping the butt in the spittoon.

Ann moved toward him. "Surely Hester told you my intent is righteous."

"Hester swore on her deathbed that you were evil and that you didn't know how to love. Is that true?"

"I can't believe she'd say such a thing."

"I assure you she did. Is it true that you don't know how to love?"

"Of course not!"

"Then you have loved?"

"Yes."

Nate had watched Ann unconsciously close the gap between them to less than four feet. In the flick of an eye he could reach out and snatch her to him. A tempting possibility. "Who?"

"That is none of your business."

"I'm making it my business."

She met his accusing eyes without flinching. "What about the money? Set your price. I have only a small amount at the present, but I'm certain I could obtain more from Beau until my father replenishes my funds."

"I said I was here for only one reason." His curt voice lashed at her. "Richard."

"I will never give you Richard! If you were truly sincere about this, you would see the advantages of leaving him with me. What do you have to offer? You're a drifter. You would drag him from one place to another, or eventually pawn him off on someone to rid yourself of the responsibility. You don't want Richard. You just don't want me to have him!"

"I'll give you two weeks."

"You can't do such a terrible thing," Ann said angrily.

"I never claimed to be a saint."

"How can I possibly prove I want only what is best for him?"

Nate rubbed his jaw. In her anger, Ann seemed to have come alive. She stood proud but tense, her green eyes sparkling. His gaze settled on her full, tempting lips. No matter what his opinion of her might be, his desire was undeniable.

"I take it you would do anything in your power to keep me silent."

"Anything."

Nate reached out and pulled her to him. Her lips parted in denial, but his mouth covered hers. At first she struggled, but as the kiss deepened, she became compliant to the point of leaning against him. Her arms were raised to circle his neck when she suddenly jerked her head back, apparently realizing what she was doing. He made no effort to hold on to her. "Obviously not anything," he said, a smile playing at the corners of his mouth.

"You're despicable," she accused, still reeling from his kiss. "If I ever have the opportunity, I will get even with you for having taken such unwanted liberties."

"Admit it. You enjoyed the kiss."

"I did not. I found it to be nauseating."

"What a liar you are. Two weeks, Duchess. If I'm not convinced by then that you would make Richard a good mother, I will tell everyone who his real mother is, then I'll take him away. Do I make myself clear?"

Ann was horrified. Nate's face had become set in stone. There was no humor now. "You could take the money," she tried again.

"You still don't understand. I don't want your money, sweetheart." His grin was cold. "I want to see that loving nature you claim to have."

Ann sucked in her breath. "Are you saying..." Angry, she made a complete circle before facing him again. "Are you saying you'll remain silent if I come to your bed?"

Nate strolled over to where she stood. No, he hadn't meant it that way, but it would certainly be the quickest way to find out what the real Antoinette Huntington was like.

Ann tried swallowing, but the lump in her throat made it impossible. She could feel his breath on her face and smell a pleasing odor of earth and sun. "Surely you wouldn't expect me to—"

Nate brushed a finger across her cheek. "Why not?" When she flinched, he was reminded of her reaction earlier when she had thought he was going to strike her. He tilted her chin with his finger and looked deeply into her sea-green eyes still flashing with anger. "You can say no."

"Can I? And if I do, how much would that influence your decision? If you are determined to use me, then it will be only after you have told Beau that Richard is mine."

"Don't make threats, Duchess. I don't scare easily. As for using you, isn't that what you're doing with Richard?"

"I'll have you shot!"

"I don't think Beau would allow that. From the beginning, you've looked down on me with preconceived opinions, and I certainly wouldn't want to disappoint you." He turned his back on her and walked away. "The only way I would want you in my bed was if you came willingly."

"Willingly?" she asked with disgust. "How would you know if I came willingly or because of Richard?"

His chuckle was humorless. "Believe me, I'd know."

"Ha!"

"And until you come to me willingly, I'll spend my time observing and guaranteeing nothing. So you see, it all goes back to how much you're willing to sacrifice to secure your...or I should say, Richard's position."

Ann rushed forward. Nate just managed to catch her wrist before she delivered the slap to his face.

"Why don't we get it over with here and now?" Ann seethed, his strong hand hurting her wrist.

Nate yanked her to him. His kiss was punishing, but Ann felt no pain. She was engulfed in the passion his lips created. She hated her weakness, but he made her feel fluttery inside. She could think of nothing but the delicious sensation he was creating. She didn't want the kiss to end. Too soon he pulled away, leaving her standing alone.

"What you need, my dear, is a good man."

Ann's chest swelled with indignation. "The one thing I do not need is a man in my life."

"Didn't your husband satisfy you, Duchess?" His words were little more than a whisper. In the past hour he'd learned more about her than she realized. "Did you shrink away from me because your husband liked to use a fist?"

"What took place between my husband and me is none of your business," Ann said defensively, "nor does it have anything to do with your decision." She couldn't bear the marriage to be brought out into the open for others to view.

Ann headed for the door but was brought up short when Nate grabbed her arm and spun her around.

"You're not going anywhere unless I release you." He ran his thumb along the contours of her full lips.

Ann became very still. "Why are you doing this?"

Nate suddenly wondered the same thing. He released his hold on her arm.

"I will never come to your bed willingly," Ann stated, practically spitting out the words.

"Afraid you might discover how much of a woman

you really are? Believe me, sweetheart, you're closer
to doing it than you know.''

''Have I your permission to leave now?'' Cynicism
dripped from each word.

''Be my guest. By the way, was it your husband
who made you believe you have nothing a man could
want?''

Ann marched to the door. She started to reach for
the knob, then hesitated. Was it locked?

''I didn't think you'd want someone to walk in on
us,'' Nate excused. ''Would you like me to see if the
hallway is clear?''

Ann nodded and stepped aside.

Nate unlocked the door, opened it and stuck his
head out. ''You're safe,'' he said with a chuckle in
his voice.

''You, sir, are the lowest form of a cad.''

''Absolutely.''

Ann hurried down the hallway.

''Remember, two weeks,'' he called after her.

Nate stood in the dark by the open bedroom window, listening to the crickets chirping outside. In the
morning he'd go see Richard. This had been an enlightening day. The moment he had set foot on the
train in New York, he had been hornswoggled. A realization he was still having trouble coming to grips
with. The lies had been nonstop. He was looking forward to hearing Matthew's version of what had happened when Edmund had been killed. But there was
one good thing that had come out of all this mess.
Learning that Albert was a woman had taken a heavy
burden off his back. His masculinity was secure.

All the qualities he had so disliked in Albert now

seemed to fit perfectly on Ann's slender shoulders. The duchess was a beauty, short hair and all. The pink gown she'd worn hadn't left any doubt as to her sex.

Hearing a noise outside, Nate looked up and caught a glimpse of Matthew strolling toward the trees. Were his thoughts also on Ann? The woman had everyone turning in circles.

Nate moved back into the room and began undressing. That Ann had felt desire for him was one thing. To get her to acknowledge it and give herself freely was another.

He removed his shirt. At this point in time, leaving wasn't even a consideration...unless Richard wasn't being treated well.

He dropped his trousers. Thinking about the different times Albert had come within a breath of having a fist planted on his jaw caused Nate to chuckle. Remembering the look on Albert's face when he'd been shoved out of the stagecoach door right onto the laps of the ladies of glory brought forth a roar of laughter. How long had it taken the women to find out Ann wasn't a man?

"Mr. Huntington?" a male voice called softly.

"Yes," Matthew replied, "it's me."

"I found just the man you're looking for." Tex glanced around to be sure no one could see him talking to the Englishman. "His name's Chico. For the right money, he'll do anything you want, including murder."

"You've done well." Matthew handed Tex some money.

"He said he'd meet you here in two nights, at the same time." Tex disappeared into the night.

Matthew headed back to his quarters. From the first time he'd set eyes on the young man, Matthew had known Tex liked to make money without having to work. In two nights, he would set his plans for Antoinette into motion.

Chapter Seventeen

Edmund's hands and face were covered with blood as he forced Ann onto the bed, his cruel laughter ringing in her ears. Desperately she kicked and clawed, but he was too strong. She buckled with pain as he mounted her. To Ann's horror, as he pulled away he turned into a skeleton with flesh hanging from his bones. Ann screamed as someone repeatedly called her a murderess.

Ann awoke with a start and jolted upright. It took a moment before she realized it had all been a dream. She rubbed her eyes and climbed wearily from the bed. She'd had little sleep last night and it was already light outside. She went to the commode, poured water from the pitcher into the bowl, then doused her face. Some of the water splashed onto the front of her nightgown, giving welcome coolness.

The dream had left her feeling terribly alone. But she had made her choice and there was no turning back. If Richard didn't become the duke of Gravenworth, what would have been the purpose of all she had gone through, or Hester's death?

Feeling as refreshed as could be expected, Ann

moved to the chifforobe and pulled out her clothes for the day. The sun had just cleared the horizon and there was still a blessed coolness to the air.

After dressing, Ann went into the nursery for her morning visit with her son. She was horrified when Blossom told her that earlier that morning, Nate had spent nearly a half hour with the boy.

"You let him hold Richard?" Ann asked angrily.

Blossom grinned. "No worry. Diablo fine man, great warrior."

"He wants to take Richard from me. Don't ever let him touch Richard again." Ann's uneasiness increased when Blossom nodded her agreement but broadened her smile.

When Richard fell asleep, Ann returned to her room. She glanced around her chamber. She was tired of trying to avoid Matthew and Nate, and she certainly didn't need Edmund's ghost giving her a bad time. She thought of Star. The mare needed to be exercised. They could both use an outing.

Nate and Beau sat on the corral fence admiring the Hereford bull that had just arrived from England. They had been spending a great deal of time together talking about everything from Indians to buffalo grass. And Beau had developed a healthy respect for the man once called Diablo. In fact, he liked him better than any white man he'd ever been acquainted with.

Beau took his hat off, shoved his hair from his forehead and put the hat back on. "I get the feeling you and Ann have known each other in the past."

They climbed down from the fence and started walking.

"Have you noticed that the lady hasn't quite taken a liking to me? Sometimes I miss the quiet times when I lived with the Cheyenne."

Beau nodded. "Last night I had a dream. I was racing with the wind and warring with my enemies. I traveled hundreds of miles with nothing but land and buffalo as far as the eye could see."

"Those were good times and bad. Are you saying you want to become an Indian again?"

Beau chuckled. "No. It was a dream of times past. I'm content. But every now and then..." He stopped and looked at Nate. "Tell me, Diablo, do you think you could still mount a wild horse and break him without a rope?"

Nate's eyes lit up with interest. "I know I can. Can you?"

Beau grinned. "You forget. I was a Cheyenne dog soldier."

"I haven't forgotten."

"A thousand dollars says you can't."

"And a thousand dollars says you can't."

Beau cocked an eyebrow. "Can you pay?"

"Prior to coming here, I had been in New York attending my mother's funeral and settling the estate. My father was in shipping and had fleets in America as well as in England. I'm as rich, or possibly richer than you are. Oh, yes. I can pay your thousand dollars many times over."

"Good, because I plan to win." Beau roared with laughter.

"Let me know when you're ready to test my skills."

"How about tonight after everyone has gone to bed?"

"Where?"

"The farthest corral from the house."

"I'll be there."

Still laughing, Beau headed toward the blacksmith shed while Nate went the other direction. It suddenly occurred to Beau that Nate hadn't answered his question about knowing Ann previously. Beau chuckled. Nate was a sly one.

After an invigorating ride and having handed Star's reins over to the young stable helper, Ann felt in complete control. The ride had allowed her to take a good look at her situation. She had concluded that Beau could keep Matthew in hand. As for Nate, she would try using a little ladylike pleasantness instead of snapping at him.

Ann had just turned the corner of the stable when she saw Beau and Nate separate. "Nate," she called, her vow to be nice already forgotten.

Nate came to a standstill and turned. Seeing Ann headed toward him, he moseyed over to the shade at the side of the stable and waited.

"I do not want you seeing Richard," Ann ordered when she stopped in front of him. "Nor is charming Blossom going to avail you of a thing."

"I wanted to be sure Richard was being properly taken care of," he calmly explained.

"Now you know, so there is no reason for you to see him again."

"Is that all you wanted?"

"No, there is something else." Ann suddenly remembered she was supposed to be pleasant. Her voice softer and her body more relaxed, she said, "I know you're a fair man, and I'm certain that during the following two weeks you will realize that I also care about his happiness, as well as his future. When you acknowledge and accept that, you will clearly see that you must tell the others I am Richard's mother.''

Nate raised an eyebrow. ''My, my, how your opinion of me has changed.'' The duchess was actually attempting to charm him. He casually moved in front of her, causing her to turn her back to the wall.

''I admit I have been a bit hard on you.'' She smiled sweetly. ''I've had a lot of things to contend with. We started off wrong. Let's try starting over as friends.''

''I can't think of anything I'd like better.''

''Good.''

''But my terms haven't changed, nor will they.''

''But friends are supposed to be forgiving,'' Ann said through clenched teeth.

''It's been too long since our last kiss.''

''What? Have you listened to a thing I've said?''

''Every word.'' He leaned forward and gently sucked at her bottom lip while teasing it with his tongue.

Ann refused to be swayed by his advances...but the sensations he created were not like anything she had ever experienced before. As if in a distance, she heard moans of pleasure. She suddenly realized the moans were hers! She turned her head to the side.

Anticipating her next move, Nate placed his hands on the wall on either side of her, preventing her from leaving. ''Why do you continue to fight your desire, Ann?'' he asked softly. ''Why can't—'' he kissed her nose ''—you admit—'' he kissed her eyelids ''—that you want me—'' he kissed the corners of her mouth

"—every bit as much as I want you?" His lips captured Ann's, demanding she join in the pleasure.

Her blood was turning to liquid silver. She hated herself for being so weak, but she couldn't turn away.

"Let go, Ann," Nate whispered, his lips tickling hers.

Ann was about to throw all caution to the wind when she heard children laughing. To her relief and sadness, Nate backed away, humor dancing in his dark eyes.

"Do you make a habit of accosting women?" Ann snapped, trying to hide the passion that he had so easily ignited. She straightened her dress. "What are you smiling at?"

"Too bad those boys showed up."

"What do you mean?"

"Who is going to save you next time, Duchess?" He tipped his hat and walked away.

Ann closed her eyes, but it did no good. She couldn't sleep. She had a new and serious problem. She was no different than Hester or other women. No matter how she fought it, Nate was becoming increasingly irresistible. It was humiliating and degrading. Even more so because he was well aware of her reaction to his kisses. She climbed out of bed and soundlessly walked to the open window. A soft, cool breeze was blowing, causing a spark of her old self to come alive.

Without taking time to think, Ann climbed out the window. It was late and no one would see her. She luxuriated in the feel of the breeze blowing her hair and clothes, the sweet smell of night jasmine adding to the spell. Overhead was a multitude of stars winking at her. Maybe it was only for a moment, but for the first time in many years, she felt completely free.

Lowered male voices suddenly caught Ann's attention. It sounded like Nate and Beau talking. Curious, she stepped farther away from the window. Was Nate telling Beau that Richard was her child?

Feeling someone beside her, Ann spun about. Danny held a finger to her lips, motioning for Ann to be silent.

"You never said anything about doing it in the dark?" Nate protested.

"Did you think I was going to make this easy? What are you complaining about anyway? There's a full moon, so you've got plenty of light to see by."

Hearing the men walking away, Ann turned to Danny. "What is going on?"

"I don't know, but I intend to find out why my husband slipped out of bed as soon as he thought I was asleep. He's been acting strange all evening." Danielle raised her finger to her lips again. "Let's just see what these two are up to. Beau has ears like a hawk, but hopefully he's too busy talking to Nate to be listening."

Ann's interest was also piqued, and she hurried after the petite redhead.

Danny and Ann followed the two men for some distance. When Beau and Nate stopped at a large corral on the south end of the compound, the women hid in the shadows. There were other men gathered around the fence, including Matthew. Apparently they had been waiting for Nate and Beau to join them.

Inside the corral were two large, stiff-legged mustangs. Their withers twitching and their ears laid back, they darted from one side of the corral to the other, never taking their eyes off the men.

"Like you asked, boss, I picked the meanest ones I could find," the foreman said.

Beau nodded. "Want to change your mind, Nate?"

Nate laughed.

"And would you care to join us?" Beau asked Matthew. "The wild mustangs were brought in yesterday. We can still get you one."

"Certainly not." Matthew snickered.

Danielle and Ann squatted, trying to make themselves as comfortable as possible.

"What are they going to do?" Ann asked.

"I have no idea," Danny replied.

Ann watched both men strip down to their buckskin britches, then pull off their boots. Never had she seen such total masculinity. Their bodies were perfectly molded and their hard muscles rippled in the moonlight. They reminded her of two Greek warriors going into battle. Why would they want to fight each other, Ann worried? But when they climbed through the fence poles and stepped into the corral, it seemed fighting was not what they had in mind.

The mustangs kicked up dirt as they scattered to the opposite side.

Danielle's hand flew to her chest. "I know what they're going to do," she gasped. "They're going to break the horses."

"But that's impossible. They have nothing to work with."

"Beau told me about it once, but I've never seen it done. Oh, Ann, they could be killed."

"Then run out and stop it."

"I can't."

"I can." Ann started to stand, but Danielle pulled her back down.

"You don't understand, and I can't explain. But I know that if we show our faces and make a scene, both men would lose face. I wish someday someone would explain to me why men have to act like men."

Ann's breathing became shallow as she watched each man pick a horse, then begin stalking it. At different times Beau or Nate waved their arms and called out to the frightened animals as they moved closer and closer. Other times they crooned soft words to their horses, as if talking to a baby.

As the sorrel darted past Beau, he ran his hand across the withers, back and along the rump, the horse missing him by inches. The bald face reared on Nate then came back down biting and bucking. Nate had to dive out of the way.

Ann sat speechless, watching two magnificent men show their prowess. Raw passion stirred her blood as Nate grabbed a short mane and leaped on then off the bald-face's back. Beau grabbed an ear and bit down on it, bringing the sorrel to his knees. Then in one swift motion, he swung upon the stallion's back. He was bucked off, but easily landed on his feet.

Time seemed unending. Sweat glistened on sleek bodies and muscles bulged as each man started to take control of his animal. Then, after seemingly hopeless odds, bucking, kicking, biting and falls, Beau, then Nate had the mustangs trotting around the corral, obeying every direction given them, and acting as though they had never known a wild day in their lives.

As both men laughed from sheer joy, Ann heard Danielle release her breath. And as Nate and Beau leaped to the ground and hugged each other, Danny rose to her feet and headed back toward the house.

"Danny, are you all right?" Ann asked after they were far enough away that the men couldn't hear.

Danny nodded. "I'm fine now. It was magnificent, wasn't it?"

"I've never seen anything like it." Ann was still breathless with excitement.

Danny squeezed Ann's hand. "Are you all right?"

Ann feigned disinterest. "Why wouldn't I be?"

Danielle laughed softly. "If you're trying to fool anyone, it's only yourself."

Once back in bed, Ann pulled the sheet over her. Her nipples were sensitive and her body alive. Her hand moved down her stomach and paused. This couldn't be happening. What had Nate done to her?

"There's no use pretending to be asleep, love," Beau said as he climbed in bed. "Did you enjoy the show?"

"You knew we were watching?"

"We knew the minute you started following us."

"You swine!" She took a swing at him.

Beau didn't try to avoid the blow.

"You could have killed yourself." Danny started crying.

Beau wrapped her in his arms and kissed her head.

Danny snuggled against his chest. "I want to ask you to never do it again, but I know better."

He wiped away her tears.

"And I guess if you did agree, you wouldn't be the man I fell in love with." She raised his hand to her breast and said seductively, "By the way, you were magnificent."

Chapter Eighteen

Ann sailed into the dining room, not expecting to find Matthew eating breakfast alone.

"Good morning, my dear," Matthew greeted. "I don't believe I've ever seen you up so early, or looking more ravishing."

"How generous of you," she replied coldly.

Ann picked up a plate from the sideboard and began dishing out the delicious-looking food from one of the various sterling platters. "Where are the others?" she asked with a hopefully deceptive indifference.

"According to the servant, Nate and the Falkners ate at dawn and have since departed the premises." Matthew mopped his neck with an eloquent gesture. "Even at seven in the morning, the heat here is insufferable. I'll be glad when we return to England."

"When I return, it won't be with you." Ann brightened. How wonderful it felt to finally speak her mind without fear of retribution. "Danny told me of your underhanded lies. Did you honestly think they would believe you?"

"Except for the part about the poacher, I told the truth."

"Come, come. Your naiveté is grinding. Don't you think telling Beau and Danny that you love me was a bit implausible?"

"I'm sure you've known for years how I've felt," Matthew said smoothly.

Ann placed her dish on the table, then poured her coffee. "Your declarations are wasted." She fingered her cup, her hands surprisingly steady. Perhaps she had shed her fear of Matthew, however, Nathan Bishop was an entirely different matter. She had a feeling the rogue would do as he pleased no matter what or who stood in his way.

Matthew set his empty plate aside. "I would think your spirits would be quite high after seeing to Edmund's demise."

Ann's hand paused in midair, the bite of egg falling unnoticed from her fork onto the tablecloth. "I would never have done such a thing!"

"Try to remember to whom you're talking, or have you already forgotten that I was there?"

Ann speared another bite with her fork. "I'm surprised you didn't ride out with the others."

"I derive no pleasure from the American style of living." Matthew brushed a crumb from his tweed jacket. "Furthermore, I fail to understand how Beau could expose us, or his lovely wife, to a highwayman."

"How do you know he's a highwayman?"

"He was identified by that guide who brought you here. I must admit, however, that for a highwayman he does seem to be an amiable chap."

Like Matthew, Nate apparently liked to spend his

time charming people. "We're alone, Matthew. This is an excellent opportunity for you to make your threats or state your proposition." Ann waited expectantly.

"Very well. I want you to return with me to England as soon as possible. We can be married by the ship's captain."

"We will never marry." Ann took her time chewing a bite of ham. "Why don't you leave, Matthew?" she finally asked. "There is no reason for you to remain. Richard is the duke of Gravenworth now. There isn't the slightest hope of you acquiring the title."

"Unless it's proven he's not yours." Matthew peered down his nose at the lovely creature seated before him. "We both know Richard is Edmund's bastard. Don't stick to this farce, Ann, or you will rue your decision. There is more than one way to get you out of this house and I could care less about the bastard."

"Beau warned that he'd see you dead if anything happened to Richard or me."

"Money can buy a lot of favors."

"He's not interested in money."

"I wasn't speaking of Beau."

Ann carefully placed her fork on the plate. "What are you saying?"

"I'm saying that I have no desire to remain here any longer than necessary."

Ann stood so quickly her chair fell backward. "I will inform Beau of your threat."

"And I will deny it as I have denied that bastard is your son."

"No matter what you do, it will change nothing. Richard will be the duke of Gravenworth. I will be sending a letter to my father, informing him that he is now a grandfather and the dukedom has been secured.''

''If the new duke lives. I suggest you tell our host the truth and that you do it very soon.''

Ann hurried out of the room. Matthew's threat had frightened her. Richard's life was in danger. If only adoption could make Richard the legal heir to the title, there would be no worries. Unfortunately, English law did not permit a bastard or an adopted child to inherit the title of duke.

She had to try again to make Nate see the importance of her being Richard's mother. If that didn't work she would let him have his way with her.

Safely ensconced in her quarters, Ann retrieved the book from the shelf that she had placed there yesterday. Only minutes later she snapped it shut. She couldn't concentrate on anything except what she was contemplating doing.

Other women thought nothing of bedding a lover, so why was she so reticent? Pride and self-worth. She would be allowing Nate to get away with blackmail! And what about the way he had treated her in the past? Had she already forgotten how much she hated him?

Well, she was just going to have to swallow her pride. The situation had to be handled and the sooner the better. Besides, all she had to do was enter Nate's room, lie on the bed and spread her legs. His lust would do the rest. Nothing could be worse than what she had gone through with Edmund. Five…ten… fifteen minutes at the most was all it would take for him to satisfy himself. Then it would all be over. She would be rid of Nate and, upon having proof of

Richard's parentage, Matthew would return to England.

After supper that evening, Ann went directly to Nate's room. She was exhausted, but it wasn't just from lack of sleep. All afternoon and during supper she hadn't been able to think of anything except what she was about to do.

She thought about turning up the lantern, but changed her mind. If she must do this dirty deed, she preferred the room to be dark. She sat on a small, uncomfortable chair. The doubts she'd suffered earlier had returned with a vengeance. Even her pulse was racing and her face felt damp from her nervousness. But she couldn't change her mind now.

Ann soon found herself watching the wag clock. Time crawled...her tension grew. She had tried to tell Nate she would be waiting, but he had kept his distance and an opportunity hadn't presented itself.

An hour passed.

Ann ran her fingers through her hair. If she didn't hurry up and get this over with she would surely go insane. How long did it take to have a cigar and drink? What could the men be talking about for so long? Probably cattle and horses since that had been the main topic of discussion during supper.

Ann steepled her fingers. The underhandedness to obtain a title were all ploys she had heard about and lived with all her life. She understood them and knew how to deal with them. It was her feelings for Nate that were foreign and continually left her in a quandary. One part of her found Nate irresistible. In her mind, she could still picture him breaking the mustang last night. But another part of her hated him.

Perhaps it was the danger he seemed to exude that made her want to test the water. Foolish woman!

She glanced at the clock hands again. Another half hour had passed. She couldn't stay any longer.

The door suddenly opened, causing Ann to leap to her feet. Though the light was dim, she could clearly see Nate's frame filling the doorway.

"My apology. Had I known I had a guest I would have made a point of being here sooner."

"I've come to once more appeal to you to help me."

"Oh?"

Ann wished that he looked more like the weasel she had met in Grand Central Station instead of tall, strong and very masculine. It would have made everything so much easier. "I want you to forget about our agreement."

"I didn't know we had an agreement."

"You said that if I came to you willingly—"

Nate raised an eyebrow. "Is that why you're here?"

This was her opportunity to say yes. She opened her mouth, but the word didn't come out. No matter how determined she'd been, she suddenly realized she couldn't go through with it. She raised her chin and looked him straight in the eye. "No," she lied. "I wanted to tell you that I love Richard very much and I couldn't stand to have you steal him away from me."

Nate sat in what had become his favorite chair and stretched out his long legs. "Steal? I couldn't steal Richard even if I wanted to."

Ann moved toward him, hope blossoming in her bosom. "What are you saying?"

"To begin with, I don't know of another wet nurse that I could use to replace Blossom." He reached over and pulled a cigar from the humidor. "And getting Blossom out of the house would be a bigger feat than I'm capable of. She'd make so much noise that anyone within ten miles could hear her. And if I did manage to get her, Richard and myself out of here, she'd slow me down to the point that even Matthew would be able to find us. Then there would be Beau and every other hand on the ranch to contend with."

Ann was almost afraid to believe what she was hearing. Nate wasn't going to take Richard!

Nate struck a match, held it to the end of the cigar and took several puffs. "There is only one way I could leave with Richard."

Ann's excitement plummeted. "How?"

Nate gave her a cocked grin. "Don't you know?"

"No."

"I tell the truth about the boy."

Ann slowly walked to the door and left the room.

Nate frowned as the door closed behind his visitor. For a brief moment he had felt sorry for the duchess. He blew a perfect smoke ring. Ann hadn't learned how to hide her feelings behind a stoic face, and he had clearly seen the battle she was fighting within herself. She was tempted to let him make love to her, but her pious integrity was standing in the way. She definitely didn't know how to act around a man intent on seducing her, nor did she flirt or play little female games. No, in many respects, Ann was still a virgin.

His leg comfortably looped around the saddle pommel, Nate continued sitting off to the side with Beau and Matthew, observing the three-year-old steers the cowhands were rounding up. He tipped his hat down to block the morning sun.

"Mighty fine looking herd you'll be delivering to the forts," Nate commented to Beau.

Beau chuckled. "That's how I keep the contract."

Hearing a whine, Nate looked to the ground. The whippet was tugging with all his might against the rope Nate had placed around his neck earlier. He laughed. "The dog wants to do some herding on his own."

Matthew grunted. "Why do you suppose Sir Drake always follows when you mount a horse?"

"Maybe he thinks he's a cattle dog," Nate replied.

Matthew clicked his tongue. "The blasted animal has never liked me."

"Do you like him?" Nate asked.

"Absolutely not."

Nate grinned. "There's your answer."

Matthew shifted in the saddle. He much preferred his English saddle to the Western counterpart. "I wonder what Ann would say if she knew how Sir Drake was being treated?" he stated with considerable snobbery. "Until now, he's led a very pampered life."

Nate chuckled. "If Sir Drake persists in following me, he's going to learn not to chase everything he sets his sight on. If he doesn't, he'll end up tangling with some critter that thinks he's a meal."

Beau agreed.

Nate swung his leg down and jammed the toe of his boot into the stirrup. "I have no idea how Ann would feel about it, and I don't particularly care. Tell me, Beau, do you have a problem with me putting a rope around the mutt's neck?"

"None whatsoever."

"I wish you would quite calling him a mutt," Matthew complained.

Nate gave a quick snap to the rope, making the whippet stop his tugging. "Well, if you gentlemen will excuse me, I believe I'll head back to the house." He smiled.

"I'll ride back with you," Matthew said.

"Tell Danny I'll be a little late for supper. I want to find out why I haven't seen young Tex bringing in anything. He's probably sitting under some tree letting all the others do the work. Then I'm going to have a talk with his pa." Beau tipped his hat then nudged his horse forward.

From the bored expression on Matthew's face, Nate knew the Englishman was ready to head back. In fact, Nate had counted on it.

Feeling a momentary slack on the rope, Sir Drake lunged toward the nearest steer. When he reached the end of his tether, his momentum caused him to be jerked up into the air.

Nate shook his head. "You're as stubborn as the woman who raised you." He kicked his mount into an easy lope, the dog finally trotting peacefully alongside. With the dog's tail tucked between his legs, he looked cowed. Nate knew better. Sir Drake was always ready to take on anything, no matter how big it was. Maybe that was what Nate liked about him.

"Why do you continue to remain on this ranch?" Matthew asked as they moved their horses through the tall buffalo grass.

The sharpness in Matthew's voice told Nate that the Englishman wasn't just asking a casual question. Nate settled back in his saddle, looking relaxed. "I'm almost embarrassed to tell you I came to learn about cattle. You see, I have some acreage between here and Santa Fe that I want to do something with. I don't know of a place that could teach me more than here.''

"And just how much acreage do you have?" Matthew asked sarcastically.

"A little more than a thousand."

Matthew was impressed. He hadn't expected anything nearly as big. "Are you planning to settle down?"

"Maybe in a year or two. I just haven't found a woman that I'm willing to tie the knot with." Nate glanced over and saw the pleased look on Matthew's face. It wasn't hard to tell the meaning behind the questions. Ann seemed to be the reason behind almost everything lately.

Nate tipped his hat farther down on his forehead to block the sun. "I've never had much luck at figuring out women," he said innocently. "For instance, since the day I arrived, I've wondered why the duchess accuses you of shooting her husband?"

Matthew looked at him sharply. "Is there a particular reason for asking?"

"Just curious. Who else am I going to ask? Certainly not her. All she can do is snap a man's head off."

Matthew laughed, thoroughly enjoying the comment.

By the time they arrived at the house, Nate knew all about Edmund Huntington. He knew Edmund slept with about any woman who came into his eyesight. He knew Edmund beat his wife and that Matthew had been tempted many times to charge into the bedchamber to stop the abuse, but hadn't because it would have only worsened matters. Nate knew Edmund's father had been deranged and abusive. He knew Edmund frequented a particular section of London where opium and any other depravity known to man was in abundance. Nate had seen similar places in San Francisco.

After turning their horses over to the stable boy, Matthew and Nate parted. Sir Drake headed toward the sound of Kit's laughter coming from the side of the house. Nate chuckled when the dog made a wide circle around the goose. Apparently the mutt had learned something after all.

Nate stepped onto the veranda and went directly to the huge old tree in the center. Its thick branches stretched out in all directions, giving a welcome reprieve from the burning sun.

He removed his hat, tossed it onto the bench circling the trunk, then sat. Closing his eyes, he inhaled the melodious odors of the flowers. The bright blossoms were in big planter boxes, as well as earthen pots sitting on the ground and other pots hanging from the open rafters. A couple of days ago, he'd found Danny out here cultivating her plants. She had said that this was her favorite place in the entire house. He agreed.

Nate rested his back against the thick tree trunk and relaxed. He thought of Ann calling him a drifter. She didn't know that part of his life had ended sometime ago…even before he'd joined his mother in New York. The only question had been where he wanted to live. Now he knew. As Beau's father had done, he'd turn his land into a fine ranch and a proper home for Richard. He already looked forward to his visits with the happy child, but resented being restricted to early morning sojourns so Blossom wouldn't get into trouble with Ann.

Nate picked up his hat and ran his hand around the brim. His casual inquiries with the servants, Danny and Blossom had not produced the answers he'd expected. All praised Ann, saying she was the perfect, caring mother. The next comment was usually, "Too bad she had to lose her husband."

The comments weren't consistent with the image Hester had painted of the duchess. Matthew's portrait of a confused and misused woman didn't agree, either. Nate's impression of Ann was entirely different from both Hester and Matthew's. So who was the real Antoinette Huntington? The woman who wanted money and power and cared about no one, the doting and loving mother, the woman who accused Matthew of murdering her husband to get rid of him, or the headstrong but insecure woman who had been in his bedroom trying to strike a bargain? Or was she sitting back and making a fool of all of them. Ann had been quite convincing as the impossible husband, Albert. That alone was enough to prove she couldn't be trusted. Damn if he'd let her hornswoggle him again.

Nate rose to his feet and stretched. Since Ann was so clever, why hadn't it occurred to her that she'd gone about this all wrong? How would she explain that he had delivered her baby when she'd denied ever having met him before?

Chapter Nineteen

Ann began following the narrow path she'd accidentally discovered while riding Star. For days it had been teasing her curiosity. Where did it lead? There was no doubt it was old. In most places it was obscured by undergrowth and thick brush. At times she'd had to search to be sure she was still on track. At least the effort was keeping her mind off Nate. She was disgusted with herself. He seemed to be all she could think about.

"Antoinette, I want to talk to you."

Ann felt as if an icicle had pierced her from head to toe. How had Matthew found her? She had been certain no one had seen her leave the house. Taking control of her emotions, she slowly turned and faced him.

Matthew sneezed. "Where do you think you're going?" he demanded.

Ann wanted to run. He'd catch her. She was too far from the house for anyone to see them. Her only chance of safety was to appear unafraid. "I wanted to take a walk alone." Why was he looking around the area? "Are you looking for something?"

"I thought you might be meeting Bishop."

Ann stiffened. "Why would you say that?"

"Why wouldn't I? All the other women in the house seem to be infatuated with him. I didn't like the way you were looking at him during breakfast." Matthew sneezed again.

Though Nathan had supposedly gone off with Beau this morning, he wanted to make sure it wasn't a ploy. Satisfied that there was no one else around, he settled his attention on Ann. "I want you to remember something, my dear. I would kill you before I would allow you to be in another man's arms."

Matthew spoke casually, but Ann knew he was dead serious. "As you killed Edmund?" *She would not let him frighten her!*

"Stop this foolishness, Ann. You don't belong in this savage place any more than I do."

"I've become quite fond of this so-called savage place."

"You'll quickly tire of it. You'll soon find that you miss the balls and social amenities that you're accustomed to in England. You don't belong with these people." Matthew pulled his handkerchief from his sleeve and blew his nose.

"And Richard?"

Matthew glanced up at the clear sky, trying to control his impatience. "Why do you persist?" He looked back at Ann. "We can marry and have our own children. Why would you want a bastard?"

Ann turned her back to him.

Furious, Matthew grabbed her arm and jerked her around. "I assure you, I can be quite a romantic. Unfortunately, circumstances have not permitted me to prove it." He pulled her into his arms and pressed his thin lips against hers.

Rather than struggle, Ann remained immovable.

Matthew pushed her away. "No wonder Edmund beat you," he said angrily. "It was probably the only way he knew to get any emotion from you."

"How dare you speak to me in such a manner?" Ann hissed back at him. "Dare you forget that I am the duchess of Gravenworth? You can do what you want with me, but it will gain you nothing. I have the proof that it was I who birthed Richard." Ann couldn't even see any of the outbuildings.

"Impossible. However, assuming you are telling the truth, then I shall be his father. But you must prove your statement first. You see, nothing has changed. Whatever it takes, you shall not escape me, my love."

Ann watched Matthew's gaze travel to her breasts and his eyes turn glassy. Good Lord! He was considering taking her right here on the path! She quickly turned away, pretending to examine the leaves on a tall bush. "Don't do anything foolish, Matthew," she said softly. "Should anything happen to Richard, or me, Beau will kill you."

"If he can find me." Matthew smiled. "However, I have no intention of incurring Beau's wrath," he said smoothly. He had to be careful. He had waited this long to possess Ann, and he could wait a little longer. Chico had already left for San Francisco to find the right captain with the right ship to carry off his plan. His eyes hardened. "Remember my warning, should you consider a liaison with the highwayman." He spun on his heels and left.

Ann watched Matthew disappear into the foliage.

She plopped down on the ground, trembling. For now she was safe. But what about the next time? Matthew had a plan, and he was only biding his time until he could put it into action.

Ann wanted to return to the house but couldn't bear the possibility of Matthew waiting for her. How foolish she had been to go off on her own. She had thought to take a walk in the fresh air to clear her mind of images. Images of Nate taming the horse, his face, his body, his kisses. Remembering the smell and feel of him were aphrodisiacs to her mind.

Ann looked ahead. She couldn't continue to just sit there. Standing, she decided to follow the path a little farther. It had to lead somewhere.

The brush rustled behind her. Ann spun about. Matthew had returned. She grabbed a dead limb, held it over her head and waited. But instead of Matthew, it was Sir Drake who bounded toward her. Ann laughed from pure relief. ''Where were you when I needed you?'' She reached down and gave him a loving pat.

Ann continued her quest but was disappointed when the path ended abruptly at a wide stream. Sir Drake ran to the edge and lapped the water as she studied the tall, dense foliage that followed the bank on the other side. Surely the path continued on. She nibbled at her bottom lip, her imagination alive and her curiosity eating at her.

Had this once been an outlaw or Indian trail? She would never know if she didn't ford the waterway. That would mean getting a perfectly good pair of shoes wet, or removing them and possibly cutting her feet on sharp rocks hidden below the surface. However, it looked shallow and the water running down the middle didn't appear to be too swift. After having traversed this far, it would be a shame to quit. She glanced at the sky. It was only midafternoon and it shouldn't take too long to return to the house.

Her mind made up, Ann removed her shoes. Her excitement building, she leaned down and grabbed the back hem of her skirt. Pulling it forward between her legs, she then hiked her skirt up to her knees and tucked the back hem into her waistband. Her shoes in hand, she stepped into the water. It was colder than she had expected, but the water was only ankle deep and the rocky bottom bearable.

Ann had reached the edge of the swift water when Sir Drake barked. She turned to see what he was barking at. She caught sight of a fox just before being plunged into the rapids. It was deeper and swifter than she had allowed for. She flayed her arms and kicked, frantically trying to keep from being pulled under, but she couldn't swim and her gown had become heavy and had wrapped around her. Facedown, she was taking in more water than she could hold. She was being washed downstream. She was dying!

It took a moment before Ann realized she was lying in shallow water. Coughing, sputtering and gasping for breath, she finally managed to drag herself into a sitting position, her heavy clothes making any movement seemingly impossible. Holding her stomach, she leaned to the side and heaved water time and time again.

Ann had no idea how long she'd sat there when she heard barking coming from the far side. She looked up just as Sir Drake jumped into the water. He came straight to her. After a good face-licking, he shook. Ann didn't even try to dodge the rivulets of water that shot out in every direction. Content, Sir

Drake bounded toward the bank. Ann caught sight of a wound on his neck where he'd apparently been bitten.

Ann managed to climb to her feet, but her breathing was even more labored from having to drag her skirts behind her. Relentlessly she waded toward where Sir Drake waited. The rocks were sharper now and bit unmercifully into the soles of her feet. Several times she stopped, gritted her teeth and waited for the sharp pain to subside. She blessed the sun's warmth as she pulled herself from the water and collapsed onto the dry ground. Mud puddles were already forming beneath her, but she didn't care. She was too tired to care about anything.

Blossom was so upset she could only speak in her native tongue. Worried that something was wrong with one of the children, Danny ran out of the house in search of Little Dog. Hopefully the old Indian could interpret what Blossom had been trying to say. If only Beau hadn't had to go to the fort to complete the cattle arrangements.

"Danny!"

Danny was relieved to see Nate standing by the stable.

"Why are you in such a hurry?" Nate asked as he walked toward her. "Is something wrong?"

"Blossom is terribly upset about something. I can't understand a thing she's saying. Do you speak her language?"

"I can understand most of it."

They hurried back to the house. Blossom met them at the doorway, relieved to see Diablo. She proceeded to tell him of her fears.

"What did she say?" Danielle asked. "Is something wrong with one of the children?"

"No. It's Ann."

"Ann?"

"Blossom is convinced something has happened to her. She says Ann went for a walk early this afternoon and hasn't returned. Have you seen her?"

Danny shook her head. "Not for several hours. I assumed she was either taking a nap or she'd chosen to remain in her room to avoid Matthew. He seems to be constantly at her heels. I don't trust him for a minute. Do you think he's done something to Ann?"

"I'll look for him. You ask around if anyone saw her leave."

Danielle nodded. "One of the hands told me she's been taking the mare out on rides lately."

"Not this time. Star's in her stall."

They quickly parted.

Nate found Matthew sitting on the veranda, drinking tea.

"Where is Ann?" Nate demanded.

"Is something wrong?"

"I don't know, but Blossom seems to think so. She went for a walk and hasn't returned."

Matthew frowned. "We talked earlier, but she continued on along some old path she'd found."

"Show me the path. I warn you, Matthew, if you've done anything—"

"Why would I do anything to the woman I'm going to marry?" Matthew demanded.

The sun had nearly disappeared over the horizon and every minute was crucial. Matthew led and Nate followed.

"I happened to see her disappear behind the tanning shed and followed."

"And you let her continue on alone?"

"She said she wanted to be alone."

"Did you fight?" Nate persisted.

"What we said is no concern of yours, but no, we did not fight."

They walked behind the tannery.

"There." Matthew pointed to the path.

"I'll follow the trail. You tell Danny to round up some men. I may need help to search for Ann."

"You tell Danny," Matthew said angrily. "I'm going after her, not you."

Matthew started forward. When Nate detained him, Matthew swung a fist. Nate dodged the blow.

"Dammit, we haven't time to settle this now. I can read trails—" Nate dodged another blow. Left with no recourse, Nate planted a hard fist to Matthew's stomach, causing the Englishman to double over. "Get to Danny. Have her bring men and lanterns." Nate took off running.

When Matthew could finally stand upright, he was tempted to take off after Nate. But the outlaw had been right. It was getting dark. He went in search of Danny. He and Nate would have to settle their differences another time.

What with the undergrowth and shrubs, the path would have been barely discernible to most people. But Nate could see where Ann and Matthew had stopped, where they had parted, and even where Sir Drake had joined her. But the trail was hours old. Ann should have long since returned.

Nate pushed himself harder, paying scant attention to brush and slender limbs that whipped at him. Ann knew nothing of the area or the dangers that could befall her. Besides the wildlife, Indians came into the area, knowing they were safe on Falkner land. Would they harm her?

Nate reached the riverbed. There had to have been considerable rain in the surrounding mountains for the river to be so swollen. After quickly determining that Ann had started to cross to the other side, Nate entered the water. Time was of the essence. The sun had gone down and there was little light left.

There were no signs of Ann leaving the water on the other side. Nate's gnawing concern grew, yet he refused to believe that she had drowned. He started following the bank downstream, carefully watching for anything that might show Ann had reached land. It was time consuming but he couldn't take a chance of missing anything.

Nate hadn't gone far when he thought about Sir Drake. Hopefully the dog was still with Antoinette. Nate placed two fingers between his lips and released an ear-splitting whistle. "Here, Drake," he called. "Come on, boy!" He whistled again. Sir Drake's bark started Nate running.

Night had closed in quickly, and Nate could barely make out Sir Drake standing protectively over the limp form lying on the ground. He saw her fingers twitch. Ann was alive.

Nate knelt and placed a hand on Ann's forehead. She was shaking badly from the cold, but she didn't seem to have a fever. He needed to get her warm as quickly as possible.

Ann's eyes opened. "Nate?" Her teeth were chattering, making it hard to talk.

"Yes, angel."

"I'm so c...cold."

"I know." He pulled his knife from his boot. "I have to get these wet clothes off you."

Ann nodded. "I fell in the st-stream."

When he was down to her chemise and drawers, Nate removed his shirt and wrapped it around her slender body. Satisfied that there was nothing more he could do, he lifted her in his arms and stood. She snuggled against his chest, drawing warmth from his body. Considering the strength of her determination, it seemed out of sorts that she felt so light in his arms.

Hearing Sir Drake whine, Nate looked down and smiled. "You did good, boy," he praised.

Nate worked his way back upstream, wondering where the shallowest part of the river would be. Then he heard voices and saw lantern lights on the other side of the bank. Help had arrived.

Ann raised her head from the pillow. The wooden shutters were open. It was the lack of sunlight in the room that told her it was late afternoon. She had slept all night and well into the day. She dropped her head back onto the bed. After having almost drowned, she felt amazingly good. Though she had drifted off and on to sleep while Nate had carried her, she clearly remembered the sensation of being pressed against his bare chest, his body warming her.

Ann raised her hand and felt the dry mud still caked in her hair. For the first time she was grateful that it was short. Getting the mud out would have been nearly impossible when her thick hair had hung past her hips. When she had been placed on her bed, Danny and Maria had stripped the rest of her clothing off. A quick sponge bath had followed, then she had been encased in a warm flannel nightgown and put to bed. A hot, wrapped brick had already been placed inside the covers to warm her feet. She had been too tired to stay awake a minute longer.

Ann heard a dog bark. Dear, sweet Sir Drake. He hadn't run away last night. He'd remained beside her, and had probably kept her from getting pneumonia. She needed to make sure the bite on his neck was attended to.

The door quietly opened and Ann watched Danny enter the room.

"You're awake," Danny said. She raised the hem of her skirt and went to the bedside. "How do you feel?"

Ann laughed. "Like Sleeping Beauty, except no prince kissed me awake."

"I'll go back out and let you rest."

"No, please stay. Really, I'm fine. I want to know how Nate found me."

"Like Beau, Nate knows how to follow a trail. It was Blossom who alerted me. I told Nate, and Matthew pointed out the path you'd taken." Danny clicked her tongue. "It's amazing. Your complexion is so pink and healthy that it's hard to believe what you've been through. Are you sure you wouldn't like me to leave and let you rest?"

"Positive. I'm so sorry I worried everyone."

"Since you mentioned a prince, I must say that I believe you've found one."

Ann stuffed another pillow beneath her head. "What are you talking about?"

"Nathan Bishop. He insisted on carrying you all the way. He left your bedroom only because I chased him out. Even then he paced back and forth in front in the hall like some caged animal and refused to go to bed until Blossom assured him you'd be fine. And, in all fairness, Matthew was equally concerned. There is no doubt in my mind that Nate and Matthew would have gotten into a fight had I not reminded them that you were sleeping.''

''Really?''

Danny sat on the edge of the bed. ''I was told to let them know the minute you opened your eyes.''

''I haven't made any conquests, Danny. Both men are devoid of any feelings.''

Danny smiled. ''You didn't see the concern on their faces. I think you underestimate Nate. He may appreciate women, but he also knows when to withdraw. He is a man who has kept a very close watch on his heart. I believe that this time he's having feelings that run far deeper than just concern.''

''You're a romantic.''

''True, but I still think you've captured the heart of a man who, hitherto, has been untouchable. Have you ever heard the story of Diablo?''

''I know he's a worthless outlaw.''

''Who told you that?'' Danny asked indignantly.

''A woman at the fort. And I'm sure Diablo's known many women,'' Ann commented, more to herself than Danny.

Danny's laughter drifted through the air. ''I believe that's rather obvious.''

''Obvious?''

''You can see it in his eyes and the way he looks at a woman. Nate knew how to protect himself against women…until you came along.''

''If he's an outlaw, why doesn't the law come and arrest him?''

"Until he showed up here, I hadn't heard anything about him in several years. The law could never put him behind bars because any witnesses to his crimes swore the wrong man had been arrested. He's a legend. He was always helping the needy, especially the Spaniards. Men and boys wanted to be just like him, and the women wanted him in their beds." Danny grinned. "I doubt if there is a man or woman in the southwest who hasn't heard of the infamous Diablo."

"Well you're wrong about him being interested in me. Nate only cares about Richard. It's my body he—" Ann swallowed. She had just made a huge mistake.

"Cares about Richard? Your body?" Danny asked suspiciously. She leaned forward and took Ann's hand in hers. "I know you're hiding something. Why won't you let me be your friend? I learned the hard way that things always seem better if you can talk them out."

Ann squeezed her eyes shut, fighting the urge to tell everything.

"If it's because of Beau, you have no cause to worry."

Ann badly needed a confidant.

"You don't know Beau as I do," Danny said, "or you wouldn't want to hide things from him. However, if you ask me not to repeat what you say, I'll honor that wish."

Tears slid from the corners of Ann's round eyes. "I guess I have to start trusting someone or I shall indeed lose my mind."

An hour later, after many questions and truths, Danny rose from the edge of the bed and exhaled. "Poor Ann. What a monumental task you took upon your shoulders. You've had no one. Not even Hester. As for Nate, he's a sly one. However, I still don't think I've misjudged him. Why would he try to black-mail you into his bed when he could probably have any woman he wants?''

''Because he knows he can't have me and his pride smarts.''

''Perhaps. I promised I wouldn't tell Beau about Richard, and I won't. But you're making a serious mistake. Matthew has threatened you and you believe he has a plan. Beau would make certain he doesn't fulfill his promise. What a dilemma. If you show Nate any attention, Matthew might harm you. On the other hand, if you don't find a way to pacify Nate, he could tell everything and leave with Richard.''

''Do you believe he'll do that?''

Danny smiled. ''No.'' She ran her hands down the front of her skirt to smooth it. ''If only I could talk to Beau,'' she mused.

''Danny, I love Richard as if he were my own child. I could not bear to give him up.''

''I know. But I agree with what Nate said. At this time, Richard is quite safe.'' Danny walked to the door. ''Are you hungry?''

''Starved.''

''And a hot bath?''

Ann grinned. ''Absolutely.''

Danny laughed joyously. ''I'll have your food pre-pared immediately and your tub will be filled as soon as the water is hot. In the meantime, I'll let Blossom and the others know you're all right. Dear Blossom. She sat in here all night watching after you and only left to check on Richard. Not until she was convinced you weren't going die was I able to talk her into getting some rest. You have very loyal friends.''

''Danny, I believe I will dine with you tonight. I can't let Matthew think he has me under his thumb.''

''Good for you. It will also allow the others to see for themselves that there has been no harm done.'' She took hold of the doorknob. ''Ann, just what are your feelings toward Nate?''

Ann sat up and swung her leg over the side of the bed. She felt a moment of dizziness, but it quickly passed. ''He's untrustworthy and an opportunist,'' she said quietly.

''Do you love him?''

''Certainly not. I could never love another man.''

Not for a minute did Danny believe that declaration. ''But you didn't love Edmund. From what you've told me, you've never been in love. I'm not certain that you'd even recognize it if you were.'' Danny opened the door. ''Permit me to express an opinion. If you don't want to tell Beau the truth, tell Nate. No matter what you think of him, he is the answer to all your problems.''

''But he wants to take Richard from me.''

''Because he sees only what you've allowed him to see. I'll tell the others you will be joining us for supper tonight.''

Danny quietly closed the door behind her.

Ann looked around the room, seeing nothing. Telling Danny the truth had removed a heavy burden from her shoulders. Someone else saw Matthew as he really was. But it hadn't resolved a thing. She had wanted counsel and she had received it. But as from the beginning, the decision was entirely hers. She could marry Matthew and let Nate take Richard. Then everyone would be happy. Except her. The thought of Matthew touching her and losing Richard, was more than she could tolerate. She had started all this, and she had to see it through.

That evening, Nate sat in the parlor, nursing his drink and smiling. Matthew certainly had a propensity for being in the wrong place at the wrong time.

"I can't begin to tell you how relieved I was when Thomas returned from the kitchen to inform me that I wouldn't die from poisoning," Matthew continued telling Danny. "I'm surprised I can even sit. The scorpion was between my sheets. He wasn't any longer than my little fingernail, yet it still hurts."

"I'm so sorry," Danny lied. She wished Ann hadn't sworn her to secrecy. When Beau returned tonight, she wanted desperately to tell him everything and put an end to Matthew's visit.

Matthew was still discussing the extent of his discomfort when Ann entered the parlor. Both men rose from their chairs. Nate's gaze followed her across the room as Matthew escorted her to a chair. She was tall, willowy, beautiful, and moved with a grace few women possessed. How could he have ever believed Albert was a man?

"I was so relieved when Danny said you were well enough to join us tonight," Matthew gushed. "I feel wretched. I should never have allowed you to go on alone yesterday."

Ann wanted to scream at him. But he was dangerous and she had no defenses. "As I recall, it was my decision, not yours."

"Are you sure you should be up so soon?"

"I'm fine. I want to apologize for my foolishness

and thank all of you for rescuing me.'' Earlier she'd spent time with Richard and had told Blossom how grateful she was. "I have already thanked Sir Drake.''

"Sir Drake?'' Matthew asked.

"Yes. Even though it was his yelp that caused me to fall in the water, he remained by my side, keeping me as warm as he could. Poor fellow, the fox he'd chased bit him on the neck, but he didn't complain.''

"I'll have to make sure he has an extra big bone tonight,'' Danny said.

As Ann explained what had happened at the river, Nate watched her closely from across the room. He didn't miss a single movement, nor the fact that she wouldn't meet his eyes. Why? He glanced at Matthew. The Englishman was too smug. What had he said to Ann to make her so edgy?

Chapter Twenty

Ann picked Richard up off the grass and placed him back on his blanket, but she knew he wouldn't stay there long. He was already trying to crawl, but instead of going forward he kept pushing himself backward. Richard let out a squeal of laughter and turned over on his stomach so he could watch Kit and Blossom playing tag. Kit couldn't stop giggling, which made Richard squeal all the more. Richard loved being outside and as she watched him having so much fun, she knew what she had to do. There was only one sure way to protect his heritage.

After returning Richard to the nursery for his nap, Ann left her room to search for Danny. She had only taken a few steps down the hall when Matthew stepped in through the French doors leading to the veranda. There was no question that he had been waiting for her.

Matthew grabbed her by the arms and shoved her against the wall.

Ann anointed him with a hostile glare. ''Be careful to remember I will eventually return to England,'' she threatened. "If you keep this up, I will see that you pay for any wrongdoing."

Matthew ignored her warning. "I left Beau only a short while ago. It appears you haven't said anything to him or his wife about departing for England."

"Nor do I intend to. I refuse to let you frighten me or to allow you to dictate my life. I have already sent letters to my father and uncle informing them of the new duke. I have also told Danny of your threats, and I've made certain Richard is protected at all times. Tomorrow or the following day I shall have proof that Richard is my child."

Matthew dropped his hand and stepped back. "And how do you plan to accomplish that?"

"I'll tell you and the others when I produce the proof. When it's discovered that you lied about the child being Hester's, no one will believe anything you say. It would be wise of you to take your own advice about leaving. I also suggest that when you return to England, you remove all your things from Graven-worth. You will no longer be welcome."

Matthew's lips thinned with anger. "You need not try to play your games with me, Ann. I don't believe a word you've said. When I leave, which will indeed be soon, you will be with me and we *will* be married aboard ship."

Ann turned and continued down the hall, her forearms aching where Matthew's finger had dug into them. How much longer could she continue this charade? From the way Matthew was acting, something terrible was going to happen. What frightened her most was his total confidence. He had a plan, and because she didn't know from which direction he would strike, she had no defense...without seeking help.

Matthew's gaze followed Ann until she disappeared from view. Yesterday Tex had told him that Chico would return as soon as he found the right sea captain. One or two weeks at the most, Tex had assured him. Then Matthew could put his plan in motion. It was a simple plan. Chico would kidnap Ann. Being one of the ranch hands, Tex would see that Chico left the ranch without being stopped. Chico would then put Ann on the ship in San Francisco, where she would be held a prisoner. By remaining at the house, no one could prove he was behind Ann's disappearance.

Matthew smiled. Then, sadly, when Ann could not be found, he would give up hope of ever seeing her again and leave for San Francisco to continue on to England. He and Ann would be married during the voyage. He had paid Tex and Chico well, with an agreement of more when he arrived at the ship and had made sure Ann had been well taken care of. Tex and Chico were too greedy to make any mistakes.

Matthew left the house by way of the veranda, then went directly to the blacksmith's shed.

"Good afternoon," Hector said cheerfully. "Is there something I can do for you?" He stopped working on a skillet he'd been given to repair and wiped his hands on his dirty leather apron.

Matthew looked with disgust at the blacksmith's bulging cheek where he held a wad of tobacco. "Yes, there is." He was careful not to get any soot on his clothes. "I plan to leave soon, and want to trap some animals to take back to England. I was wondering if you could make me a cage. Say...one that would hold an animal about the size of a coyote but would allow enough room to exercise, feed and drink.''

Hector rubbed his stubbled chin. ''How soon do you have to have it?''

''Naturally I'd like to start trapping as soon as possible.''

''Is tomorrow soon enough?''

Matthew gave him a tolerable smile. ''That would be excellent.'' He started to walk away.

''You got a place in mind to put that cage?'' Hector called.

Matthew returned to the shed. ''No. Do you have any suggestions?''

Hector spit tobacco juice on the ground. ''There's a big old oak sittin' by itself in a draw in the south pasture. You can't miss it. It'll give plenty of shade, there's a little creek that runs right past it, and no one ever goes out that way anymore. It's some kinda sacred Indian grounds. Your animals should be safe.''

Matthew nodded. ''Yes, indeed. It sounds like the perfect spot.''

Chapter Twenty-One

Ann tapped her finger on the arm of the chair as she and the others waited for Beau to change clothes and join them in the parlor. For the past thirty minutes she'd had to listen to Matthew entertain Danny and Nate with a dissertation on castles. It made her sick to see how perfectly he played the charming gentleman, devoid of murderous instincts. True, he had made several attempts to include her in the conversation, but she had refused to partake. So, for the present, she was being ignored.

Nate, however, had taken it a step further. Other than a brief acknowledgment when she had entered the parlor, he had completely ignored her. As before, he hadn't even given her the opportunity to inform him that she would return to his room tonight, and this time she would not act the milksop. This time, the coupling would take place. If he hadn't been gone all day with Beau, she would have already taken care of the matter.

Danny's knowledge of Nate's past and her comments on how he acted around women had continued to gnaw at Ann. She managed to give the impression she was listening to Matthew, when in reality she was comparing the way she remembered Nate on the train to his present demeanor. A metamorphosis described it perfectly. Apparently she had been so wrapped up in her own problems, she hadn't noticed how he exuded charm and was quick to flash the roguish smile that was so infectious. He knew how to turn a woman to jam and wasn't the least bit abashed about using it to his advantage.

Ann's ire raised a notch when Nate continued his cool aloofness during supper. Apparently he didn't consider her worthy of a gentlemanly acknowledgment even if he did want her in his bed. Matthew was undoubtedly elated at the way Nate was ignoring her.

Ann dabbed her lips with the linen napkin. How dare he treat her like this then turn around and steal kisses? She hated him. She hated everything about him! She despised him and Matthew for what they were forcing her to do. But Matthew was frightening her. Especially after their confrontation in the hall. She had to stop any schemes he might be plotting as quickly as possible, and there was only one way she knew to do it. Prove Richard was indeed the rightful heir.

She speared a carrot with a fork tine. Even as much as she hated Nate, she couldn't seem to keep her eyes off him. When he raised his wine goblet to drink, she caught herself staring at his long, tapered fingers as they curled around the crystal. He could easily hold both her hands in just one of his. The same hands that had so freely glided over her body when he had forced her to stand still while he searched for a weapon.

Ann looked down at the uneaten food on her plate. The woman in the train station had clung to Nate, and Hester couldn't seem to keep her hands off him. That would never happen to her. Tonight her infatuation would end. After having to put up with his body on top of hers, she would find him repugnant and never want to see his face again.

Ann looked up to tell Danny about her gift to Kit when she discovered a pair of dark eyes watching her. Nate's lashes were sinfully long for a man. Before she could look away, Nate winked. The gesture was so unexpected that the fork slipped from Ann's fingers and landed with a loud clank on her plate. The impropriety had drawn everyone's attention. A weak smile was all she could offer as an apology.

Ann wondered if Nate had known she'd been watching him. The nerve of the man to have winked at her! But if the wink had annoyed her, why did she feel warm and giddy inside? Because it proved that though he had shown no interest, she hadn't been out of his thoughts.

"Danny," Ann spoke up, "if you have no objections, I would like to give Sir Drake to Kit as a gift."

"But, Ann, Matthew said the dog is quite valuable."

Ann smiled. "In England, not the Arizona Territory. I hardly see him anymore and I know Kit has become very fond of him."

"Are you sure?" Danielle asked. "I hope you don't think—"

Ann shook her head. "I don't think anything."

"Kit will be so pleased," Danielle said excitedly. She proceeded to tell about Kit and the dog's antics and the time they spent playing on the veranda.

After supper, the others participated in a game of charades. Ann chose to watch instead of partaking, thereby making the two sides even. She used the time to reinforce her vow to not leave Nate's room until their agreement had been settled.

Thirty minutes after the game was over, Ann sat in her room brushing her hair until it glistened. She put the brush down. She was procrastinating. She didn't want to go to Nate's room. She felt as if she were turning her back on her integrity. With shaking fingers, she straightened the blue bow on the front of the nightdress. The long cloth amply covered her body, but it wasn't plain. It had trim down the front as well as the back of the bodice.

Fifteen minutes at the most, she assured herself, then it would be finished.

Ann took a deep, hopefully stabilizing breath and left her room. Her palms and cheeks were already moist from her nervousness.

Ann had since discovered that the two bedrooms were the only ones at the bend of the hall. Nevertheless, worried that she might be seen, she practically ran to Nate's chamber. She had already told so many lies she couldn't even remember them all, and she didn't want to have to think up more. Without announcing her arrival, she swung open the door and hurried inside. The lantern was turned high. She released a sigh. Nate was not in his room. She hoped that, perhaps, he would stay away all night, but she knew better.

As Nate walked down the hall, he was still chuckling over one of Matthew's rare witticisms. When he entered his room, it took a moment before he noticed

Ann silently standing near the chifforobe. Her posture was rigid and the long sleeves and stand-up collar of her nightdress certainly wasn't the most seductive costume he'd ever seen. The epitome of prudishness, he concluded. His gaze continued down to the simple slippers peeking from beneath the ankle-length gown, back to her full, tempting lips, and on up to her wide green eyes.

"I've come to consummate our bargain," Ann spouted. There! She'd said it. "And of my own free will," she added for good measure.

"I see."

"Is that all you have to say?" She watched him take his coat off and toss it onto the back of a chair, his arm muscles clearly defined beneath his shirt. "Danny said you're a noble man and—"

"Don't make me too noble or you're going to be very disappointed." Nate walked to the commode and poured himself a glass of water.

Ann stared in disbelief. This wasn't at all the way it was supposed to be. "Considering your reputation—"

Nate downed the water then turned. "My reputation?"

"Danielle told me all about Diablo." She licked her dry lips. Why didn't he come directly to her?

Nate's anger was growing by the minute. But what had he expected? She had said she would do anything to get what she wanted. She hadn't lied. "Have you ever taken a man to your bed besides your husband?"

Why was he acting so cold? "Most certainly not."

"Why?"

"Why what?"

"Why haven't you had a man in your bed? You're

still a young, very beautiful woman. Do you intend to become a nun?''

''That has—''

''Go back to your room, Duchess.''

Ann looked toward the door. No. She couldn't leave. ''I'm here because you said you would testify that Richard is mine if I let you bed me. Since you do not want to do so, I shall assume that you are forgoing your end of the bargain and will testify anyway.''

Nate glared at her. ''You can assume no such thing.'' He was about to tell her he had never said he would testify when she suddenly marched toward the bed.

''Very well, then let's be done with it. Fifteen minutes should be more than enough to satisfy your lust.'' Ann couldn't believe that she was being so forward.

''For someone who claims such innocence, you seem to be quite an authority on the matter.'' Nate didn't hide his sarcasm.

''Well...I was married.''

''Ah, yes. I guess that would make you quite knowledgeable about such matters.''

''Yes.'' As she moved toward the lantern, Ann said a quick prayer that her legs wouldn't buckle beneath her.

''What are you doing?'' Nate asked.

''I'm going to turn off the lantern.''

''But I want it left on.''

Surely he didn't expect to copulate in a lit room? She headed for the bed. Just fifteen minutes, she kept telling herself. Just fifteen minutes.

Nate watched in amazement as the duchess neatly

folded back the covers, then lay on the bed, her gown properly pulled down so as not to reveal any part of her body. Her legs tightly pressed together, she folded her arms over her waist and stared at the ceiling.

Nate's lips slowly curved into a smile. A man of honor wouldn't take advantage of the lady. Apparently he wasn't a man of honor. He unbuttoned the top buttons of his shirt, then pulled it over his head. It was time someone taught the prickly duchess a lesson she'd never forget, and he was in just the right mood to be the teacher. And there was no way in hell that she was going to leave in fifteen minutes.

"I can't say you are the most appealing woman I've seen," he teased.

Ann bolted straight up and gazed at his magnificent body and the curly black chest hairs.

Nate sat in the chair, then took his time pulling off his boots.

"We agreed that I would come to your bed, and I'm abiding by it. Now can we please get on with it." She plopped back down, again staring up at the ceiling.

"Since you're so eager to have me make love to you, I guess I should oblige." He stood and dropped his trousers.

"Make love? Is that what you call it?"

"I'm curious, angel, are you expecting to go through with this and not feel a thing?"

"I am a lady. Only men enjoy passion."

Nate's smile broadened. The more challenges she threw at him the more he was enjoying this. "Do you have anything on under your nightdress that needs to be removed?"

"You can at least show enough respect to not discuss such matters."

"Just answer yes or no."

"No." Feeling the bed sag, Ann squeezed her eyes
shut and waited for him to climb on top of her. Instead he brushed the hair from her face.

Nate propped himself up on one elbow and looked
down at her. "Look at me."

Ann shook her head.

"I don't bite."

His deep voice wasn't much louder than a whisper,
but Ann heard every word, as well as the humor in
his voice. He was enjoying her discomfort! She turned
her head toward him and opened one eye at a time.

"Making love wouldn't carry any pleasure for me
if it wasn't equally pleasurable for you."

"I have no need to hear your lies. I'm not so foolish that I don't know a man doesn't need a woman's
passion."

"I do." He leaned over and lightly kissed her on
the lips. "Such sweet honey."

Was he still making fun of her?

Nate took her hand and placed it on his chest. She
snatched it away.

"Why fight me? Take pleasure in what I can give
you."

"Your pleasure, not mine."

Nate chuckled. "Are you also going to tell me that
you haven't given any thought to our being together?" His tongue trailed a path down to the curve
of her neck before nibbling where her pulse beat.

Ann returned her gaze to the ceiling. "The only
thing I have dreamed of was seeing you hanging from

a rope by your neck. You are the lowest form of a cad to have forced me into this.''

"Poor Antoinette. I guess you're right. You're just going to have to suffer through it.'' He kissed the corner of her parted lips. "But since I'm rather particular about equally shared pleasures, I must insist you partake. Naturally it would only be pretending, but as Albert, you proved you're very good at acting.'' He took an earlobe between his teeth and tugged gently.

Ann could feel his warm, moist breath against her skin. "I can't—''

"Can't? A terrible word, *can't*.''

Antoinette clenched her fists, fighting the warm sensation his feathery kisses were creating. "If you insist, I'll try.''

"I insist. Kiss me.''

Ann leaned over and gave him a quick peck on the lips.

"Well, I guess that's a start.'' Had a man never kissed her? He felt her stiffen. "No one knows what's going on but you and I.''

Ann held her breath, refusing to acknowledge the pleasure she was feeling.

"If I make love to you, what's to stop you from making love to me? Put your hand back on my chest, Ann.''

Carefully she touched him, the feel of his corded muscles pleasing to her fingers. Nate's kiss became more passionate, his tongue playing with the inner pleasures of her mouth. Uncertain, Ann joined her tongue with his, the act creating magnificent erotic sensations. She drew a little closer, suddenly wanting to experience more. After all, it was only pretending.

When he sucked her tongue, tremors bolted through her body. She moved even closer, her body molding against his, her nipples rubbing against his chest hairs.

''Isn't that better when we do it together?''

Ann couldn't speak.

Layer by layer, Nate peeled away Ann's resistance. He had already determined that her husband hadn't been much of a lover. Ann was like a child, exploring new toys and discovering the pleasures they could give. He doubted that she was even aware of how her hands explored his body.

Nate devoured her with his tongue and kisses, drawing his own pleasure as her body came alive, yielding to a searing need she had never experienced before. He raised the hem of her gown, his hand trailing up her inner thigh. She stiffened but didn't try to stop him. As his finger located what he was searching for, Ann gasped. She was already damp.

''Tell me not to stop, Ann.''

Ann refused.

''Tell me you want me to make love to you.''

Ann was being drawn deeper and deeper into a whirlpool of desire. His body was so perfect. She could no longer fight the driving passion that was overwhelming her. ''I...''

''Tell me.''

Her yes was swallowed by his kiss. Openly admitting she wanted him had released what inhibitions Ann still had left. He was driving her mad as his mouth and hands trailed across every inch of her body. He sucked her fingers, her toes and her nipples, and her passion exploded. Her tongue trailed across her dry lips, and she moved her hips against him. When he pressed her hand down, showing her that his need was every bit as strong as hers, she couldn't stop touching.

"You're so beautiful," Nate murmured, his breathing heavy.

Ann didn't care whether or not he was telling the truth. His words were like music and she was already floating on clouds. He removed his hand from beneath her skirt. "No," she whined, not caring about her brazenness.

"There's better fruit to be had." His lips found hers, and he partook of the sweet nectar.

Ann was never aware of Nate removing her nightgown, only that when their naked bodies pressed together, she felt complete. "Yes," she moaned when he entered her. At some point her mind had stopped functioning. She'd thought herself incapable of such wild sensations and heaven forgive her, she didn't want Nate to ever stop. She was being shown the bliss of being a woman.

"You taste so good."

"Yes, yes," Ann encouraged as his thrusts became faster. Her breathing quickened. He was driving her wild with need.

With one strong, final thrust, Nate took them both over the cliff to the ultimate pleasure.

When Ann came to, Nate was still lying beside her. "What happened?" she asked.

"You fainted."

"No. That's not possible. I've never..."

He kissed her breast. "It happens sometimes."

Ann suddenly didn't know what to say or do. Should she dress and leave? She reached down and pulled the bedsheet over her.

Nate pulled it away. "Never be ashamed. You are

beautiful and your passion is a magnificent sight to behold.''

''I guess I was convincing.''

Nate kissed her palm then climbed off the bed. ''What are you talking about?''

''You told me to pretend.''

Nate roared with laughter as he went over to pour them a drink.

Ann suddenly realized the lantern had never been turned off. Yet Nate thought nothing of moving about without a stitch of clothing.

Ann took the glass he handed her and gratefully sipped the brandy. ''Was I a disappointment?'' she asked, refusing to look at him. She was holding the glass so tightly her fingers were turning white. ''I know you've had many women....'' She took another sip of her drink.

He lay on the bed beside her then took her glass and placed it on top of the bedside table. ''Hush,'' he said as he pulled her on top of him. ''There were no women before you, just as there were no men before me.'' He kissed the end of her nose. ''You were beautiful. So beautiful that I already want to make love to you again.''

''You don't want me to leave?''

''Oh, no.'' He rolled her over and kissed her stomach.

''Nate, I can't—''

''Oh yes, you can.''

''But—'' She dug her nails into his shoulders as he proved he could again make her body come alive.

Ann left Nate's room just before dawn, a reborn woman. She had never been so happily exhausted. She wasn't walking, she was floating. She giggled. She hadn't even remembered to put her slippers on.

Chapter Twenty-Two

Matthew tossed the meat into the cage, then stood watching Sir Drake. The dog growled but didn't charge at him. Matthew had lied to Hector about what he wanted the cage for, because Matthew had known Ann would throw a fit at any suggestion to pen the dog up. He frowned, remembering the battle he'd had just to get a rope around the blasted dog's neck and drag him here.

So far there had been no indication that anything was wrong with the dog...but the ten days weren't up yet.

Matthew's gaze traveled around the cage, making sure it was still secure. Satisfied, he mounted his horse and headed north. He should have already had Ann out of here, but the toad Chico still hadn't returned from San Francisco.

Matthew kicked his mount in the sides. If he had timed it right, he should reach Skunk Creek before Nathan.

Nate was whistling the *Battle Hymn of the Republic* by the time the tree line that followed Skunk Creek came in view. Smelling the water, the roan he was riding snorted, shook his head and started moving his hooves a little faster. Nate chuckled. "I don't blame you. I could use a drink, too."

Nate felt good. His ride to Prescott had been time well spent. He had sent a wire to his lawyer in New York. The lawyer had wired back, confirming the money requested would be transferred to one of the Falkner banks in Santa Fe, as well as the bank in Prescott. Nate was also pleased at the price he and Beau had settled on for the cattle he was going to purchase. Everything was in place now.

All that was left was for him to make up his mind about Ann and Richard. He had thought Ann wanted nothing but money and power. Since arriving at the ranch, he had seen her determined, untouchable, vulnerable, grateful, sad, and wild with passion. It was a combination that from the beginning had pulled at him like a magnet. But then he always had been a sucker for anything he shouldn't or couldn't have.

After making love all night, he knew her body and expressions as well as he knew the back of his hand. He knew her too well to believe Hester's lies. Once Ann had shed her inhibitions, he had discovered all sorts of qualities within her, but hate and indifference were not among them. Nor could he find any fault in Ann as a mother, and there was no reason not to believe she loved Richard. He could guess at Hester's reasons for damning Ann, but it would only be supposition.

He and Ann's passions fit well together. Last night he had awakened her and she had become his. But he no longer wanted just her body, he wanted her soul, also.

When he reached the creek, Nate dismounted and let the roan drink. Nate was about to kneel down and help himself to the water when a shot rang out, the bullet lodging in the tree behind him. He swung around and saw Matthew standing less then twenty feet away.

"The miss wasn't an accident," Matthew stated smugly. "I'm a very good shot. I'm sure you can guess as to the purpose of this."

Nate's eyes turned the color of obsidian. "I don't like anyone taking a shot at me, especially when I'm not armed."

"I really don't care about what you do or do not like. I have no qualms about protecting what I consider mine, and Ann belongs to me."

"So you're going to kill me like you did Edmund?"

"Whether I did or did not kill Edmund is not the issue here. However, I can assure you I would not hesitate to shoot you if it became necessary."

"Ann isn't your property, Matthew."

Matthew moved forward, his pistol still aimed at Nate. "Stay away from her. You're nothing more than a slug hoping to become a snail. You could never make her happy. She belongs in England with her own kind."

Nate took a quick look at his surroundings. Matthew had picked the perfect time and spot for an ambush. No one was around. "You don't scare me, Matthew. I've faced worse threats than you, and many of them were every bit as big a coward."

"Your attempt to anger me is wasted. And don't think you can hide from me later. There are too many ways to catch a man off guard and make a death look accidental.''

From the corner of his eye, Matthew caught sight of something moving. He turned to see what it was, only to discover a mouse scurrying for shelter. Too late Matthew realized his mistake. Nate was already closing the distance between them. Matthew raised the pistol but Nate was too fast. He knocked the gun from Matthew's hand, sending it flying out of reach.

''All right, you bastard,'' Nate growled. He swung his fist, but to his surprise, Matthew easily dodged the blow. Matthew was quick and wiry.

Matthew managed a few good punches, but the fight didn't last long. When Matthew lay facedown on the ground, gasping for breath, Nate placed his foot in the middle of the Englishman's back and raised his head up by the hair.

''Be grateful I don't kill you here and now. Let's get one thing straight. I intend to see Ann as often as I damn well please. And since I have no desire to keep having to watch for you over my shoulder, I'm going to leave a note with Beau. You'd better take real good care of me, Matthew, because if I die, Beau's going to open that note and you're the one who's going to take the blame for my death. Do you understand what I'm telling you?''

''I understand.''

Nate let Matthew's face fall back to the ground, then removed his foot from the Englishman's back and walked to where his horse had shied away. ''One other thing,'' he said as he picked up the reins dragging on the ground, ''don't ever point a gun at me unless you intend to use it.''

Nate tossed the reins over the horse's neck and

hoisted himself into the saddle. He nudged the roan into a gallop and never looked back.

Matthew lunged toward where his pistol had landed. It was gone! He pulled himself to his feet, his body aching from the blows he'd received, and stood watching the dust trailing behind Nate's mount. The bastard had picked up the gun and taken it with him.

When Nate returned to the house, he found Ann and Danny on the veranda working with the flowers. Blossom was watching over Richard who was watching Kit play with his metal soldiers.

"Nate, Nate," Kit screamed as he ran to him.

Nate caught the boy under the arms and swung him up in the air, much to the child's delight. Even Richard laughed.

"Ann," Nate said, after putting Kit back on his feet, "I thought you might like to go for a ride."

"Where to?"

"I thought you might like to see where your path ended. I figured that after all you went through, you deserved to see it."

Ann looked up. He had a devil's grin. She looked at Danny. Danny smiled back at her.

"I'm quite capable of tending the flowers by myself," Danny teased. "And don't worry about Richard. He'll be fine."

Ann removed her apron. "I need to change clothes," she commented as she brushed off the dirt from her skirt.

"Nonsense," Nate said. "You look wonderful. Besides, I've already got Star saddled and ready to go."

Ann didn't need a second invitation. She kissed Richard goodbye, then followed Nate.

Later, when they reached their destination, Nate swung down from his horse. Ann tossed him Star's reins, but she remained transfixed in the saddle. "Oh, Nate," she muttered as her gaze traveled along the narrow draw before her. "It's like castles built into the cliff."

Nate helped her dismount. "They're old Indian cliff dwellings," he told her as he tied the horse to a shrub. "If you hadn't fallen into the river, you would have found them yourself."

Ann walked ahead, her gaze taking in everything. "How did you know about them?"

"After rescuing you, I also became curious as to where the path led." His eyes took in her thick shiny hair that now reached her shoulders, then his gaze trailed down to her ankle-length gown and boots.

"Do you think it's safe to go through it?"

"It's already crumbling in some spots, but most of it seems secure. Just be careful."

Ann continued walking, craning her neck to see everything. "They're at least six stories high. Thank you for bringing me here."

Nate perched himself on a fallen boulder.

"You're watching me again," she called. She turned and smiled. She hadn't realized how far she'd walked.

"How did you know?"

"I can feel it." She locked her hands behind her and strolled back. "I always know. I even knew when you saw me at the fort."

"Have you told anyone we were together last night?"

Ann lowered her head. "No," she said softly.

"When you allowed me to make love to you, you gave up more than you realize."

"What do you mean?"

"You belong to me now."

"I belong to no one except Richard."

Nate chuckled. "It's not a death sentence, you know. Would you like me to prove I'm right?"

Ann folded her arms over her chest and stared at him.

"No reply? Duchess, I know you so well now. I know how to make you laugh, I know how to make you cry. I know your expressions and I know you became excited when I asked you to come with me, even though you hid it from Danny. I also know that all the way here you were thinking about being in my arms again, but you're too proud to ask me to make love to you."

Ann was embarrassed to know he could read her thoughts so easily. "That's not so," she denied.

"Are you saying you don't want me to make love to you?"

"That's exactly what I'm saying."

"Don't try lying to me, Duchess. It won't work. You want me every bit as much as I want you."

"We had a bargain, and I've fulfilled my part. Nothing more. And just when do you plan to tell Beau and the others that I'm Richard's mother?"

Nate shoved his hat to the back of his head. "I've no intention of telling anyone a thing."

"But you—"

"You assumed I would, and I never bothered to correct you. No, I'm not going to tell Beau or anyone else you're Richard's mother."

Ann picked up a rock and threw it at him. Another

followed before she took off running toward the horses. In one fluid movement, Nate leaped off the rock and had her by the arm before she could even grab Star's reins.

"Turn me loose," Ann demanded.

Nate easily contained her flogging fists. "You didn't let me finish."

With all the fury of a tiger, Ann leaned forward and bit him on the shoulder.

"Why, you little wildcat," Nate uttered before his mouth claimed her in a punishing kiss.

Ann bit his lip, but the kiss continued. She kicked at him, only to be thrown onto the ground. "I don't want you touching me," she screamed. She twisted her body from side to side and pounded his chest with her fists. Then he was lying on top of her, his knee between her legs preventing her from moving. She tried scratching his back, only to have her arms stretched over her head. Then his mouth was on hers again. She hated him! But his kiss softened and coaxed, and try as she did, she couldn't stop the fire that was already blazing within her.

Nate pulled his lips a hairbreadth from hers. "I told you, you're mine now."

Again Ann struggled, and Nate laughed. Her efforts quickly faded as she gave way to the raw passion he could so easily ignite. She wanted him, and he knew it. He answered her craving with a fervor that took her beyond anything she had known. It was, indeed, exquisite bliss.

Still in a state of euphoria, Ann lay quietly on Nate's arm, her breathing slowly returning to normal.

"Telling everyone you're Richard's mother would have accomplished nothing."

Ann sat up and looked at Nate. His eyes were closed and he looked as if he were sleeping. "How can you say that?" she asked, still clinging to the last bit of hope that he would change his mind.

Nate opened his eyes and remained silent for a moment, gathering his thoughts. "Because, Duchess," he finally said, "you play your roles too well. You made a big error when you led everyone to believe we had never met. They won't believe the truth now, but they will believe you coerced me into saying you're Richard's mother."

Ann paled. She had been so determined to prove Richard was hers that she had failed to see the impossibility. Hester's death, the fight and anguish she'd gone through to keep from having to go to Nate's bed, then the humility she had suffered for acting like a whore had all been for nothing. Even her flight from Matthew had failed. Matthew had been right. Nothing had changed. She was right back where she had started. The men had her where they wanted her. Matthew could continue making threats when no one was around and Nate had accomplished exactly what he had set out to do.

Ann snatched up her clothes and started dressing. "I want to return to the house."

Nate could see Ann's emotions mirrored on her face and could fairly well guess what was running through her mind. He considered taking her in his arms and soothing away her worries, but right now she wanted nothing to do with him. She had every right to be upset.

They rode back in silence, both lost in their own

thoughts. When they left their horses at the stable, Ann walked away, her posture rigid and her determination set in stone. As she neared the house, she saw the goose chasing some chickens that had escaped the coop. "Nate," she called in an unfriendly tone of voice, "have you seen Sir Drake lately?"

"No."

"Strange, no one else has, either."

"He's probably found him a coyote in heat. He'll show up before long." Nate made a mental note to search for the mutt. Hopefully he hadn't gotten himself in some kind of trouble he couldn't get out of.

"You can't escape your feelings or needs, Duchess," he called after her as she continued on toward the house.

"We'll see."

Nate laughed.

Chapter Twenty-Three

Two nights later, Ann stood in her dimly lit room, aching for Nate to make love to her. Even after he'd used her in every despicable way possible, tonight in the parlor she had wanted to reach out and touch him. She had wanted to feel his lips devouring her…their bodies united.

She went to the bowl of water and splashed it on her face again. She would not allow this to happen. She pulled up her gown and ran her wet hands down her stomach, trying to rid the throbbing ache. She did not belong to Nate, nor did she want him. She had a son to raise and it was time she returned to her purpose for being here instead of constantly thinking about a man who wasn't worth her thoughts.

Tiny beads of perspiration broke out on her face as she threw herself onto the bed. She was living in a hell of her own making. No. It was Nate's fault. This would never have happened if he had left her alone.

Ann's door suddenly banged open.

"Damn if you aren't a stubborn minx," Nate growled as he approached Ann's bed.

Ann gasped. "Get out of my room!" she said, her

pride speaking. But her sexual desire was still paramount. His chest was bare, and she doubted there was anything beneath the jeans he wore.

Though the lantern was turned low, Nate could see the passion in Ann's eyes. ''I don't think so.'' He scooped her up in his strong arms and started toward the door. ''I'd take you here and now if it wasn't for Blossom or Richard.''

''No!'' Ann persisted, even though she was being assaulted with waves of excitement. Nate had come after her.

As Nate carried her down the hall, Ann's heated body molded to his. She buried her face against his throat and inhaled the pleasing musky smell that she had come to know. How could she have even thought she could resist him? She wanted him more than ever. Just being in his arms fueled the passion she had already been suffering. Her body was damp, alive with wanting.

Nate entered his room and kicked the door shut.

Ann looked into his eyes, waiting, needing to feel his lips on hers. Instead, he claimed a taut dusky nipple pressed against the material of her gown. Ann moaned and arched her back to give him better access. She ran her finger through his thick hair and closed her eyes, no longer remembering why she had chosen to deny him her body. She longed for fulfillment.

Nate set her on the bed. As he dropped his trousers, she impatiently pulled her gown over her head, eager to feel his naked body against hers.

Nate lay down beside her. The other night he had turned a kitten into a tigress. Though she already wanted him, he wanted to see that tigress again. He kissed, touched and nibbled the places he knew to be the most sensitive.

"Nate," Ann said, her breathing shallow, "I want you."

"Your soft skin and sweet mouth."

"But—"

He trailed a path with his tongue down the valley between her breasts. "I want to coax and tease until your body is screaming for me." He nipped her flat stomach as his hand caressed her inner thigh. His body moved against hers as he returned to her lips. "I want to hear you say please."

"Please," Ann murmured as his hand moved higher up her leg.

Nate tugged at Ann's bottom lip, teased it with his tongue, but didn't kiss her. Already lost in the throes of desire, she began moving her hips back and forth, drawing what pleasure she could from his hand resting between her legs, while raining kisses over his body. She was driving him to the breaking point.

"Tell me you'll never stay away from me again," Nate said, finding it difficult to talk.

Ann shook her head. "Never...again."

Nate rolled onto his back. He was not just driving her wild, it was all he could do to keep control of his own need. He chuckled with delight when Ann straddled him then eased herself down on his swollen member. The flame within had become a roaring fire. She was possessed and determined. She was everything he could ever want in a woman.

"You feel so good," he crooned. Her back was arched, her sweet breasts pushed forward, as if waiting for his mouth. Her lips were open and her eyes closed as she rolled her hips on top of him. He sat up, pushing himself deeper inside her.

"Oh, Nate," Ann whispered. She wrapped her arms around his neck.

To Nate's delight, her mouth covered his hungrily as she continued to move up and down on him. "Did you miss me last night?" he asked between kisses, his voice husky.

"I...thought I would...lose my mind...I wanted you so badly. I..."

Nate could no longer control himself, and he had heard what he had wanted to hear. She was his completely. He rolled her over on her back. She wrapped her legs around his waist. Her breasts had taunted him all night, and he ravished each one as he took Ann with him to the clouds where they soared like eagles.

Later Ann watched Nate walk across the room, stark naked, to get them a drink of water. He'd told her he didn't wear nightclothes, not even in the winter. He combed back his hair with his fingers, causing his arm and back muscles to ripple, then doused his face with cold water from the pitcher. She never tired of watching.

"You should have told me you wouldn't say anything about Richard being my child," Ann said, after they had shared the water and Nate had returned to the bed. "You forced me to come to your bed, believing—"

Nate chuckled. "I've been called ruthless when I want something bad enough." He brushed her hair from her cheek. "I was willing to do whatever it took to get you in my arms. I'm not going to say I'm sorry. I'd do it again if I had to."

Ann's pulse became erratic. Was he saying he loved her? No, she was fantasizing. But maybe he could learn to love her. "Nate, why don't you go to England with me?"

"Why do you have to go to England? Why can't you remain in America?"

"Richard has to be proclaimed duke of Gravenworth."

"Is money and power still that important to you?"

Ann rolled over so she could face him. "Money and power have nothing to do with it, Nate."

Ann snuggled against his warm body and placed her arm over his chest. "You said you know me well. That may be true, but the woman you know in America is not the duchess of Gravenworth. Nate, from the time I was a baby, I was raised knowing my obligations and that they took precedence over everything. My desires came second. I accepted those obligations when I agreed to marry Edmund."

Ann raised her head. "Nate, can't you understand what I'm saying? I can't turn my back on all the tenants for whom I'm responsible. When Richard grows up, he will bear the same responsibility."

Nate remained silent and Ann lay back down. She should have waited to talk about her return to England. No matter what she had tried telling herself about remaining in America, she knew there had never been a choice. She would return to England. It was her birthright.

The following afternoon Nate and Ann went for a ride. As soon as they were far enough away from worrying about prying eyes, they made love.

Much to Nate's delight, Ann had completely shed her inhibitions. She came to him free and wild and not at all abashed at admitting her need for him. She wanted to learn and experience everything. She even took pleasure in running about in the grass naked. Antoinette Huntington had discovered a whole new life.

For the next two hours he and Ann made passionate love in the tall grass. If they weren't making love, they talked.

"Are your parents still alive?" Ann asked at one point.

"No. My father died when I was seventeen. I was on my way back from my mother's funeral when I got on the train. Tell me about your mother and father."

"My mother passed away when I was seven. The sadness has long since been buried with memories." Ann waved away a pesky fly. "My father is tall, very attractive and has the eye of many women. I have one brother, two years my senior."

Fond memories brought a smile to her lips. "When I was young, I was forever sneaking away so I could follow Piers about...much to his aggravation. Because he continually insisted that I was too young to tail after him, I became determined to prove I was every bit as good at doing anything he could."

She laughed playfully. "My father wasn't at all pleased with my boyish behavior. Determined that I should have only ladylike mannerisms, he was constantly changing nannies and tutors. On more than one occasion he threatened to send me to a convent if I didn't start acting with proper decorum."

"I would like to have known you then." Nate ran a blade of grass down Ann's bare stomach. "I have an uncle in San Francisco. Years back he gave me a bit of advice.''

''What was that?''

Nate reached up and pulled Ann down on top of him. ''He said to beware of women. Especially Englishwomen.'' He kissed the curve of her neck.

''He did not.''

His hands cupped her hips and he moved her around on him.

''I have never been good at taking advice.''

During the following weeks, Ann and Nate took every opportunity to be alone. For now, Ann didn't have to worry about Matthew. He continued to remain in his room trying to overcome his sneezing, runny nose and his itchy eyes.

Most of the time Ann and Nate made love at the old Indian dwellings that Ann was so fond of. Their nights were spent in Nate's quarters. Ann worried constantly that someone would catch them, while Nate could have cared less.

But time was running out.

Ann couldn't bear the thought of having to leave Nate. She loved him far too much to lose him. But soon she and Richard would have to return to England.

Try as she might, Ann couldn't make Nate understand that too many people were dependent on her, and that her father had his own responsibilities and couldn't be expected to handle her tenants and obligations as well as his own.

Toward the end of the week, as Nate and Ann lay satiated in one of the rooms of the old dwelling, Ann decided to broach the subject of England again. She knew Nate didn't want to discuss it, but she couldn't allow it to drop.

Ann sat up and looked down at the man she loved. Nate playfully trailed a finger down her breast and over the nipple.

"Have I told you that you have perfect breasts?"

Ann's pride swelled. Where Edmund had made her feel ugly, Nate made her feel like a queen.

Nate pulled her back down on him and ran his tongue over the tempting nipple. "Mmm," he muttered, "you taste just right."

"Stop it," Ann said lovingly. She pulled away and sat back down on the ground. "I have something to discuss."

Nate laughed. "All right. What is it you have to say?"

"I didn't tell you that in England you could have anything you want."

Nate groaned and rolled onto his back.

"Nate, I'm trying terribly hard to make you want to come with me."

"I already have everything I want," he said gruffly. Nate was fighting his own demons. He had never loved a woman so deeply and it frightened him.

"Apparently I misunderstood." Ann glanced around the small room, needing to contain the emotions she was feeling. "I didn't realize I was so naive. I thought..." She looked down at the ground. "You're right. It wouldn't work. My father would insist we marry."

Ann cleared her throat. His silence was overwhelming. "I'm sorry. Though you've never said it, I had foolishly assumed you loved me." She turned away from him, trying to fight back the tears that were threatening to explode. This was Diablo. How could she have even thought that, just because they were lovers, he would be in love with her? She was embarrassed. She hurt. She wanted to die. "I should have known better...I—"

Nate took one of her hands. "Shh. You've no reason to apologize, angel." He pulled her back into his arms

"Having just made a complete fool of myself...I think we should—"

"Ann, I love you." He kissed the top of her head. "It just took me awhile to realize it. I started questioning my motives for getting you in my bed after I found you cold and motionless by the river. I would have killed any man who tried taking you away from me that night."

"You would have done that?" Ann said in awe.

"In the flick of an eye."

"And now?"

Nate chuckled. "And now, I'm even more dangerous."

"I think I loved you the first time I ran into you."

"How much do you love me?" Nate asked, his humor gone.

"Are you asking me to prove it?"

"Come away with me."

"You know I can't do that," she said. "But we can be together in England. We could always come back for visits."

Nate sat up. He had a driving need to have her prove her love. Not for money, not for power and not for Richard. For him. "Ann, say to hell with England. Let Matthew have his title and you come away with me. I know we would be happy. Richard could grow up just like any other boy. There's nothing in England that you can't have here.''

"I can't,'' Ann stood, again fighting the desire to cry. He hadn't understood a thing she had been trying to tell him.

"Then have someone run the place for you.''

"Get a manager? He could take everything, besides robbing and mistreating the tenants. If you love me as you say, why can't you go to England instead of me staying here?''

"I won't be a kept man.''

"No,'' Ann said anxiously. "It wouldn't be like that.''

Nate stood. "I believe it would.'' He began pulling on his clothes.

"Nate,'' Ann pleaded, "why are you being so stubborn. There is nothing to keep you in the colonies.''

He looked at her, anger and suspicion eating at him. They were at an impasse. He wanted to take her in his arms and tell her he'd go to England. But first he had to prove to himself that once there, she'd decide she didn't love him after all, she had simply wanted to secure Richard's title.

"I could say the same thing. You have nothing in England,'' he snapped at her.

"You know that's not true,'' she retorted.

"What I know is that you would give up everything to make a child—who isn't even yours—a duke. Richard is only a baby. He can't possibly rule over his so-called tenants. So don't try telling me you're doing this for him.''

Ann wanted to say a man doesn't become a proper duke just because he has a title, and that it takes years of training. But what good would it do? She reached for her clothes. There seemed to be no resolution.

After supper, Matthew hurried to his room. Danny and Ann retired to the parlor while Nate and Beau went onto the veranda to enjoy a smoke and drink.

"Beautiful night," Nate commented after lighting his cigar.

"Not as far as Matthew's concerned. Danny tells me he sat for hours leaning over a steaming bowl of water with a towel draped over his head, inhaling whatever it is that Thomas puts in the water. Cook told Danny that he's even tried mustard plasters and anything else that's suggested."

Nate laughed. "Couldn't happen to a better man. Unfortunately, he told Ann he was starting to feel better."

Beau nodded.

Nate turned and faced his friend. "I know there's something on your mind tonight besides Matthew, so why don't you just spit it out."

"I was in my study most of the day, and never saw hide nor hair of you or the duchess. Danny confessed that while Matthew has been in his room all week, you and Ann have been going out on long rides."

"Ann's not a spring maiden keeping watch over her virginity, Beau. She's a widow. What she does is her own business."

"As a friend, I'm asking you to tell me what's going on."

Nate strolled over to the tree bench, sat down and took several puffs on his cigar. "Very well. Your suspicions are quite accurate. I seduced her."

"Seduced or forced?"

"That depends on your interpretation of force."

"What the hell is that supposed to mean? Dammit, Nate, did you physically force yourself on her?"

"Nope. She willingly climbed into my bed."

Beau rubbed the back of his neck. He was at a complete loss as to what Nate was talking about. "Are you saying she likes her romps with men?"

"Absolutely not."

"What the hell is this? Some sort of guessing game?"

"I just don't care to discuss it. I seduced her, but it backfired. I fell in love."

Nate didn't expect Beau's sudden peal of deep laughter.

"*That* should make Danny happy," Beau finally managed to say. "She's said all along that the two of you were a perfect match. So the infamous Diablo finally let a female bring him to his knees!" He couldn't stop chuckling.

A slow grin settled on Nate's lips. "I don't know that you have anything to laugh about. Danny managed to do the same thing to you."

"Don't you see? That's what's so damn funny. Another good man has joined my ranks!" Beau looked at his friend. "Have you asked her to marry you?"

"Nope."

"I know you're a grown man, Nate, but let me give you a word of advice. Don't let Matthew stop you from staking your claim. Because of damn pride, I almost lost Danny to another man. Thank God, I finally came to my senses."

"It hasn't been Matthew keeping me from her."

Beau frowned. An owl had hooted three times. Never a good sign. Something was going to happen and it wasn't going to be good. "So Ann was your quest?"

Nate nodded. "There are, however, two major problems. She's determined to return to England. Secondly, I'm not sure if she loves me or just thinks she does."

"You have a suspicious nature. But then so did I."

Nate smiled. "But mine's inbred. A friend of mine put it very well. He called it bitter roots."

Beau went over and sat beside his friend. "Since you seem to be in a talkative mood, would you care to tell me how you and Ann knew each other before coming here?"

Nate chuckled, not at all surprised at Beau's perceptiveness. "I'm not inclined to be *that* talkative."

"But you do admit knowing each other."

Nate's smile broadened. "Let's talk about it a couple of years down the road."

Beau knew it was useless to pursue the matter any further. "I received another wire from those buyers in Chicago."

"And?"

"I've decided to go talk with them. They want to buy stock from me for breeding purposes. Seems they're interested in starting their own cattle business."

"How long are you going to be gone?"

"Two weeks at the most. Can I count on you to watch after things?"

Nate nodded before finishing his drink.

Chapter Twenty-Four

Feeling better than he had in days, Matthew rode out to check on Sir Drake and to make sure Tex had been feeding him properly.

After tying his horse to a tree branch, Matthew walked the few feet to the cage. He watched Sir Drake run around, lie down, then do the same thing again. The dog's countenance was now anxious. His eyes were bloodshot and his appetite depraved. He had neglected his food, yet hungrily devoured his own excrement. There was no longer any doubt that the fox that bit him had been carrying rabies.

Matthew wondered if there was a way he could use this to his advantage, but dismissed the thought as quickly as it had entered his mind. Someone was going to have to put the beast out of his misery, but it wasn't going to be him. Everyone knew the dog didn't like him, and would undoubtedly accuse him of murder.

Matthew mounted his horse and headed back to the house. Though he'd never cared for Sir Drake, there was no reason for the dog to suffer any longer. Hopefully, by the time he reached the house, Beau would have returned from a sudden business trip to Chicago. If not, Danny would have to handle the problem.

As soon as Matthew had the horse secured at the hitching post, he hurried into the house.

"Nelly," Matthew called to the little maid who had kept him company last night. "Has Mr. Falkner returned?"

Nelly giggled. "No, sir, he hasn't. Will I be joining you again tonight?"

"I can't be bothered right now," he admonished. "If I want you I'll send for you. Where is the duchess?"

"Last I heard she was in the nursery with her son," Nelly replied with a pout.

"And your mistress?"

"Her and Diablo are outside somewhere."

"His name isn't Diablo!" Matthew left the house.

After asking several men, one of the hands informed Matthew that Danny and Diablo were in the stable. Matthew gritted his teeth. Soon he wouldn't have to listen to that name again.

Matthew entered the big, magnificent stable that could compete with any England had to offer. He walked down the brick center. As he looked in the stalls lining either side, some of the fine horses stuck their heads out the compartment openings and nickered, while others paid no attention. He inhaled the familiar odors of fine leather tack and freshly laid hay. He was reminded of his own stable and suddenly felt a deep longing to be back in England. Where the hell was Chico? He'd had enough time to locate a dozen willing captains. He passed Star's stall and frowned. One way or another he was going to find the owner of the mare and offer a price that couldn't be refused.

Hearing Danny's laughter, Matthew hurried forward.

"She's so beautiful!" Danny laughed again. "Nate, have you ever seen anything so perfect?"

Matthew reached the large stall. Danny, Nate and several others stood off to the side, admiring the new foal. The filly tried standing on long, wobbly legs, then fell back down. The mare nudged her encouragingly.

"This is indeed an auspicious occasion."

Everyone turned to see who had spoken.

"Unfortunately," Matthew continued, "I must interrupt. Danny, I need to speak to you in private."

"Is it something that can wait?" Nate asked.

"No."

Matthew's solemn look convinced Danny she should go with him. She resented the intrusion. When Beau returned from Chicago, she'd try again to have him make Matthew leave.

"What's so important, Matthew?" Danny asked impatiently when they were off to themselves.

"Sir Drake has rabies."

Danny stared at him in disbelief. "We've all been looking for him," Danny uttered.

"Are you certain," Nate asked.

Matthew looked up, not realizing Nate had had the audacity to follow.

Danny fell back onto a bale of hay. "How terrible. Kit's going to be upset, but I can take care of that. But Ann...she believes Sir Drake saved her life."

"I'll go to her," Nate said, "then I'll ride out and see for myself."

Danny shook her head. "No, go to Sir Drake. If he

does have rabies, you'll put him out of his misery, won't you?''

Nate nodded.

''I'll tell Ann.'' Danny looked up at Matthew, surprised to see concern on his normally stoic face. ''We owe you our gratitude. I shudder to think what might have happened had you not recognized the symptoms so early.''

''I am very pleased to have been able to repay you in some way for your generous hospitality.'' After giving Nate directions to the cage, he said, ''Now if you will excuse me, I shall go to the veranda and have my tea.''

After Matthew left Danny took her time going to the house. She needed time to think about how she was going to break the sad news to Ann.

Matthew sipped the tea Thomas had prepared for him, and nibbled at the petit four. Any fool could tell Ann and Nate were having a liaison. If only he knew where Beau had placed the note from Nate, the highwayman would be dead. But he'd already searched Beau's office and Thomas had riffled through Beau and Danny's chambers. They had found nothing.

He removed the cozy from the teapot and poured another cup of tea. With Beau gone, now was the perfect time to put some sort of plan in action. Ann was going to be enormously upset over this last catastrophe, so she wouldn't be looking for trouble. He could no longer rely on Chico. The Mexican had obviously absconded with his money. But with Tex's help—

''How dare you!'' Ann accused as she charged out the French doors. ''Lies! All lies!'' She marched straight to him and slapped his face. ''How could you do this? You know there's nothing wrong with Sir Drake. You only want to hurt me.''

Danny, who had followed Ann to the veranda, held her breath. As Matthew stood, she could see the set of his tight jaw.

''That is enough, Ann,'' Matthew ordered.

''Never give me orders again. You have no authority, you have no title and—'' She took a deep breath, trying to gain control of herself. ''If Nate shoots Sir Drake,'' she hissed, ''I shall see that you—'' Her face suddenly lit up as she looked toward the end of the veranda. ''Oh, my poor Sir Drake,'' she crooned. Seeing his condition, she moved forward. ''What has he done to you?''

Matthew twisted about. Somehow, Sir Drake had escaped his pen. He was frothing at the mouth and snapping at anything. Matthew threw himself forward, shoving Ann away just as she was about to reach out to touch the dog. He felt the fangs pierce his leg.

Nate had galloped his horse hard to report back that the dog was missing. As soon as he had informed Ann and Danny, he planned to round up the ranch hands and scour the area. He had just stepped onto the veranda when Matthew shoved Ann away and Sir Drake had bitten him. Nate could see the blood on Matthew's trouser leg. Nate pulled his forty-five and shot the dog. Ann's hand was over her mouth, her face ashen. Danny stood speechless.

''I demand you shoot me,'' Matthew said quietly to Nate. ''No man should be forced to endure such a death.''

''No,'' Danny spoke up. ''He can't do that. You don't know for sure that you'll be infected.''

"I see." With a pompous dignity befitting royalty, he walked to the French doors. "Then lock me in the old jail among the trees tomorrow."

"You can stay in your room," Danny persisted.

"And what if I suddenly start biting at everything? Do you think I would have the willpower to remain in my room?"

"I'll have your leg attended to first."

"I'm afraid, my lady, that I shall have to manage that myself. No one should touch my blood."

"Very well," Danny finally agreed. "The jail hasn't been used in years, but I'll see that it's cleaned and properly outfitted as best as possible. It's old and the floor is hard-packed dirt. Are you sure you wouldn't prefer to be locked in a room?"

"I think not. I may grow to like it too much."

Ann could only stand and listen. This was all her fault. If only she had listened instead of accusing. "Matthew," she finally whispered, "I once called you a coward. I was wrong."

"You've been wrong about many things, my dear. But were I brave, I would take my own life."

When Beau returned, he found Matthew sequestered in the old one-room jail. It was Nate who told him what had happened. On the same day, Danny delivered a note to Matthew. As soon as she left, he tore it open and read the contents. The writing was scribbled and the words misspelled, but it wasn't difficult to decipher.

"I got captn. evrything redy. u no were to fine me. Chico."

Matthew's bitter laughter echoed around the four thick walls. Chico's return was a bit late.

* * *

As the day's passed, Ann withdrew more and more into herself. Her headaches were unmerciful and the nightmares unbearable. She refused to leave her quarters and wanted to see no one but Blossom and Danielle. She especially didn't want to see Nate.

Danny tried telling Ann that not Nate, nor anyone else, blamed her for what had happened, but Ann remained adamant. Ann couldn't rid herself of her blame. Had she not taken that walk, Sir Drake wouldn't have been tangled with the fox and Matthew wouldn't have been bitten. Even after all her belittling accusations, he had sacrificed his life for hers.

Though Danny had kept Ann informed as to Matthew's condition, eventually hearing about him wasn't enough. Ann had to see for herself that, so far, there had been no signs of him having contracted rabies.

"Matthew?" Ann called when she reached the one-room wooden jail.

Ann heard a shuffling sound from the back of the cell.

"Matthew?" she called again. The figure and cot were hidden in the shadows.

"You've waited a long time to pay a visit. Unless I've miscounted, this is the thirteenth day I've been in this blasted hole. The others have visited me at least twice a day. Why haven't you?"

Ann twisted her fingers around the rusty steel window bars. "I've come to realize that I couldn't live with myself if I didn't thank you for saving my life, and tell you how very, very sorry I am for having caused this misfortune."

"Is that so? 'Misfortune' doesn't seem quite a worthy word for my affliction. In other words, since it is apparent that I shall die, you are now willing to bestow a kind word and even show a degree of compassion." He stepped from the shadows. "How very gracious of you. And on top of all that, you want my forgiveness."

"I don't blame you for being bitter. How terrible it must be having to stay here day after day... waiting." Ann looked for any signs of madness. Even in such bleak surroundings, his clothing was meticulous, he was shaved and his hair combed. He looked tired, but that was to be expected.

"Matthew, I did not realize Sir Drake was rabid. I thought it was something you had made up. I would not have wished this misfortune on anyone."

"And pray tell," he said crossly, "why would I do that?"

"You already know the answer. I refused to give up Richard and return to England with you so I thought you were getting even with me."

"I still believe you are making a grave mistake by not heeding my counsel, but there is nothing I can do about it now. You have won your battle, Ann. The bastard will become the duke of Gravenworth."

Ann didn't feel the least bit victorious. "Perhaps you won't be infected by the disease."

"Perhaps, but not likely."

"Danny said there have been no signs. Beau has sent again for a doctor from Prescott. As you probably know, the family doctor is bedridden with gout. Beau told his men that this time they were to deliver one, no matter how much he protested."

"And just what good can a doctor do?"

"We can hope. Is Thomas supplying you with everything you need?"

"He furnishes what I need by way of an extended stick. He's afraid to come near me. Why all of this sudden concern, Ann? Why are you really here? Surely you don't expect me to believe you've only come out of concern or to ask forgiveness?"

Ann lowered her head. "No, that wasn't the only reason." Pictures of the English meadow and a large stag flashed in her mind. She looked up. "Please, Matthew. I must know. Who killed Edmund? You or I?"

Matthew's hard eyes held hers for what seemed like an eternity.

"I did." He pretended to dust lint from the lapel of his jacket. "As soon as I saw you drop your rifle and the horrified look on your face, I knew you thought you had committed the crime. I assessed the situation and used it to my advantage. Love does strange things to a man."

"Love? You never loved me."

"Always. I'm going to die, Ann," he said with just the right touch of flippancy. "There would be no reason for me to lie now."

Ann wondered how, during all those years, she hadn't known. "I wouldn't bother you, Matthew, but you are the only one left who can answer questions that have remained in my mind. May I ask one other thing?"

"By all means. Next time I might not be able to answer."

Ann hesitated, trying to find the right words. "Do you know why Edmund hated me so, or why he beat me and never laid a hand on Hester? Was I such a disappointment that he couldn't bear the sight of me?"

Matthew released a heavy sigh as he moved forward and placed his hands over hers. "I believe Edmund loved you...as much as Edmund was capable of loving."

"How could you say that?"

"He didn't know how to show love. He had been taught that such things were signs of weakness in a man. He beat you because of that weakness and because you would never allow him to be your master."

A single tear dropped from her eye. Finally she knew the truth. It had never been her fault.

"You never crawled."

"Like you?"

He resumed his devil-may-care attitude. "And others. At least I made him think so. I liked the conveniences my position offered and was quite willing to put up with his madness."

Ann realized that she'd never really known Matthew. Was his pompous demeanor actually a façade, a mask to hide behind? "Did you murder Edmund for the title?"

His sudden, cruel laughter frightened her. "You said one more question."

Ann tried to pull her hands from the bars but he wouldn't release his hold.

"Do you realize that if I sank my teeth into your hand and drew blood, you would be put in this cell with me? Think of it. We'd be together for eternity."

Terrified, Ann's mind was racing for a way to get him to take his hands off hers. "You were going to tell me why you killed Edmund."

Matthew chuckled. "You're wrong. I had no such intention. However, if you persist, I killed him because of you, my dear."

The moment he released his hold, Ann hurried away.

That afternoon, a doctor was delivered to the ranch. Danny informed Ann that the old physician was apathetic, stating coldly that nothing could be done about Matthew's condition. He'd also said that it could take as long as fifty days before any symptoms began to show. Matthew's depression, restlessness and fatigue could be signs, but then it could also be due to his circumstance. He refused to even go near Matthew and insisted he be taken back to town. His wish was granted.

The same reasoning could not be applied to the fever and excitability that came two days later. Matthew had rabies. It was already starting to affect his nerves.

It seemed that the worse Matthew's condition became the more Ann's health declined. She was the cause of Edmund's and Hester's deaths, and now Matthew would be added to the list.

Ann hardly ate and her loss of weight was showing. She refused to even see Danny. The only companions she wanted were Richard and Blossom. Everyone in the house was worried. Nate brought another doctor from town and, at Beau's insistence, Ann did allow him to examine her. He could find nothing wrong.

Though worried, angry and bitter at Ann for turning him away, Nate had abided by her wishes. However, thanks to Blossom, each day he'd received a report as to Ann's condition. But when the doctor had said he could find nothing wrong with Ann, Nate had reached the end of his patience.

It was midmorning when he charged into Ann's

dark room. He went directly to the windows, opened the wooden shutters, then went to where Ann lay in bed.

"Get up!"

Ann tried covering her face with the blanket, but Nate yanked it away. He was furious when he saw her hollowed eyes. Her body was little more than skin and bone. "Dammit, Ann, how could you do this to yourself?"

"Go away."

"I'm not going anywhere and I suggest you don't pull that cord to summon a servant. Can you get up or do I have to carry you?"

"Why are you doing this?" Ann put her hand to her head. "Can't you see I'm sick."

"Sick? From what? I love you, Ann, and I'll be damned if I'll let you or anyone else take you away from me. I want you out of this room and in the sun. I want you eating, even if you think you can't swallow a single bite." He yanked the heavy quilts from her thin body. "One way or another, I'm going to prove to you that—"

"Nate, I'm going to die."

"I refuse to believe that."

"I've been told in a dream that if Matthew dies, so shall I. It's happening."

It hurt to see the terror in her eyes. "Only because you're allowing it to, sweetheart." Nate scooped her up in his arms.

"I can walk," she protested weakly.

Nate paid no attention. It felt too good to have her once again in his arms. He carried her out of the bedroom, through the hallway French doors and onto the veranda. A table had been set with juice, fruits, sorghum and biscuits. "This morning, my love, we're dining together." He placed her in one of the chairs then sat in the other.

"I can't eat any of this!"

"We're going to sit here and you're going to eat, even if it takes all day."

Danielle and the servants peeked out the door and smiled. If anyone could make Ann well, it was Nate.

That night, with a lantern in hand to see her way, Ann slipped out of the house. She heard Matthew's heart-wrenching groans long before she reached the small jail. This time she didn't grab the bars.

"Matthew?" Ann called. The rank smell from inside was overpowering.

"Ann?" His voice cracked and was barely audible.

He rushed at the window, causing Ann to jump back. She raised the lantern higher. He squeezed his red eyes shut and tried to hide his face with his hand, but Ann had seen what was left of a once proud man. He was frothing at the mouth, his face was twisted and his body jerked. She lowered the lantern. "I'm sorry," she whispered.

"Listen to me, Ann. I'm…I'm becoming paralyzed and the convulsions have started. I've begged the doctor, Beau and Nate to kill me. Ann, have mercy. I beg you, put me out of my misery. Don't let me die like this."

Ann ran away. She couldn't bear to see Matthew suffering so. She suddenly stopped and listened. The silence was overwhelming. Had she heard a shot? She spun around and ran back to the cell. Again, silence. Slowly she lifted the lantern high enough to partially see the floor of the cell. Matthew lay on his back, arms stretched out, his face peaceful. He had been shot between the eyes.

Wide-eyed and her head pounding as picture after picture flashed in her mind, she backed away. The stag...Edmund sliding off the horse...Indians...Hester dead on the floor—

Ann dropped the lantern and placed her hands over her eyes, trying to block the visions. "Oh, merciful God, please..."

Matthew's grotesque face...

Scream after scream ripped from Ann's throat. Finally she fell to the ground, engulfed in blessed blackness. Unconscious, she didn't see the lantern flames already hungrily eating the dry grass and licking at the small jail.

Chapter Twenty-Five

"Come in," Nate called upon hearing a knock on his bedroom door. He was surprised to see Danny enter. The look on her face warned him of trouble. "I'll take a big guess that this has something to do with Ann."

"She has asked Beau to make traveling accommodations to England for her, Richard and Thomas."

"I see." Since the fire at the jail three nights ago, he'd tried every way he could think of to talk to Ann. She'd refused to see him except when others were about. The wild, free spirit he'd released within her had died with Matthew. Now there was only sadness in her eyes. He knew he was losing her.

"She's in the parlor," Danny said, "waiting for you."

Ann stood in the parlor, staring out the window. Lightning suddenly streaked across the sky, followed by a loud clap of thunder. There had been a similar storm the day she'd chosen to return to Gravenworth and fetch Hester. It was like an unending circle. It all seemed so long ago.

She glanced down at the ruby-red apple on the small plate. It looked ridiculous with only one bite taken out of it. At least her health had improved, thanks to Nate. The headaches and nightmares had even ceased. How pathetic that it had taken poor Matthew's death to force her into seeing what she had to do, yet she couldn't even return his body to England. The jail had been burned to the ground.

Ann knew the moment Nate entered the room. Though his movements were soundless, she had always been able to sense when he was near.

"Were you going to tell me you had asked Beau to make arrangements for your return to England, or was I supposed to find out after you'd left?"

"I had planned on telling you this morning."

"Why wait until now? You know where my bedroom is."

Ann turned. How strong and magnificent he looked, and how desperately she needed to feel his arms around her just one last time. "It had to be somewhere where we couldn't make love. My thinking becomes muddled when I'm in your arms." If only they could return to what they had shared before Sir Drake bit Matthew. "You're angry with me."

"Why should I be angry? Could it possibly be because you're leaving, or that you haven't even let me near you since Matthew's death? How can I help you when I'm not even allowed to speak to you? Ann, love is more than just sex," he lashed out at her.

"I know I haven't been fair, but I had to sort things out in my head. You couldn't have helped."

"You didn't give me a chance to try. I used to say that only fools rush into love. I should have listened to my own advice."

Ann sat in a chair and motioned for him to sit, also.
"I prefer standing."

"Nate, I have some things I must tell you and it isn't going to be easy for me. Would you please sit instead of moving about the room like some restless cat?"

Nate remained standing. "I've been waiting to tell you I'll go to England with you. Beau said I'd never understand what you've been talking about unless I went there."

Tears slid down Ann's cheeks. "I love you, Nate, but you can't come with me."

"Lady, you certainly know how to twist things around to your advantage." Nate started toward the door, then suddenly spun back around. "Am I now supposed to graciously leave and let you go peacefully on your way. Well, sweetheart, I'm damn well not feeling in a gracious mood. I want to know how you can say you love me in one breath and in the next tell me I can't be with you."

Ann flinched. His low, quiet voice left no doubt as to his anger. "I'm trying to. If you would just sit—"

Lightning lit up the room, followed by shattering thunder.

Nate plunked down on the Queen Anne sofa and waited.

"Nate, can't you see? This has nothing to do with you or our love. It's me. It's what *I* have to do." Her fingers toyed with the lace on the handkerchief she held. "I need to heal."

"What are you talking about?"

"My guilt—"

"It was my understanding that Matthew told you he shot Edmund." Nate still wondered if the dying man had said that to take the guilt from Ann's shoulders.

"Finishing what I had set out to do and my own self-worth are negligible at this time. Since Edmund's death, one catastrophe has followed another. I haven't even had an opportunity to learn who the real Antoinette is. I must return to my roots. England. Only there, and without interference from others, can I learn to forgive myself for the deaths I have caused. I need to learn to like myself again. I want to be happy for what I've accomplished instead of sad for what I didn't accomplish. If we stayed together now, I would surely end up destroying our love. I don't want to do that."

Nate remained silent. He didn't want to hear what she was saying. Probably because he understood how she felt.

Ann sighed. "Before Matthew died, he confessed that he murdered Edmund. Do you know why he did it?" She didn't wait for an answer. "For me. So you see, Edmund, Hester and Matthew's deaths all revolved around me." She sniffled, then wiped her nose.

Nate wanted to go to her and kiss her troubles away, but he knew it would only cause her more sorrow. He had already lost her, and it hurt like hell.

"I'm a murderess, Nate. Not once, but three times."

"Dammit, Ann," he said quietly, "don't do this to yourself." He raked his fingers though his hair, frustrated at being so helpless. "Ann, you didn't kill any of them."

"I was the cause of their deaths."

"Ann, we can work this out together."

She looked down at her hands. "This is something I must do alone. As I am, I'm no good to anyone, not even myself. I have to learn to live with my sins, Nate, and pray for God's forgiveness. Maybe someday I'll look toward tomorrow instead of continually looking back at the past as I do now."

Ann looked up at him. "Nate, I can't do this without your help. You must let me go." She slowly stood and returned to the window, fighting her desire to go to him.

"What about Richard?"

Ann watched the rain pound the ground outside. "I know how much you love him. Blossom admitted you had continued your morning visits."

"I'm taking him with me and raising him myself," Nate said.

Ann turned and smiled sadly. "Yes, you could do that. You could also tell Beau I'm not Richard's real mother. But if you really love me, don't let everything I've done become meaningless. Let Richard take his rightful place as the duke of Gravenworth."

"It's because of what you have gone through that makes me wonder. You have no more worries now. Matthew is dead. I'm the only one left who knows the truth, and once you're rid of me, you'll have everything you consider rightfully yours."

"Do you think leaving is easy for me? I love you!"

"Really, or have I just been the biggest fool walking?" He spun on his heels and left the room.

Ann's eyes filled with unshed tears.

That night Nate headed for the stable, his bedroll tucked under his arm. He hadn't told anyone he was leaving, and he hadn't visited Richard. It was best to leave things as they were.

It only took a minute to saddle the big gelding he'd purchased from Beau.

As Nate rode off, he didn't look back. He had lost. He'd thought that there would never come a day that he'd let Ann go. He had been wrong. But it wasn't the first time he'd felt as if his gut had been torn from his body, and it undoubtedly wouldn't be the last. Life never seemed to change. Sometimes you won, sometimes you lost. But this loss hurt like hell.

Chapter Twenty-Six

Gravenworth, England
One year later

Antoinette quietly set her teacup down on the saucer and gave the two women standing before her, her full attention.

"I had no choice, Your Grace," the younger woman whined. "He took me right there on the floor, 'e did. I swear I was fightin' 'im when Miss Curry walked in the storeroom. I'm a good girl, Your Grace. I don't fancy any foolin' around."

"I heard giggling, not fighting!" the housekeeper expelled. "This one's a troublemaker. A real wild one."

Ann remembered Nate once calling her wild. "Who was she with, Miss Curry?"

"A stable boy," the housekeeper answered.

There was nothing pretty about the girl, and she had the most unruly mop of carrot-red hair Ann had ever seen. "Take the issue up with me in the morning."

"But—"

Ann gave the elderly lady a stern look. The two women left. Ann knew she should have handled the matter and been done with it, but she just wasn't of a mind to do so. All morning she'd felt listless, something that, as of late, seemed to be occurring with more frequency.

She looked out the window. It was such a beautiful sunny day, something she probably wouldn't have even taken notice of when she had first returned to England. How differently she looked at things now, thanks to her dear father. One day, as they were taking a leisurely ride across the lush green countryside, she had admitted to her father the guilt she carried over the deaths of Edmund, Hester and Matthew. To her surprise he had called it a foolish waste of her time. "During the war, I slew many enemies of the crown and I blasted well didn't spend the rest of my life condemning myself for it. Death eventually comes to us all. The trick is to take the most from the good that life hands us, and accept and try to forget the bad." With that he had dismissed the entire subject, considering it not worth a conversation.

Over the months she had thought a lot about what her father had said, and finally she found herself looking ahead instead of behind. When sweet, laughing Blossom had died of pneumonia four months after their arrival in England, Ann had been crushed. But thanks to her father's wise words, she had been able to turn her sorrow around and think of all the good things Blossom had brought into her life. A sad smiled played at the corner of her lips. And though she would never love any man the way she had loved Nate, she knew in her heart that returning to England had been the right thing to do. She was now the accepted dowager duchess of Gravenworth and her son the duke. Everything had gone exactly as she had planned so long ago.

Ann stood and stretched. The letter she'd received from Danielle this morning had her thinking of the past. As usual, Danny hadn't mentioned Nate. She pursed her lips. But that wasn't Danny's fault. Prior to leaving the ranch, she had requested that Nate's name never be mentioned again. What a fool she had been to think it would help her broken heart mend faster. At this very moment she ached to know if he was well, if he had kept in touch with Beau, had he remained in Arizona and if he had found another woman to take her place.

Convinced a stroll would lighten her spirit, Ann left the solarium. Once outside, she inhaled the clean air and welcomed the sun's warmth on her face. Since her return, the castle always seemed chilly.

Taking her time, Ann wandered across the wide brick courtyard, down the terraced stone steps, and proceeded to browse through the immense flower gardens. Everything was in bloom, making her feel as if she had entered a fairyland. She offered compliments to the gardeners and closely examined a variety of blossoms, becoming lost in their absolute beauty. How could anyone remain unhappy amid such perfection?

Ann had no idea how long she had been gone, but by the time she returned to the courtyard, she was feeling much better. Seeing her father's horse tethered, she hurried forward. She found her tall, distinguished father in the great hall, standing near the huge fireplace. He was laughing at his grandson's antics on the wooden rocking horse. The boy's nanny stood off to the side, watching fondly.

"Father," Ann greeted, "what a pleasant surprise. How long have you been here?"

"Only a short time."

Richard slithered off the horse and ran to his mother. Ann swung the giggling boy up in her arms and made funny faces at him. "Did your grandfather awaken you from your nap?"

"Absolutely," Jonathan acknowledged. "He's much too old for naps. Why, he'll soon be two and ready for his own pony.

Ann smiled. "Nonsense." She placed the wiggling child back on the floor.

"Edmund was a handsome one and I do believe Richard is looking more like his father with each passing day."

"Your Grace," the nanny spoke up, "it's time for His Grace's meal."

Ann nodded. The nanny whisked the boy away.

"Come sit with me, Antoinette," Jonathan said as he made himself comfortable in one of the deep chairs. "It's been too long since we've talked."

"Oh?" Ann chose a small chair across from him. "Is something wrong, Father?"

"I'm worried about you. I understand you declined an invitation to Lady Percy's ball next month. Correct me if I am wrong, but I do not believe you've attended a single social affair since your return."

Ann's back stiffened. "There is no need for you to worry about me, Father, I'm quite well."

"You should be around others, laughing, dancing and enjoying yourself. Surely you're not going to tell me you are grieving for Edmund?"

"I'm not that much of a hypocrite." Ann clasped her hands in her lap and adopted a pose of perfect serenity. "In time I'll undoubtedly desire to mingle with others, but for now I'm content."

"In time? You've been back over a year now." Jonathan looked keenly at his daughter. "You liked the New World, didn't you?"

"Very much."

A sudden warmth had filled her eyes, the likes of which Jonathan hadn't seen since her return. "I'd thought to go there sometime, but lost interest when my brother, Beau's father, died. In his letters, Gerard always said it had a different beauty from England and that it was endless."

Ann relaxed as she thought of the miles and miles of virgin land she'd seen. "Oh, Father, you can travel forever and each day's scenery is different."

"Ann, my sweet," Jonathan said softly, "you've never talked much about the New World. You said it was too painful. Do you think you could talk about it now?"

Ann studied one of the big stained glass windows, the evening sunlight making the vibrant colors come alive. "Yes," she said with a wide grin. "I'd like that."

Father and daughter talked late into the night. By reversing roles and making Hester the husband, Ann was able to tell Jonathan most of what had happened. It hurt to continue the lie about Richard, but she had long since accepted her fate. Only two others knew his real heritage, and that was the way it would remain.

When Antoinette had finished, Jonathan was still trying to recover from the reality of the obstacles Antoinette had encountered while trying to reach her cousin. That she had survived was a miracle in itself. Though he chose not to say so, he was exceedingly proud of how she had handled the problems.

Jonathan rose from his chair and walked to the sideboard where the whiskey decanter sat. He knew his daughter too well to not recognize that she had left out parts of her story. He still didn't know why she had been so discontent since her return. True, she was happier now than when she had first arrived, but why hadn't that silent longing in her eyes ever left.

"Antoinette, why have you stayed in England?"

Ann was taken aback by the question. "You know why. Richard is the duke of Gravenworth. He has responsibilities." She released a halfhearted laugh. "Have you already tired of me, Father?"

"You know better than that. I'm curious as to what happened to that man...Nathan Bishop. Interesting chap. He sounded like a man I'd like to know."

Ann sipped the wine he handed her. "Oh, he's still out there somewhere." She didn't know what else to say.

"You mean that after all you went through together you haven't kept track of him? Haven't you asked Beau or—"

"No," she answered a little too sharply. "Where he is isn't of any importance to me. I haven't seen him in over a year."

Jonathan raised a suspicious gray eyebrow as he poured a glass of whiskey for himself. "You talked about Richard's obligations, as well as your own. As no-account as Edmund was, no one could ever fault his business sense. I've checked all his holdings and they are in excellent shape. He also had the intelligence to have only the very best of men watching after his investments. Your estate is not losing money. Quite the contrary.''

From the reports she had been receiving, Ann wasn't surprised.

Jonathan strolled to the fireplace and momentarily watched the flames lick at the big log. ''We've been sitting and talking for...I don't know how many hours. We have laughed, scowled, and at times we've even been teary-eyed. But never, since your return, have I seen you as alive as you've been while recounting your adventures.''

''What do you mean?'' Ann raised her glass and a servant immediately refilled it with wine.

''The Nathan Bishop you spoke of, were you in love with him?''

Ann was shocked at his perceptiveness. ''I don't know what that has to do with anything.''

''You didn't answer my question.''

Ann raised her chin. ''Yes, I loved him.''

Jonathan was beginning to understand. ''He didn't want to come to England?''

''I didn't want him to come.''

''Why?''

''He wouldn't have been happy here, and I needed time to think.''

''But that was his choice to make, not yours.''

''Father, I really do not care to discuss this.''

''Perhaps you discovered you didn't love him as much as you may have thought.''

Ann leaped to her feet, nearly spilling her wine. ''That's not so!''

''Then why are you here and he's there?''

''Is this an inquisition?'' Ann asked angrily. ''You

know why I'm here. I do not take my obligations lightly.''

Jonathan's features softened. ''Antoinette, I am not a blind man. You haven't been happy since your return. Now that you've told me most of what took place while you were gone, I understand why you haven't attended any social functions. Your heart is in Arizona Territory and, I suspect, with this man you call Nate.''

Ann turned her back to him, not wanting him to see the tears that filled her eyes. ''I never knew how wonderful or painful love could be until I met him,'' she confessed.

She spoke so softly that Jonathan could hardly hear her, but he heard enough to know the depth of her pain. ''And does he love you?''

Ann nodded.

Jonathan handed her his white handkerchief, wrapped his arms around her and let her sob, something he hadn't seen her do since she was a child.

When the sobs had diminished, Ann told Jonathan of her parting with Nate.

''My dear, go back to Arizona Territory and the man you love,'' Jonathan said softly.

Ann looked up at him, tears still standing in her big eyes. ''But it's been over a year. What if he—''

''You'll never know until you face him again.''

''But the estates—''

''Are being very capably handled. I shall inform you if you're needed. I'm certain that you and your family will make many trips to England over the years, and Richard will benefit from them. When he gets older he can spend the summers here.'' He smiled. "Between your uncle, brother and I, Richard will become a most magnificent duke."

"But our bitter farewell—"

"All lovers have arguments. That's what keeps everything interesting. If his love was true, it will not have faded. Besides, you're much too beautiful to be forgotten." He nodded for the servant to bring his things. "I shall make arrangements for your passage in two weeks. Meanwhile, I suggest you set the servants to packing first thing in the morning." He chuckled. "Richard's things alone will take up half a ship."

Ann wiped her cheeks. "Thank you, Father. I shall always love you."

"And I you, my dear." He took the cloak the servant handed him and placed it over his shoulders.

"Father," Antoinette called as he made his way to the large French doors, "do you really think this can be done?" She held her breath.

"I know it can. I loved your mother above all else and she would never forgive me if I prevented you from experiencing the love we shared."

Ann stood at the ship's rail, paying scant attention to the light sprays of salt water brushing her cheeks. Slowly but surely, the sun and her England were disappearing in the distance.

Ann was suddenly overwhelmed with a sense of giddiness. The past two weeks had kept her constantly busy. But now, for the first time, the reality of what she was doing had hit her. She was returning to the land and the man who had stolen her heart. Something she had come to accept as never happening.

A movement in the water caught her attention.

Looking down, she saw several dolphins racing alongside the ship. She craned her neck to watch their sleek silvery bodies keeping pace with seemingly effortless movements. Was it true that such animals had saved sailors' lives? The sun had gone down and she lost sight of them.

For the hundredth time, Ann wondered if she was doing the right thing? What if Nate never wanted to see her again? She had already decided not to discuss Nate until she was settled at the ranch. There were things she needed to know before trying to find him.

Chapter Twenty-Seven

Ann was already eagerly scanning the dock as the ship berthed. She hadn't thought of San Francisco as being large, and therefore was surprised to see the piers teaming with life. Stevedores were busily unloading ships, passengers hurried to board vessels preparing to sail, while others had come to see them off. Then there were those who had congregated to welcome the passengers debarking from the ship she was on. Even though she knew it would be impossible to pick out Beau or Danny, she continued looking. What if they hadn't been able to come? Worse yet, what if they hadn't received her letter?

Then she saw Beau, standing a good head taller than most and steadily making his way toward the lowered gangplank. Ann's heart soared as she hurried along the deck to meet him. Now she was home.

After making arrangements for her many pieces of luggage to be delivered to the Palace Hotel, Beau took Ann, Richard and Maggy to the hotel where Danny and Kit waited. Ann could not remember a happier reunion.

After two weeks of rest and gaiety in San Francisco, the entourage headed for the Arizona Territory and Beau's ranch. Compared to the trip she'd made from New York, she was traveling in the lap of luxury. There was even a bronze tub on one of the wagons, and there was no shortage of water. Beau knew all the streams and water holes. After the evening meals, the boys played while Beau, Danny and Ann reminisced. Beau mentioned Nate's name several times, but Ann made no comment. She couldn't bring herself to talk about Nate in front of Beau. She still preferred talking to Danny privately.

When Ann finally caught sight of the ranch house, tears welled in her eyes. Returning to Gravenworth had brought forth memories of Edmund's hatefulness and Matthew's determination to keep her there. Here she had known happiness and freedom.

As the days passed, Ann and Richard settled into Ann's old rooms. On a particularly warm day, Danny and Ann stood by the corral watching Kit exercising his new pony.

"He looks as if he was born on a horse."

"He's his father's son, which sometimes scares me."

Ann leaned against the corral rail. "I still can't believe I let Beau talk me into letting Little Dog take Richard on his first hunting trip! He's only two years old! I can't stop worrying. Thank heavens, they'll return today."

"Ann, try to relax. I know that's difficult, because I know how upset I was when Beau let Little Dog take Kit on his first trip. I had thought Kit would come home crying and wanting to be with his mother after such an ordeal. Like Richard, it was the first time

Kit had gone away without either Beau or me. But Kit loved it and has never forgotten what he learned. Now he looks forward to going out with his father and Little Dog twice a year. It will be the same with Richard. I hate to admit it, but Beau was right. They learn to be men.''

"Men? He's a two-year-old boy!"

"Look, Mommy!" Kit called.

Danny turned just in time to see Kit leap off his pony. "Indian Joe," Danny called, "if you have to, tie Kit to the saddle! I don't want him doing that again. He could be trampled!"

"Yes, ma'am," the lanky Cheyenne called back, his mouth spread in a big grin.

"Kit's much too adventuresome and Beau encourages it." Danny rubbed her hands on her buckskin britches and frowned. "The Cheyenne are great warriors and renowned for their riding abilities. I think Joe's trying to make Kit a great warrior like his father was." She watched the quiet man put Kit back in the saddle and tie the leather straps around his waist. She was certain Joe would remove them the minute she and Ann returned to the house.

"I'll never forget the night we watched Beau and Nate break those wild mustangs," Ann said, the remembering making her misty-eyed. "It was the most magnificent sight I have ever seen."

Danny studied her friend for a brief moment. "That's the first time you've spoken Nate's name. Ann, I can't stand it another day. Was I all wrong? Did you love Nate? I thought you were so perfect for each other. Did you return to England and forget about him?"

The puff of dust Kit's pony kicked up landed on

Ann. She raised her handkerchief and wiped the grit from her eyes.

"Are you all right?" Danny asked.

"Of course I am." Ann laughed. "I ceased being the delicate English flower the day I headed for Arizona Territory over two years ago."

Danny laughed and took her by the arm. "Come on. Let's get out of the sun and have some lemonade. I warn you though, I'm not going to drop my questions about Nate," she continued as they headed for the patio. "After all this time, I think I deserve to know just what happened that night he left."

"There's no mystery. When he joined me in the parlor, I told him that Richard and I would be returning to England alone. We didn't speak after that."

They stepped onto the patio and sat on the bench circling the huge tree, welcoming the shade. "Did you ever see Nate again?" Ann asked.

"About five months later." Danny couldn't miss the pleased look on Ann's face.

The maid came out with a pitcher of lemonade and two glasses.

"Thank you, Elizabeth," Danny said to the young girl before taking a long, welcome drink. She made herself comfortable against the tree trunk. "Beau understood why you had to leave, but I don't think he agreed with your decision to go. I thought you loved Nate and would have at least asked about him in one of your letters."

"I didn't ask about Nate because I was afraid of the answers. But returning to England was the right decision. Not only for Richard's sake but for me, as well. I had to rid the demons from my head before committing myself to anyone."

"Did you plan on returning all along?"

Ann shook her head. "I was certain I would spend the rest of my life in England, helping Richard become a great duke. And when he did take over his responsibilities, I knew too many years would have passed to regain Nate's love."

Danny tossed her hands in the air. "I'm completely confused. If you didn't plan to return, what difference would the answers to your questions about Nate have mattered?"

Ann looked at the mountain range surrounding the valley. They looked blue in the distance. She released a tired laugh. "Let me start from the beginning. I have always had a tendency to see things in a broader scope than necessary. Fortunately, my father is very good at putting things back into proper perspective."

Danny drew her knees up and rested her feet on the bench.

"My father can also be very wise. He allowed me time to straighten my mind out and get Richard established before…"

Danny listened attentively as Ann poured out her heart. When Ann grew silent, Danny was still lost in the wonderful love story that had just unfolded. "I told Beau you were right for each other!" she finally blurted out. "You came here to see if Nate still loves you!" She jumped to her feet. "How romantic."

"Not entirely. I came to see you and your family, also."

Danny threw her arms around Ann and hugged her. "I know that."

"Mommy!"

The women turned in unison. Richard was running toward them, Little Dog right beside him. Ann stretched out her arms and her giggling son ran to her.

"Mommy! Fish!" Richard turned in her arms and looked back at Little Dog. "Show."

Little Dog dutifully pulled a fish from his pocket.

"Mine," Richard said proudly.

Everyone laughed.

Ann wrinkled her nose. "You smell. Let's go tell Maggy you need a bath."

"Ann," Danny called as the duchess headed for the house, "Nate is turning his land near Santa Fe into a fine horse ranch."

Ann missed a step and almost dropped Richard. "You've talked to him?"

"He's been here on several occasions," Danny teased.

Ann continued on into the house. She still couldn't draw the courage to ask the one question she wanted to know. Later. She'd find out more later.

It was several days before Ann chose to reopen the conversation about Nate. Kneeling on the patio floor next to Danny, their aprons and gloves already covered with dirt, Ann sank the trowel deep into the rich dirt and loosened the soil in the flowerbed. "Why haven't you said anything more about Nate?"

Danny shrugged her shoulders, pretending disinterest. "I figured you'd come back around to it when you were ready."

Ann took a deep breath. "Is there another woman in Nate's life? I'd understand if there was," she added hurriedly. "After all, he never expected me to reenter his life. His reputation—"

"Ann!" Danny sat down on the stone floor and

stared at Ann, who was digging a hole to hell. "Ann, are you going to let me answer your question?"

Ann's hand paused. "Do I want to hear the answer?"

"As far as I know, Nate has not taken another woman, but we haven't seen him in months."

Ann plopped down on the floor. "Danny, after I left, did he ever... Did he ever mention my name or say anything about missing me?"

Danny leaned forward and patted Ann's hand. "After Nate left, it was nearly five months before we saw him again. One day he came riding up to the house, wanting to tell us about the horse ranch he had started. He has never mentioned the night you parted. At least not to me, and I doubt he would have said anything to Beau."

"Oh, Danny. I thought I could live my life without him, but I was wrong. I have missed him so terribly."

Danny nodded. "But you have to think of how he must have felt when you left. You're the only woman he ever wanted, but you made it clear you would not be returning. He has had to make a life for himself without you. He's a proud man and not likely to let you break his heart again."

The two women fell silent.

Ann wiped the dirt from her face with the back of her glove, then rose to her knees. Grasping a bulb, she dropped it into the deep hole she'd dug. "Until Nate tells me face-to-face that he no longer loves me, I refuse to believe that we can't still have a life together. I know how deeply I hurt him, and I really don't know how he feels about me now." She shooed a fly away. "I've given a lot of thought as to how I should approach Nate, and I've decided on a letter. I can't embarrass him by suddenly coming back into his life. He'll need time to accept my return and decide what he wants to do about it. If he chooses to turn his back on me, I'll have to think of some other way to win his love again.''

Chapter Twenty-Eight

Though Nate had returned from Santa Fe over a week ago, it wasn't until now that he discovered a page missing from his breeding journal. Knowing how careless his housekeeper could be, he started shuffling through the clutter on his desk. She had probably moved it somewhere, but where? Lifting a woven flower basket she had set down and forgotten about, he spied a letter.

Cursing under his breath and swearing to find a new housekeeper as soon as possible, he tore open the letter. The perfect female script caused him to glance down at the signature. Refusing to believe his eyes, he looked again. His face turned red as his hand slowly curled into a fist, crushing the paper he was holding. How dare Ann try to contact him! She was out of his life and that was where he wanted her to stay. He tossed the paper into the trash basket and stomped out of the house.

Five minutes later, Nate returned. Angry with himself for his weakness, he snatched up the crumpled letter and smoothed it out on the desk as he sat on the straight-backed chair. Why was Ann writing him after all this time?

My dearest Nathan,
How surprised you must be at receiving this letter. It seems a lifetime since we parted. At the time I was confused, heartbroken and convinced we would never see each other again. How naive of me to have thought that by being apart I could learn to accept being without you. So, my dearest, I have returned to find out if the love we knew still exists. I know when I left I hurt you deeply, but if we can recapture the happiness we previously shared, I swear I will never leave you again. However, if too much time has passed and you no longer harbor feelings for me, I will understand. But if, by chance, you do still love me, please come to me as fast as your horse will carry you.

Yours forever, Ann

Nate returned the letter to the trash and went back outside.

But even after two weeks had passed, he couldn't stop thinking about Ann waiting at Beau's ranch. Memories flooded back of Ann passing herself off as Hester's husband; the look on her face when he had tossed her out of the stagecoach and left her to the mercy of the ladies; the view of her riding out of the fort a hero, with Richard and Blossom trailing behind; the look on her face when they made love; her laughter; and even her temper. Did he still love her? More than he cared to admit. Did he want to go to her?

Yes. Did he trust her? No. Did he believe that she really loved him? No.

Though he was determined not to allow Ann to make a fool of him again, the nights without sleep were having their effect. Finally he'd had his fill of nothing but memories and fighting with himself. He'd go to Ann and once and for all get her out of his system. He'd listen to what she had to say then leave. Having made up his mind, two days later he rode away from the ranch before the sun had peaked over the horizon.

As the miles passed beneath his horse's hooves, Nate began to seriously wonder if Ann had told the truth about still loving him. She had loved him once, why not still? He pushed his horse to a faster pace. What if she had given up on him coming after her and had returned to England? Calling himself a fool, he pushed his mount to a full gallop.

Both horse and rider were bone weary when Nate finally brought the gelding to a sliding halt in front of Beau and Danny's house. Nate was already out of the saddle before the dust could settle. He went directly into the house yelling, "Beau, Danny, Kit? Where is she? Where is Ann?"

Danny came hurrying down the hall, a smile spread across her entire face. "I was in my room and I still heard you." She threw her arms around him and gave him a big hug. "Beau and Kit rode into Prescott for some supplies."

"I'm not here to see Beau and Kit. Where is Ann?"

"She went for a ride. I offered to go with her but she said she needed to be alone. Oh, Nate, she's heartbroken. She thinks you no longer love her."

Ann really loved him! A surge of joy ran through Nate's veins, the likes of which he hadn't experienced since before Ann had left for England. "It's going to rain," he commented more to himself than to Danny. Then he turned on the heels of his boots and headed back toward the door.

"Where are you going?" Danny called.

"I think I know where Ann is."

Ann slowly made her way around the rocky rubble while looking up at the magnificent cliff dwellings. Brush was everywhere.

In a most unladylike manner, she plopped down onto one of the boulders and stared at the once proud structure. Like Nate's love, the old dwellings had deteriorated with time. Tears filled her eyes as she thought about the hours she and Nate had spent here, making love, talking and getting to know each other. They had been such special days when nothing mattered but being with the man she loved.

Why hadn't Nate come for her? It had been almost a month since she'd sent the letter.

Ann suddenly sat up straight. Almost afraid to turn for fear she could be wrong, she slowly turned to see if Nate was near. He was sitting tall and proud on a magnificent gray horse, studying her. How long had he been sitting there? As he dismounted with the ease of a man well-known to the saddle, she felt as if her breath had been cut off. Her gaze traveled the length of him as he walked toward her. It was as if time stood still. He hadn't changed at all. He was still the most magnificent man she had ever seen.

"I would never have thought it possible, but you are even more beautiful than before," Nate said. He stopped less than a foot away. His eyes couldn't get enough of her.

"I didn't think you were coming." Ann hadn't expected to feel shy and hesitant, but she suddenly didn't know how to approach him.

"I almost didn't."

"I didn't know if you still—"

Nate pulled her into his arms, wanting to hurt her as she had hurt him. But when her arms willingly circled his neck and she pressed her body against his, he realized that the woman who had left him no longer existed. The woman he'd fallen in love with had returned. The old confidence and determination shone like a bright beacon. But it was the look of pure love he'd seen on her face when she turned and looked at him that was his undoing. Unable to wait a moment longer, he claimed her full lips in a smothering kiss. All thoughts of the past or future were erased as their passion burst into a smoldering flame. They couldn't undress each other fast enough.

"Oh, Nate," Ann said, her breathing already labored, "I've waited a lifetime for you to make love to me again. I love you so much." She gasped from sheer joy as he plunged deep within her. They didn't even notice when it sprinkled rain, nor when it stopped.

An hour later, Ann lay with her head resting on Nate's shoulder, his arms wrapped protectively around her. Though she didn't want to break the spell of contentment, she was concerned that even when they were making love, Nate hadn't spoken any words of love.

"It's gone, isn't it," she finally said, fighting back her tears.

"What's gone?"

"Your love for me. I've lost you."

Nate leaned down and gave her a good nip on the shoulder.

Ann swung around and faced him, her eyes flashing with anger. Hearing his chuckle, she sat up and reached for her clothes. "Is this your way of getting even with me? You take what I was willing to give then leave?"

He pulled her back down on the ground and pinned her arms and legs until she stopped struggling. "God, you're beautiful when you're angry."

"Let me go."

"I thought we'd stay here until nightfall and make love. We have a lot of time to make up."

It was the twinkle in his eyes that she recognized first. He was teasing her. His slow smile sent her heart pounding against her ribs.

"Did I forget to tell you I love you?"

"Yes."

His tongue played with an inviting nipple. Never again would he agree to let her leave him, even if it meant kidnapping her, taking off to the mountains and becoming hermits. "Are you ready to marry me and settle down on my ranch?" He toyed with the other nipple.

"I'll marry you today if you want."

Nate's laughter echoed through the old dwellings. "I'd welcome it, however, it isn't possible."

"Why?" Ann asked suspiciously.

"Because, my darling, when I left the house, I heard Danny joyfully mumbling something about the wedding arrangements she had to make.'' He kissed her nose. "Have I told you how much I love you in the last five minutes?"

"No, it has been at least six. I would rather you show me."

"You are indeed a wanton woman."

"You've made me that way."

Nate laughed with joy. The bitterness of the past no longer existed. In his family only love and happiness would abound.

He suddenly looked down at her. "You're not planning on living in England, are you?"

Ann smiled. "Richard and I shall live at your ranch with you." She'd wait until after they were married to inform him there would have to be occasional visits to England.

"I shall make you the Queen of Santa Fe. I never told you, but I am a very wealthy man."

"Nate, you have to promise you will no longer rob people. I couldn't stand constantly worrying that you'll be put in jail."

"It's an inheritance, my lovely."

Ann wanted to question him further, but his hands were already setting her skin on fire.

Epilogue

After handing his daughter over to Nathan, Jonathan took his seat in front and watched the ceremony. It was a huge wedding with people coming from as far away as England. Everyone seemed determined to witness the union of the lady and her outlaw.

Jonathan's chest swelled with pride. Antoinette had never looked as beautiful or as happy as she did at this moment. Her cream silk gown was covered with pearls and diamonds, showing her to be the duchess she was, and the pearls and diamonds woven through her thick hair were her crown. He winked at Richard, who was standing proudly with the ring that had momentarily been placed in his safekeeping. Richard winked back.

Jonathan cleared his throat. It was a good thing he hadn't discovered his daughter planned to marry a highwayman until after he'd arrival in the colonies. Had he known beforehand, he would never have permitted her return. But Nathan's criminal background seemed to bother no one but him. In fact, he was highly respected and treated as if he were some sort of legend. And, in truth, after coming to know the man, Jonathan had to admit Antoinette had chosen wisely.

As the couple said their vows, Jonathan was reminded of his own wedding so many years ago. He had loved his wife with all his heart and still did. That was why he had never considered taking another wife. And when Antoinette and Nathan turned to face the guests as husband and wife, he saw that same undying love in their eyes. He was content. He glanced around. Convinced all eyes were turned toward the happy couple, he wiped a tear from his eye, then chuckled. The sun was bright, there was laughter and joy in the air, and his daughter had just been married. A man couldn't ask for a better day. He moved forward to offer his congratulations.

* * * * *

Start the year right with
Harlequin Historicals' first
multi-author miniseries,

KNIGHTS OF THE BLACK ROSE

Three warriors bound by one event,
each destined to find true love....

THE CHAMPION, by Suzanne Barclay
On sale December 1999

THE ROGUE, by Ana Seymour
On sale February 2000

THE CONQUEROR, by Shari Anton
On sale April 2000

Available at your favorite retail outlet.

HARLEQUIN®
Makes any time special ™

Visit us at www.romance.net   HHKOTBR

3 Stories of Holiday Romance from three bestselling Harlequin® authors

Valentine Babies

by

ANNE STUART

TARA TAYLOR QUINN

JULE McBRIDE

Goddess in Waiting by Anne Stuart
Edward walks into Marika's funky maternity shop to pick up some things for his sister. He doesn't expect to assist in the delivery of a baby and fall for outrageous Marika.

Gabe's Special Delivery by Tara Taylor Quinn
On February 14, Gabe Stone finds a living, breathing valentine on his doorstep—his daughter. Her mother has given Gabe four hours to adjust to fatherhood, resolve custody and win back his ex-wife?

My Man Valentine by Jule McBride
Everyone knows Eloise Hunter and C. D. Valentine are in love. Except Eloise and C. D. Then, one of Eloise's baby-sitting clients leaves her with a baby to mind, and C. D. swings into protector mode.

VALENTINE BABIES

On sale January 2000 at your favorite retail outlet.

HARLEQUIN®
Makes any time special ™

Visit us at www.romance.net

PHVALB

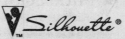

Every Man Has His Price!
HEART OF THE WEST

At the heart of the West there are a dozen rugged bachelors—up for auction!

This January, look for
Shane's Last Stand
by **Ruth Jean Dale**

Dinah Hoyt was chosen by the good citizens of Bushwack, Colorado, to "buy" former Bushwack resident Shane Daniels at auction…and then talk him into using his celebrity to save "Old Pioneer Days." Everyone knew that she and Shane had once been close. But no one knew exactly how close, or what had become of their teenage love affair…not even Shane. And if Dinah had anything to say about it, he wasn't going to find out!

Each book features a sexy new bachelor up for grabs—and a woman determined to rope him in!

Available January 2000 at your favorite retail outlet.

HARLEQUIN®
Makes any time special ™

Visit us at www.romance.net

PHHOW8

This season, make your destination
England with four exciting stories from
Harlequin Historicals

On sale in December 1999,

THE CHAMPION,
The first book of *KNIGHTS OF THE BLACK ROSE*
by **Suzanne Barclay**
(England, 1222)

BY QUEEN'S GRACE
by **Shari Anton**
(England, 1109)

On sale in January 2000,

THE GENTLEMAN THIEF
by **Deborah Simmons**
(England, 1818)

MY LADY RELUCTANT
by **Laurie Grant**
(England, 1141)

Harlequin Historicals
Have a blast in the past!

Available at your favorite retail outlet.